The Butterfly Tree

The Library of Alabama Classics,
reprint editions of works important
to the history, literature, and culture of
Alabama, is dedicated to the memory of
Rucker Agee
whose pioneering work in the fields
of Alabama history and historical geography
continues to be the standard of
scholarly achievement.

The Butterfly Tree

Robert Bell

With an Introduction by
Thomas Rountree

THE UNIVERSITY OF ALABAMA PRESS
Tuscaloosa and London

Library of Congress Cataloging-in-Publication Data

Bell, Robert E.
    The butterfly tree / Robert Bell ; with an introduction by Thomas
    Rountree.
        p.   cm. — (The Library of Alabama classics)
    ISBN 0-8173-0560-2
    I. Title. II. Series.
PS3552.E523B88   1991
813'.54—dc20   91-15402

British Library Cataloguing-in-Publication Data available

INTRODUCTION

Thomas Rountree

The cradling elements that build for the birth of a novel are similar to the architecture of a bird's nest: a randomlike layering and weaving of materials that somehow hold together in the right way at the right time. The delicate structuring is so firm that its vital internal spaces and arrangements remain largely a mystery, but some of the twigs and bits of grass or thread can be identified and pondered. So it is with the elemental weavings that supported the incubative imagination which grew into Robert Bell's *The Butterfly Tree* (1959).

As he remembers it, words were vastly important to Robert Bell even before he could read. Born on Wednesday, 13 October 1926, in Tarrant City, Alabama, he was fortunate to have a mother who read to him and his two brothers and who told them stories from her own vivid imagination. In those days before television, they learned to visualize from words alone. And aside from the picturing quality of frequent movies (especially Saturday westerns and serials), the other more prevalent unprinted means of entertainment—radio—would have forced them to "see" things and concepts almost entirely through words. Except for some mood music, when one listened to an episode of "Lux Radio Theater," "Red Skelton," or "First Nighter" (the little theater off Times Square) it was the sound and import of words that brought the excitement of other lives and places into one's own life and locale. The time was possibly the twilight of the age-old dominance of oral tradition as a means of communication, and it was a favorable one for an alert future wordsmith to register the fullness of words around him.

Naturally enough, in his boyhood and adolescence books became just about the most important things in the world for Bell. He literally read the entire children's department of books at the Tarrant City

Public Library and could hardly wait to turn thirteen in order to use the adult department. His own modest library held works by Thornton W. Burgess and Louisa May Alcott, serial novels about the Hardy Boys and Nancy Drew, and the popular "big-little" books available from every dime store (thick little books of four-by-four-inch pages which alternated between text and drawings). He read runs of comic books concurrently with *Jane Eyre* and *Uncle Tom's Cabin*, and at fourteen he went through the many pages of *Gone With the Wind* within the library's seven-day lending period. In contrast to such voracity, he built one model airplane and did not learn to drive until he was twenty-six.

His verbal interest and ability took firmer direction at Phillips High School in Birmingham, where understanding teachers were ready to help and where he became a devoted student of Latin. It was from Latin that he remembers learning the mechanics of English and about word origins. Because he discerned that algebra was a sort of utilitarian language in its own right, that and Latin became his favorite course subjects, leading to a revelation that words could unlock secrets. Perhaps, he thought, there was a formula among the thousands of books at the Birmingham Public Library, and he sought it in all kinds of volumes. Although he never found *the* formula, he discovered other wonderful things, including a renewed urge to write.

Earlier in junior high school he had had a crush on a girl who was born an hour after him and who wanted to be a writer. When writing of course became his ambition too, he began penning great sagas that never got past the first chapter, but he did complete a little play that was produced for a weekly assembly program. Now for his senior English class he wrote a long and gloomy story about Viking brothers who fell in love with a girl who turned out to be their sister, and he composed a highly romantic masque called "Echo and Narcissus," an early indication of his long-lasting interest in mythology.

Although his studies at Birmingham-Southern College were interrupted after just one school quarter by army service, he returned there afterwards and took classical Greek, French, and German. Good luck gave him as freshman composition professor Richebourg McWilliams, a remarkable man of Black-Belt uprightness and erudition who liked Bell's writing and became his adviser. McWilliams proved ultimately to be a permanent and major influence, for Bell completed his degree there though he and his family had moved to Fairhope on Mobile Bay in 1947.

No one could have known it at the time, but the Eastern Shore region was the most immediate "twig-rich" locus for Bell's novel-to-be. The area has long been known for its distinctive red cliffs and gullies, its inviting summer shoreline, and its abundance of plant and animal life, including small life like that of the monarch butterfly during its seasonal migration to Mexico. Different people have different favorite spots for the most spectacular display of the little travelers: among the small, gnarled live oaks of Cedar Point on the lower western bay, along the causeway crossing the upper bay, variously here and there on the Eastern Shore, and around Fort Morgan farther south. Unarguable, however, is that during October and November the bright black-and-orange butterflies reach the bay area by thousands upon thousands. Nonetheless they had to wait for a work of fiction to create a myth-like legend about their congregating activities.

But at least as important as the natural setting for the still not quite nascent novel was the kind of people in the Fairhope area. Even before the rural section was settled as the Fairhope Single-Tax Colony in 1894 because it was found superior to sites in four other states, the two-man search committee from Iowa (James Bellangee and S. S. Mann) predicted that it would attract many friends from the North. But it did more than that, for the democratic and reasoning tenor of the early settlers, coupled with later developments like the founding of Mrs. Marietta Johnson's innovative School of Organic Education in 1907, made the community an intellectual and cultural center that from one place or another attracted unusual individuals who were sometimes as delightfully eccentric as a butterfly's flight. By the 1940s and 1950s (though also before and since then) Fairhope was a folksy and cosmopolitan community with a sympathetic tolerance for the occasional nonconformist, for the intellectually and artistically inclined.

It was because of this juncture of people and place that for quite some decades the Eastern Shore has been Alabama's equivalent to

California's better-known Carmel-by-the-Sea, and Robert Bell became an observing part of it in the late 1940s. He slipped into deep and lasting friendship with Andrew Dacovich, an appreciative native of the area. But beyond observing, he was also developing his interest in Greek mythology, for Dacovich remembers that on his first visit to Bell's home Bell took him to his bedroom to show him a huge six-foot-high piece of cardboard on the wall. Thereon was written *Zeus* along with the genealogy of the gods and goddesses all the way down to the minor deities and heroes. It was perhaps this preoccupation that enabled him to see the types inherent in the specific persons of the Fairhope area—the tolerant but individualistic natives; the flux of naturalists, writers, and other kinds of artists; the retirees and returnees who often had fascinating backgrounds that they were willing to share while pursuing additional backgrounds. Later he would fictionally concretize some of these composite types into new individuals as part of the ambience and essence of Alabama's "Carmel," but that had to wait on further experience.

Working for Holton Corporation as the chemical engineer's assistant, he often came home splotched with dyes, his wrists perpetually itching from embedded particles of fiberglass. But far more important, he was interviewing successfully for a General Education Board fellowship to study at Harvard. During his year there he came to know Boston in a way that would later be of use as one setting for *The Butterfly Tree*. At the same time his literary experience was being sharpened by some of the best-known scholars and writers of the time: Douglas Bush, Kenneth Murdoch, Carvel Collins, Howard Mumford Jones, Richard Wilbur, and Kenneth Kempton. The endless reading for Jones' course excited him about realists and naturalists such as Crane, Dreiser, Norris, London, and Howells; stirred him with the language and verbal coloring of Lafcadio Hearn; and left him in awe of Henry James. The works of Hemingway and Faulkner moved him significantly less than those of Steinbeck and Kate Chopin. Meanwhile he was enjoying the publications of Truman Capote and writing fiction himself for Kempton's class. The very first short story that he submitted to Kempton was later published (1959) in *Descant* with the title "Touch-and-Run." The guidance and encouragement by Kempton were so important that Bell recalls him and

Richebourg McWilliams of Birmingham-Southern as the most powerful influences in his literary development.

Returning home in June 1951 with an M.A. degree from that marvelous year in the North, he became conscious of the Fairhope area from a new perspective. Though he missed the Boston life and the freedom of being on his own, his continued friendship with Andrew Dacovich deepened and he came to know naturalist Winifred Duncan, who gave the two men sculpture lessons. At the same time Bell began working at night as reference librarian for the Mobile Public Library. After work he frequently had coffee with the Mobile *Register*'s Borden Deal, a fellow unpublished fictionist who would later become a prolific novelist. The next summer he attended library school at Columbia in New York City, carrying on that study the following summer at Louisiana State. During these two years of deepening and discovery, he began a localized short story that kept wanting to overflow its length so that he realized its universals and characterizations called for the fuller presentation that only a novel could accommodate. The creative spurt, however, was short-lived.

In spite of his true ambition to write the novel, he made no progress until in 1955 he moved to Fort Worth as assistant director of the Public Library, and even then in a curious way he had to talk himself into it. He began to know many creative people in the city, and he kept telling them he was writing a novel. When they stopped appearing impressed, he decided he had better shut mouth or open workshop. He did the latter, getting himself on a schedule with the long-dormant material and staying with it. By September 1957 an interested New York agent was writing him that the manuscript was the best-written one that had come to the agency that year.

The job of writing was not yet over, however. When Lippincott accepted the work during the first quarter of 1958, both Bell's agent and his editor were referring to it as a most exciting first novel. But editor Lynn Carrick wanted significant revision to pare down many descriptive passages and the long monologues. Completing this work by the end of July, Bell had essentially behind him the creative effort which, according to agent Maurice Crain, editor Carrick considered to be a virtuoso performance by a talented new writer. What remained was the lengthy and complex business of getting the volume ready for publication, a process that elicited repeated excitement and praise from Lippincott's personnel in the advertising and sales departments.

As Bell's agent and editor had anticipated, the reviews were mixed when the novel reached the public in the spring of 1959. Yet, the closer the reviewers were to the Southern locale of the novel, the more fully appreciative they seemed to be. In the New York *Times* (7 June 1959) Frank H. Lyell, while noting the main character's "awakening to some of life's verities and mysteries," observed that the "novel's bitter-sweet mood and languorous pace are appropriate to the setting and the introspective bent of the characters." Even so, he found that much of the book was "a somnambulistic dreamworld" where precise meaning was "frequently obscured by Mr. Bell's murky prose." In contrast, Mrs. Dan Benton of the Baldwin (Alabama) *Times* (16 April 1959) admired the way the book "transforms the everyday sights, sounds, experiences, and people" of the Eastern Shore into a "classic vividness," doing so "in some of the most beautiful and literate prose-poetry that has come out of the South in many a year."

Quite a number of reviewers pointed to the symbolic, allegorical, or fantasy nature of the story and related it variously to realism. In the New York *Herald Tribune* (12 July 1959) Donald Wetzel was so taken by the warm humor and excellent description that he summed up the novel as one "of a superior quality," but nonetheless he was left somewhat confused and unconvinced by the mixture "of fantasy and reality." Although astounded that the work was by a librarian, Richard H. Dillon of the San Francisco *Chronicle* (26 July 1959) sensed a fusion of what for Wetzel was so disparate: "This is realism at its most theatrical and psychological." While yet others thought the book too symbolic for their tastes, an initialed review in the *Times-Picayune* of New Orleans (12 July 1959) discerned something authentic in "a fantasy which succeeds at its best in remaining tremulously earthbound"; and it concluded that the novel was "distinguished by a flair for language and an identification of landscape with human emotion which has in varied degree characterized the poetic novel in English, whether in Emily Bronte, or Thomas Hardy, or Virginia Woolf."

One of the most balanced reviews came from Sidney A. Williams in the Dallas *Times Herald* (3 May 1959). Trying to look at the novel in terms of what it was meant to be, he confined himself primarily to sympathetic but reasoned description of the book's content, saying finally that *The Butterfly Tree* responds rightly to the question of whether the main character finds the "meaning behind meaning" in searching for the tree: "It is an answer climaxing the suspense of the search, a search made breathless by the fascination of Mr. Bell's story and the intense poetic imagery of his style." Still, the most fitting review to conclude with is probably the initialed one in the Abilene (Texas) *Reporter-News* (26 April 1959). That critic discovered the novel's characters to be "very much of this earth" and pointed to the kind of volume in hand: "a book for leisurely reading, for the savoring of words and the lilt of cadences . . . which are felt rather than seen."

One sort of "review," doubtless common to many novels, was a regional scrutiny to try to find local people represented among the characters of *The Butterfly Tree*. It may be true that, as Henry James once said, a creative artist is someone on whom nothing is lost; yet, consciously or unconsciously, a writer of fiction also transmutes his material—including people—into new beings who may have multiple sources (creative imagination a major one) but who tend to be utterly themselves. According to Bell's memory, only Margaret Claverly among his main characters had a real-life prototype, and that prototype served marginally.

Winifred Duncan had performed successfully during the first quarter of the century with the famous American dancer, Isadora Duncan. She became so influenced by dance and the dancer that she changed her last name from Ward to Duncan, but her many interests and talents could not be satisfied by one medium. As one of a troupe entertaining servicemen during World War I, she found herself one night sitting alone on the darkened barracks steps of a camp in Georgia, for the first time really listening to the small insect voices that seemed to come from teeming little worlds within the big one. It was right then, she would tell friends later, that she became a naturalist, an interest which would last a lifetime and would lead her, for fieldwork, to establish a home in Fairhope sometime after World War II. At times she would make months-long visits to Mexico, and she published two "popular" science books: *Webs in the Wind* (1949) and *The Private Life of the Protozoa* (1950). To many she was a frank but scientific eccentric.

Bell's character Miss Claverly is also an eccentric naturalist, but there are differences. Duncan was fascinated by spiders, Claverly by butterflies; Duncan was partial to household cats, Claverly to household bloodhounds; Duncan made temporary trips to Mexico, Claverly a permanent one to New York. There is no hint of Duncan's early life in Claverly's, and apparently Duncan was not engaged in a legendary search like Claverly's for the butterfly tree. In spite of some general parallels, the two are different individuals—a fact inversely supported when, after Duncan read the novel, her only comment to Bell was that he had attributed some very dubious scientific speculation to her. In fictionality the speculation belonged to Miss Claverly, who either had grown into or simply was herself.

While the reviewing was taking place, gratifying letters were arriving from friends and strangers. Playwright and fiction writer James Leo Herlihy wrote from Key West to thank Bell for "a beautiful book—gentle, sad, humorous, lovely." Howard Harrington, manager of the Detroit Symphony Orchestra, sent word of his "joyful experience" with the novel and extended a standing invitation for Bell to be a guest at one of their concerts. More than a year after *The Butterfly Tree* was published, a letter came from new fellow Lippincott author Harper Lee, whose *To Kill a Mockingbird* was riding the best-seller lists and was only a few months away from winning the Pulitzer Prize. For quite some time, she said, she had been trying to get up enough nerve to write him. She singled out *The Butterfly Tree* from twenty-five years of reading novels and called it a masterpiece. Though his book did not go into a second printing, it was clearly making an impact on people who counted and who made themselves known.

Perhaps these insightful readers were reacting in large part to the timeless quality of the novel. For, while it can remind us incidentally of a happy time when passenger trains ran with multiple regularity, it has that timeless quality in abundance. It does not hinge on any war, social movement, political upheaval, or natural disaster. Even so, the writer and the writing came together during a certain time that may have a subtler relevance here than for other novels.

It has long been commonplace to speak of "the complacent fifties" or, after poet Robert Lowell's trenchant phrase, of "the tranquillized fifties"; but retrospect suggests that neither convenient tag encapsulates the decade. The period began with a three-year war (the Korean Conflict) which for the first time our government disconcertingly had no intention of winning though many lives were lost. After the rapid spread of communism in the 1940s, the Cold War was a global threat as convincing and palpable as the poised forces in divided Berlin, for by the time the hydrogen bomb superseded the atomic one in 1953, many people were building and stocking shelters at their private homes. With the end of 1954 Senator Joseph McCarthy's disturbing witch-hunt tactics regarding domestic communism petered out into wonder about senatorial immunity and, more important, heightened the nagging, unsettled questions about communism vs. capitalism. While the *Angst* and sense of absurdity peculiar to existentialism prevailed primarily for those intellectuals who had heard of it, much more common both North and South was the growing division about racial segregation and then about integration. To a large extent, underlying the decade's divided sense of self was a phenomenon seldom cited: the immense number of ex-servicemen and women from World War II who had just finished college on the G.I. Bill. The many who were the first of their families ever even to think of a higher education were now pulled contradictorily between a newer kind of life and the older one of family ties and ways, and the other family members often felt a converse tension. Added to this and epitomized by James Jones moving from locale to locale in a trailerhome while writing *From Here to Eternity* (1951) was a new and slowly uprooting mobility brought on by developed methods of travel and by increasing job transfers. When Russia's Sputnik I thrust through the atmosphere in October 1957 to become the first earth satellite, it resulted in a further shaking of an American sense that was the opposite of complacency, for the entire period was really one of ambivalent unease and uncertainty. The 1950s might better be called the decade of doubt.

In regard to this background, the development of Bell's central character Peter Abbott suggests what T. S. Eliot calls an objective correlative: a pattern of events or a situation which awakens in the reader a reverberating emotional response that the author desires to evoke without resorting to direct statement. In achieving this, Bell presents Peter as a fully rounded, individualized character that is also representative in a two-fold way. Peter is a sensitive, receptive person who accepts with reservation the legend of the butterfly tree from separate people who (except for the sharing twins Karl and Karen) are apparently unaware of the others' knowledge. As he grows to know these unusual, compelling characters and their belief, he demonstrates an uneasiness and uncertainty toward the legend and, in varying and lessening degrees, toward his new friends. After accompanying or following these believers on searches that prove futile, he arrives at true doubt only then to encounter the butterfly tree himself. For a brief while he is an absolute believer. But in ways that readers deserve to discover for themselves, Peter comes to wonder whether he has found *the* butterfly tree or simply *a* butterfly tree. He is again in profound doubt. It is significant, however, that he struggles to an acceptance of uncertainty, partly because he has no other choice.

Peter, then, experiences a personal pattern of doubt which reflects the universal and ever-present uncertainty that can be felt in any place at any time. That general representativeness is all the more convincing because of other timeless effects in the novel, for what transpires in Peter's Moss Bayou is so fundamentally simple (in spite of the nearly prodigal poetry of the telling) that it could have occurred almost at any point in the history of Fairhope or any similar conjunction of people and place. The other way Peter's experience is representative lies in the fact that Bell lived and Peter was created in the 1950s. The doubt of the real world (where people had no choice but to live with it) is distilled into the microcosmic world of nature, personality, and legend that is Moss Bayou.

Peter's representativeness may lead readers to wonder if the novel is related to classical mythology. After all, Bell has a long-standing interest in the subject and has published three successful books on it: the twice award-winning *Dictionary of Classical Mythology* (1982), *Place-Names in Classical Mythology* (1989), and *Women in Classical Mythology* (1991). It is true that in the novel Karl Heppler has a male beauty reminiscent of a Greek god or hero, and he suddenly and unexpectedly rescues Peter from difficulties a couple of times. Something oracular dwells in the linked names of, and the mystical encounters with, the befriending strangers who disappear after giving each main character (except Peter) glowing but vague instructions about the butterfly tree. However, if the oracle likeness holds in these instances, the voice of oracle for Peter is secondhand and has spoken differently to him. And there is the legend about the tree. But superior physical beauty, oracular speech, and legend can be met in other realms than classical mythology, and it is worth remembering that Bell himself is sure that no mythological or legendary parallels were intended.

Actually, other avenues of appreciation are more prominent in the novel: the plot based on the four seasons, the mature discovery of selfhood, the local and universal qualities of the main characters, the speech patterns, the thematic elusiveness of things (time, dreams, desire, seasons, loss, beauty, self), and of course the evocative and poetic style.

In spite of its timelessness, from a historical point of view the book is an imaginative construct out of the past. Like a reader looking back, the novel too makes use of important time-gone-by, but here the impelling past is not that of an oft-treated lost ante- or post-bellum way of life, nor is it that of an overstressed Southern decadence. It is not something merely to be recaptured. Rather, it is mostly a time-snagged but vitalizing part of the myriad present and what will follow—not loss so much as enduring, repetitive continuity. For Bell's readers as well as for his characters, this past is both something long gone as fact and something still possible—still promising—in the present and the future.

We readers may sense something unusual in the final product, as if the poetic evocation of people and place and temporality were that of a Thomas Wolfe who had discovered the marvels of the Eastern Shore while achieving a greater emotional and verbal control. Yet *The Butterfly Tree* is Bell's own unique rendering, and all an introduction like this one can do is to circle and point toward what is at the nestled center: like Bell's character Miss Billy, the novel creates its own timeless magic of a special locale that happens to be in Alabama. Ultimately it is a magic that each reader must and can discover for himself.

Acknowledgments

For kind and valuable help, I wish to thank Andrew G. Dacovich, James A. Damico, and Caldwell Delaney of Mobile, Joseph C. Mele and Robert M. Phillips of Fairhope, and especially Robert Bell himself, now of Davis, California.

Mobile, Alabama

PREFACE

The writing of *The Butterfly Tree* occasioned a great change in my life. Part of this change was physical, inasmuch as the novel was begun in Mobile but largely written in Fort Worth. This physical interruption brought about a kind of emotional alteration, and distance from the locale of the novel gave the writing a nostalgic intensity it otherwise would have lacked. The truth is that the novel would never have been written if I had not moved to Fort Worth. The genesis of the novel was a short story hastily written on my daily Greyhound commute between Fairhope and Mobile, after seeing, one morning, a swarm of butterflies on a bush on the Mobile Bay causeway. Later, I decided that I needed something larger than a short story to explore the possibilities I had opened. I then read a book on novel-writing, assigned each of my characters a manila folder (as the manual had suggested), and started to write during my lunch hour every day in a dusty little supply room in the basement of the Mobile Public Library, where I worked. This was about 1953.

This went well enough for a while, but the necessary spark had so far not been ignited. Then I fell in love, which event coincided with the resignation of my boss, who moved with his family to Fort Worth, and with my temporary assignment as head of the library. So the manila folders went on the shelf, while I went neurotic in an effort to run inexpertly a woefully underfunded institution and a not entirely reciprocal romance. A year went by, during which I was replaced as acting director and was free to accept a job offer from my former boss at the Fort Worth Public Library at the beginning of 1955.

Fort Worth was cold and lonely, and I still remember it that way, even though summers could bring temperatures well over 100 degrees and even though I eventually made many lifelong friends there. The love affair fitfully survived but finally was as cold as I felt the city to be. After the final gasp of my ill-fated liaison, my second autumn in the city, I pulled out the somewhat battered folders and with a strictly observed schedule of writing, weight-lifting, and moderating a Great Books discussion group at the library, I underwent the second part of my earlier-mentioned change.

As I said, this novel would never have been written had I not gone to Fort Worth. There my homesickness became almost palpable. My characters were virtually extensions of the landscapes I described so lovingly. The book, while operating on several levels of meaning, came to be most of all about a love affair with a place. This place, the eastern shore of Mobile Bay, was shown in all four seasons, each of them committed to a character in the novel. This celebration of place was not consciously imitative but certainly had antecedents in Alabama fiction, notably in such writers as Howell Vines and Julian Lee Rayford.

Had *The Butterfly Tree* never been published, I still would have experienced a vast satisfaction. Writing a novel, finishing a novel, was to me the greatest possible achievement. For a long time I was unable to write the final chapter. Perhaps there was an unwillingness to part with the characters who had come to be very real to me. Perhaps I could find no easy way to pull the threads together on the four parts of the story that was, after all, a single odyssey. One night, after weeks of inertia, I went to the Hi Hat Lounge in Fort Worth, took a back booth, and drank draft beer while I wrote the finale in one sitting. Not a single word of the last chapter was ever revised.

A vastly important part of the time and place of *The Butterfly Tree* was my association during those years with certain individuals who turned out to be necessary in the development and eventual fate of the book. I read almost the entire novel as it came through, chapter by chapter, to my artist friend, Lirl Treuter, who had a spiritual affinity with creatures great and small. Almost as an obbligato to my writing, she raised a real monarch butterfly from a chrysalis during this time. It tore its wing shortly after its emergence, and she delicately patched it with silk gauze and rubber cement. When it could fly again it would come at her call. I phoned the Fort Worth *Press* about this, and they ran a picture of her and the butterfly, as did several other papers across the country. Not surprisingly, she was born on St. Francis Day. I found her reactions and perceptions most valuable and followed several of her suggestions regarding tiny but important shades of meaning.

Two other friends turned out to be vital in a more direct way. Frank Self and Kenneth Kaiser read the manuscript and immediately insisted that I send it to Annie Laurie Williams, the famous literary agent, who came originally from Dennison, Texas, and was a friend of one of Frank's acquaintances from his native Terrell. Frank got permission from his friend to mention her name in a letter he sent to Miss Williams, who then wrote him that she would be happy to see the novel. Miss Williams and her husband, Maurice Crain, were enthusiastic about the book and soon interested Lynn Carrick of Lippincott, who shortly accepted it for publication. Carrick did not require too much editing, but he did insist that I cut about 30,000 words. I have forgotten all that was cut, and one day I want to reread the manuscript, which is held by the Mobile Public Library.

My inner world was thus changed, but a number of things happened to me after the publication. I had many letters, of course, mainly from friends all over the country. Two of my well-wishers were James Leo Herlihy (later known for *Midnight Cowboy*) and Harper Lee, whom I later met briefly when passing through Monroeville. I meanwhile had moved to San Francisco to take a job as executive secretary of the Book Club of California, an organization of bibliophiles. There, the novel opened a few doors for me in California's literary world. Among my friends were the historians Oscar Lewis and Richard Dillon (who had reviewed *The Butterfly Tree* for the San Francisco *Chronicle*) and the world-renowned printers, Jane and Robert Grabhorn (who long afterwards were the subject of my doctoral dissertation).

Two years later I moved back to the South and became co-owner of the Banquette Bookshop in New Orleans, and I lived off and on in Fairhope. One day I was home, and the man who was reading my meter knocked at the door. He asked me if I was the Robert Bell who wrote *The Butterfly Tree*, and I said yes and how did he know. He said, "I reviewed it for the New York *Herald Tribune*." He was Donald Wetzel, himself a novelist, who had moved to Fairhope to devote himself to writing. And, finally, only a few years ago I finally met Andy

Warhol, who designed the dust jacket to my book before he achieved everlasting importance. Lippincott had long before given me his original drawing used for the cover and four that were not used.

In the final chapter of *The Butterfly Tree*, I ask: "Where does one go from a butterfly tree?" Of course, that question was posed in a more or less universal way, the answer to be sought by each individual reader. As for myself, I suppose I am in a better position to answer that question now than I was in 1958. I finished a library degree at LSU and returned to San Francisco to earn a doctorate at the University of California, Berkeley. During the years it took to complete this I was a lecturer at the University of San Francisco and at Berkeley, and I was an assistant professor at the University of South Carolina. After completion of the degree I came to the University of California at Davis, where I have been ever since. I have compiled three dictionaries of classical mythology, all published by ABC-Clio of Santa Barbara, California, and Oxford, England. I have traveled to many countries, particularly to Greece, which I have visited about a dozen times. I wrote another novel, *Angels Forsake Us*, but it never made it to publication. At present I am working on still another one, *Letters to Jeffrey*, which I hope to complete after I retire in March of this year.

ROBERT BELL

Davis, California
February 1991

FOR HUB AND JESSIE BELL

Summer

1

THERE ARE four buses that leave Mobile daily for Moss Bayou.
No matter what time the trains get in from New Orleans or
Birmingham, you still have to wait around half the day for one
of these buses if you want to get to Moss Bayou. And a good
many people do, for Moss Bayou is a lovely, easygoing resort
town (though not as popular as it once, was), located as it is
where Magnolia River runs into the bay with worlds of giant
live oaks and sandy roads that wind forever under the trailing
Spanish moss.

There are pleasanter places to wait than in the Mobile bus
station, but you dare not leave, for the buses aren't too regular,
and if you miss one there is a long wait till the next one. Inside
the bus station you have to sit on the peeling leather seats,
watching the slow, dreary drift of people and listening to the
caterwauling of babies and the thock-thock of pinball machines.
Swamp girls sit reading comic books while they reach dreamily
into popcorn bags. Sailors in wilted white uniforms with dirty
seats mill around in pairs, looking halfheartedly at the girls or
poking among the magazines on the long racks opposite the
ticket windows.

The periodic calls on the loud-speaker seem to bespeak the
weariness, the half-dreamed crumbling eras of lost time, in the
wistful place names where people leave the bus by sand roads
—Theodore, Irvington, Hermits' Crossroads, St. Elmo, Grand Bay,
Kreola, Chunchula.

Time-dimmed names played with the edges of his memory,
and some of it came back; but it was long ago, even for twenty
years old. The remembered part was the part that was not

important, but things were usually like that. In this case the
unimportant was a memory of running in the shallow water
along a bleak and endless stretch of sand that sickle-curved
beneath a cliff, and with him were two other children, a boy and
a girl, both blond, both a couple of years older. That was all;
but they had, these children, run on forever, for there had been
no beginning to the memory nor an end. To him that was
what the mention of Moss Bayou always called up. Oh yes,
he had remembered her, too—the great-aunt, who was never
called anything at home but Miss Billy.

But now the immediacy of getting somewhere, leaving somewhere, being between times and things outcrowded the wisps
of remembering, and he looked back at the clock which had not
advanced but one click since the last time he looked.

"Bus for Mertz Station and Fowl River loading at end of
platform," the tired voice of the loud-speaker announced. A few
women in print dresses thrust magazines into tops of grocery
bags and nudged their way out the door. The pinball machines
rang bells and flashed lights but never stopped.

When finally the Moss Bayou bus was announced, it was
scarcely with relief that he went aboard. The bus driver was off
having coffee and had left the almost airtight bus sitting in
the hot sun, and with all the Saturday folk aboard he had to
stand.

He hung on the edge of the overhead luggage rack and leaned
against the end of a seat. Here in the bewildering anonymity
among the impersonal backs of heads he was fully conscious of
himself, since there was no one else he could know in this time
between times. He, Peter Abbott, had come here. It was summer,
his twentieth summer, and it was hotter than he could ever remember. His being here was improbable and the result of
many improbables, more than ever because it was true.

His reflection in the window was not altogether convincing,
because it, too, was something of a stranger among these other
strangers. Objectively, it was a nice image—the right height
and weight, nothing overdone. The face, which he couldn't see,
he knew was a pleasant face, but that's as far as he could go.

It was hard to be objective about something as close as one's face, which one shaved and washed every day. It was the one thing that couldn't be disguised fully, especially the eyes—brown eyes in this case. He felt to see if his hair was lying flat all over. It was black hair and close cut, but he knew that the part in the back always stuck up.

Heat-weighted time later the bus was leaving Bankhead Tunnel behind and crossing the causeway which led to the eastern shore. The bay at low tide looked thick and molten. He shifted his weight back and felt the heat breathe around him. There wasn't a dry stitch on him, and he could feel his under-shorts twisted in a wet rope around his loins. The long hot road with water on either side seemed to be cutting him off from the things he should—and possibly should not—be remembering. The room he had left there on the hill, for example, overlooking the night city of freight tracks and winking lights. There he had begun to know about love and most of all loneliness, for they were becoming for him somehow indistinguishable. Ann, who laughed at him with the eyes that looked deeper within him than he did himself and maybe even knew him a little better, had gone with him to the train, and they had stood there with the knowledge that they would probably never see each other again, at least not in the same way. Thoughts of her were out of place in this vast stretch of heat and water, for theirs had been a winter love—music together in the quiet room, lying on the bed looking out at the lonely lights.

The bus climbed a hill, and then the road turned south. More little villages with pretty names—Jackson's Oak, Daphne, Montrose, Sea Cliff, Fairhope. This might have been the end for roads. People will say that roads, like rivers, never really end, but they do. They end in places like Moss Bayou, simply because they have nowhere else to go. And that's when they can no longer be called roads. They have tailed off to sand paths (oh, yes, you could bring a car along them, but you wouldn't) where crape myrtle wilts in the sun, and old trees brood through beards of Spanish moss.

"You may sit here, young man," and he wasn't sure the voice

spoke to him. When he looked behind him, he saw a little woman who looked as if she didn't quite belong with the other people on the bus. She was piled up in the seat with all sorts of <u>para-phernalia</u> and had been taking two seats instead of one, apparently just becoming aware that several persons were standing.

"Can't bear to see anyone uncomfortable," she said. "Sit here." Since she had almost commanded him, he didn't try to refuse. Stooping and edging his way, he moved onto the <u>laden</u> seat where there was a black flat case which rattled glassily when he moved it. "Careful, dear—slides." And there was a butterfly net propped against the seat. Rather, it passed for one. It was made out of a clothes hanger and cheesecloth. Besides these, there were several bundles and odds and ends that looked as if they had been salvaged from a junk yard.

She was unique—old, but old in a curious and wistful sense, not like the old people he had met before. Her hair was a curious straw color, and she had it cut to hang straight down all around with bangs across the front. She was wearing blue <u>serge</u> slacks, a blue satin pajama top, and a string of <u>lusterless</u> imitation pearls, as well as several bracelets. She was eating a banana caramel, and she offered him one. "Wonderful things," she said when he refused.

"Where are you going?" she asked.

"Moss Bayou," he answered.

"So am I, but that isn't strange since I live there. Do you?"

"No, I am going to be there awhile, though. I guess you can say I live there."

"Oh? Have you been there before?"

"Once," he started to say, and in an instant the blond children splashed through the shallows again, and as suddenly stopped. He answered aloud, "No—never."

"Well, it's a rare and beautiful place. If a person is still capable of being changed, it will change him; if he cannot be, it will make him more definitely what he is."

"How?" He wondered for a second which kind of person he was, but he knew as suddenly that there was really no way of knowing.

"How? My dear, who can tell? It depends on what is supposed to turn out for one, I suppose. In fact, I know this is the case. Except that the place is a sort of catalytic agent; it brings about the reaction sooner than most places."

"You said slides. Slides of what?"

"Life, my dear, life stripped down close to its beginnings. Even this life has been altered somewhat in these surroundings, hastened to its limits of destiny, plus its genetic potentialities, of course." She scratched under an armpit and looked closely at him again. "Where is your home, then?"

"Birmingham—" he said, leaving the word suspended.

"Hmm." She popped another caramel into her mouth and lapsed into silence as the bus hurtled between oaks and pines across a cement bridge.

He really didn't live anywhere, he remembered, for there wasn't even any longer his secret room which overlooked the blinking city at night. Where he was going wasn't even a part of memory, and as for those who would be waiting for him or missing him, well that was rather vague, too.

He couldn't think that Aunt Martha in Birmingham would be missing him. She would clean up the house as usual and take an afternoon nap. Afterwards, she would sit on the screened porch with Uncle Bob and talk about the grocery store which they ran. Since it was Saturday they would probably listen to the Grand Ol' Opry and then go to bed. His being there or not being there would make little difference.

It had, as a matter of fact, been on their suggestion that he had decided to come to Moss Bayou to live indefinitely until he could finish school. He could, they had said, live cheaper in a small town, and the money he had saved from working since high school plus his mother's insurance money would go further. Besides, Miss Billy, the great-aunt, had for many years offered to let him live with her—ever since his mother's death when he was eight. But Aunt Martha had held out for letting him finish grammar school and high school where he had started, and he would always associate a certain statement with her: "Well, it's the least we can do for Madge, poor thing."

So now this great-aunt was the immediate person in his life. She had answered Aunt Martha's proposal immediately, renewing the invitation. She lived alone and would like, she said, to have someone else there. Stories moved around about her among the other relatives that she was strange and funny— funny in an unflattering sense, but her letters were always cheerful and quite normal, always two pages on both sides.

He had himself received one of these letters from her. It was gracious and full of the things he would find to do in Moss Bayou and the things they would do together. He reread the letter in the rattling bus, sighed, and returned it to his hip pocket. In many respects he dreaded this unknown storybook character and instinctively knew she would try to baby him. Old ladies always did.

The road was all sand and trees, speckled shade of trees. Giant oaks lined it on both sides, and gullies plunged away into the thick tangle of vines and woods. You couldn't see the water to your right, but there was a water-sense about the road. The pines thinned out that way, and the sun seemed concentrated in liquid shadows against the western horizon. Yet it was still heavy afternoon. To the left, old houses leaned into the woods, ancient houses secure against time, weary of time, concealing strange forgotten secrets behind their peeling shutters and flaking paint.

Suddenly the bus was in Moss Bayou, in a little one-room bus station. When he got off the bus, all he saw was a long street bordered on each side by white stucco buildings, a few cars parked in front of them, with windows reflecting the sun. Heat danced crazily above the paving, and the dusty palms on the edge of the sidewalks dangled wilted fronds over the curbing. There were people on the street since it was Saturday, especially in front of the movie house, where dozens of barefoot young'uns waited for the place to open. He wasn't quite certain where to go (the letter had not been altogether clear), and he stood there a moment with his suitcases resting on his feet.

The first sight of that town raked the thin scab from his memory, and it was a feeling of sadness that the three children splashing in the water had finally stopped and would run no more. The long street moved with people and rippling shadows of things, busy things, in the heat. If one stood there and sought a way to go, why not follow the street; there was nothing else to follow and it must have an end.

So he followed the street, casting a small shadow, for the sun seemed selfish even with that little shade. Down by the pump a child splashed water over himself and over the sidewalk, where it dried quickly. Past the post office, where some old men sat by the door spitting tobacco juice into an azalea bush, questioning the processes that make weather hot and time deceptively motionless, yet had made them old. It didn't take the town long to run out, the store buildings, at least, and then there were houses again, long comfortable-looking houses that managed to look old and cool in spite of the sun-drifted heaviness of things. White houses looking final and content with histories. Long galleries with trailing tropical plants and lost perspectives of unsunned rooms and disappearing staircases. Somewhere after a turn down the street he saw a glimmer of water, gold-flaked through the trees; the frond-dragging palms bent with the curve of the road which heat-danced ahead of him, charging the sky with its electrical glare.

Another street crossed a block or so above the bay, and someone had thought to put a street sign, a little concrete post, Baycliff Road. This was it, then, the end for roads in Moss Bayou, not-quite-forgotten place, not-quite-remembered road. He turned onto an avenue of magnolias and old heavy houses brooding a thousand mysteries, not-telling houses almost hidden. This street curved, too, following the unseen line of the cliff which hung over the bay, winding with the shore line, gradual, sinuous like the curve of beach which it paralleled. This then was the place where all his memories from now would start, where another summer would be rolled away with the other late ones which were becoming indistinct.

He walked now freely, easily, for the road, the long-imagined, not-quite-remembered road, ran through the tangle of trees as if it were tunneled there. The old houses angled away from the

road and were part of the road. Adrift in the treetops, the afternoon shimmered suffocatingly; locusts and honeybees strummed
the silence, increasing the depthlessness of it. Everything was
suspended like the noiseless count of years that crumbles old
houses to ruin.

A breeze unsettled the tree-caught afternoon, shifting the day
to new meanings. Then by a simple intuition Peter knew he had
arrived. There was suddenly another old house, looking tranquilly
toward the bay, but it was an old house that had something a
little droll about it: the chimney had settled at a rakish angle,
and some of the shingles were loose on the roof. A front shutter
dangled like a broken wing, and the ragweed and sand spurs
had devoured the front lawn. A few bricks were still left to form
what had perhaps been a walk, and they were strewn beneath
a hunchbacked trellis up to a set of sagging steps and a long
gallery that elbowed around the house.

On the gallery a lady sat, fanning herself against the afternoon heat and watching the occasional life that slipped by
under the summer oaks. At last, here was the end of the road,
the final perspective that had been deepening and coloring with
the hours. He sighed half-regretfully as he considered what he
must surrender. All the subtle passing of his life had at this
moment assumed a tangibility for him; the nothing that had
ever happened to him became a very important nothing, and
all at once he didn't want to change it. He walked slowly up to
the steps.

"Peter? As I live and breathe, I believe I conjured you up.
I was sitting here with my eyes closed, and the next minute you
were here in my messy front yard. Mercy, put your things down
and sit here." She patted him and rocked back into a screenless
window. "Eulacie, bring something coolish. He's here. Now don't
try to talk, dear; you must be a sight more than tired. That trip
could kill a person. I vowed when we buried Papa I would
just sit tight and let that be my last trip to Birmingham. My,
you've certainly tripled in size. I wouldn't have known you
without the pictures Martha sent me, and, of course, I was
expecting you. Lord, I would have been embarrassed if you had

turned out to be the paper boy—although, I'm not sure he comes any **more.**"

At that moment, an enormous Negro woman erupted from the porch door, half-carrying half-nudging a tray. "Lord, honey, you must be Peter I hear so much about. You don't carry the family resemblance none, but I always say it must wear thin. Gets me when the bastards in the families gets more credit for family resemblance than the real flesh-and-blood."

"Eulacie, do we still get the *Press-Register?*"

"Now, how'm I to know? Might not after the way I holler at the boy for throwin' them on the porch roof."

"Peter, have some—what is it, Eulacie? Child, you haven't said two words, but I guess you are tired. I would have been at the bus station, of course, but you just can't be sure about these buses. We were planning to meet the one after this; it's cooler then." She flipped open the fan and started fanning herself again.

Peter drew a breath and took a glass that Eulacie had poked at him. Eulacie continued to talk.

"I was in Birmin'ham summer before last. My sister was havin her organs removed—forget what they call 'em. We went to the Ben Hur on Fourth Avenue—that's a colored club. Use to be call the Bloody Bucket when the white folks had it. Some lady cut up her husband there one night, and they call it that in her honor."

"Peter, do you remember Moss Bayou?" This time Miss Billy waited.

"Well—"

"Lord, he'll love it. Like Mama say, you can't get it out of your blood, like certain diseases I could mention."

"No, I don't remember much that far back. I do remember swimming in the bay, and—"

"And?"

"And you, a little."

"My, ain't that somethin'." Eulacie was sitting on the porch railing, which swayed dangerously above a ragged petunia bed.

"Well, you were so little. I think it is amazing that you

remember anything at all. Your mother was so pretty then. She
wore those <u>knickerbockers</u> and a sun helmet, and your father
came over from <u>Pascagoula</u> two or three week-ends."

"I don't guess we'll ever hear from him again." Peter felt that
he was mature enough at last to be objective about something
that hadn't really mattered for a very long time.

"No, when birds flies, they flies." Eulacie apparently knew
that Peter's father had deserted him and his mother after that
long-ago summer and had never been seen again.

"Peter, I think you probably want to get your clothes off
and maybe go to the bathroom. I still say that is a long trip.
Eulacie, show him up. I'm going to bring some of those nice
dahlias for the supper table."

Eulacie creaked off the railing and flapped across the porch
in her run-down-at-the-heel slippers. Peter followed her, a little
dazed at his strange welcome.

Eulacie hummed throatily to herself and rattled the glass on
the china cabinet as she crossed to the foot of the stair.

"Peter, honey, you don't need much imagination to see why
I have trouble makin' them stairs, so if you'll just go up into
the room on your right, you are home, and I'll let you know
when supper is ready. Toilet cross the hall, and anything else
you just yell for." She lumbered into the kitchen.

It was a curious lost feeling to enter the door of a room that
would soon be home. It might have been the room where he
slept those gone years ago. Outside the window the afternoon
still hung at its height, silhouetting inside things with its
brightness. He walked to the window and saw that the room
overlooked the bay through tall pine tops. Away off, on the
Mobile side, smoke spiraled to the sky, lending remoteness.

Fatigue fell on him like weights, and he went and lay backward across the bed, watching an outside tree shadow tremble
without any wind across the bookcase. His suitcases were in a
heap on the floor, and he let his shoes fall one at a time beside
the bed. Time and heat and soft voices of gentle ladies mingled
with the mellow chuckle of Negro voices. Thin dusty stillness
slanted through a knothole and danced on the bed, and nothing

mattered all at once, for this was the end of a road for a time, and for-a-time took on the dimensions of forever.

Downstairs, Eulacie's singing voice rolled the silences apart in a tragic canebrake song, filling all the secret corners of the house, suspended in the antique interior. He came awake, and it was late dusk. The singing shifted and lifted high into a colored honky-tonk song, shattering the emulsifying quiet and speaking of immediate unimportant things. Ending in a wail, the voice seemed to be calling him.

"Pe-e-ter, supper ready." Numbed, aching, he groaned fully awake and sat up. "Peter, come you on now. Supper ain't goin' to wait."

"Peter," a voice was at the door. "Dear, you can come back in a little while. You need to eat now." It was Miss Billy, sounding soft and far off.

He came out, putting his shirt tail in. Miss Billy had apparently been asleep, too, for she was a little dreamy and not so talkative. They floated, each still somewhere else with dreams, into the bright kitchen, which halfway opened on to the gallery. A long unpainted table with benches sat on the screened gallery looking out over a garden.

"Lord, can't we sleep. I had to hit Miss Emmajean twice to get her shut up. Just can't make the day without a little sleep." Eulacie rubbed her big back and moved to bring something else from the stove to the table. Obviously she had been up for some time, for the table was spread with a white cloth, and a big bouquet of dahlias sprayed out over the china.

"My best china, dear; I believe in using what you have while you have it. My cousin in Demopolis had a whole closet of the most divine china, and one day for no reason the whole thing collapsed and broke every dish. She hadn't even used most of it. Imagine!"

"Lord sent His judgement." Eulacie busied herself with the food and then sat at the table with them.

"Why, I use them and use them, and if I break anything, I give the pieces to little Miss Emmajean and she goes on using them, playing house underneath the magnolia."

"Emmajean your little girl?" Peter asked Eulacie.

"*Miss* Emmajean," Eulacie corrected. "Her first name Miss, and Emmajean her middle name. Miss Emmajean the last thing I got around to call my own."

They ate, and the dusk deepened to night, night opening the day-sleeping flowers and bruising their perfume over the gallery and through the house. Scent of magnolia shrubs and four-o'clocks blended with katydid noises. Eulacie was telling Peter about Miss Emmajean, for it was her favorite story.

"That told, that told. Wide-eyed gal shake that wide-eyed thing, and he gone. Fsst! After he gone, that Smoky, nothin' matter much. I went off to the Tensaw to Mama's to have Miss Emmajean. Used to walk in the cool along by the water. Got to think like the water, become deep and clear like the old river, with the snake-doctors skitterin' over it." Her big black hands moved across the dahlia tops. "A day come, walkin' slow along the bank, laid down under a thick-top tree and talk with Jesus; talk on till Miss Emmajean interrupt the conversation. Right on the Tensaw."

Miss Billy scraped back her chair and stood up, pulling her blouse down at the waist. "Come, Peter, we'll go for a walk and then you can go to bed for good. You must be tired."

"He'll last," Eulacie huffed, interrupted in the middle of her favorite narrative. "He'll last; too young to wear down for long." She reached into the sugar bowl and popped a lump into her mouth.

"Eulacie, one of these days you are going to eat so much sugar you'll crash right down through the floor. The termites have already eaten all there is to eat, and it won't take much more. A lady in Mobile did, you know," she turned to Peter, "and they have called her house Termite Hall ever since."

"Humph, ain't goin' to start that diet stuff. One of my girl friends left off bread and desserts and lost, lost—got all the way down to a hunderd and ninety pound. Not for me, unh unh."

"Peter, I hope you like the front room. I think it is the nicest one in the house, the way it overlooks the bay. I would have moved into it myself except that I like the garden window, and," Miss Billy's voice strayed dreamily, absently, "I'm not sure she would come to any other window."

"Who?" Peter was suddenly interested.

The room throbbed for a moment with the night-singing voices of the garden. Somewhere on the night air someone practiced on a flute, distant, Pan-like music, like a nagging sadness. Peter was aware that Eulacie hurried to change the subject.

"Paper say heat wave comin' this way. Better be glad you got that bay-front room. Mama always say if she have that room she never leave it."

"Well, come along, then, Peter." Miss Billy led the way down the back steps and around the house.

The moon was up as they turned onto the street, and it rose above the pines and made cut-glass of their needles. The old houses were now more mysterious than ever, drawing the dark trees and trailing vines into their alchemy of forever. From somewhere the mysterious music stole wistfully out on to the street, and muffled voices floated across the lawns. Night was a magic time, for the old houses seemed to resemble more fully what they had once been, alive with lights, with people whirling in the large rooms. Barbecues and resort parties. Here a light, a voice, a hint of music called back the decades, and the houses bloomed on the summer evening like the flowers that open by night and lie sleeping during the heavy hot afternoons.

Then they left the houses behind when the road swung out in a curve above the bay, where the cliff began to slope gradually until it would eventually run into the Magnolia River. They crossed a wooden bridge, and their footsteps fell in solemn echoes into the great depth of the gully.

"Gives me the all-overs to cross this bridge. Someday it is going to collapse in a good big rain, and I'll probably be on it. You couldn't hire me to cross it if there wasn't a rail. Height is the only thing I'm really afraid of."

"Look at the fireflies, Miss Billy." Peter stopped midway of the bridge and watched as thousands of fireflies drifted from the kudzu thicket below and put out their lights halfway up. They looked like bubbles rising in a black lake. Miss Billy stopped and watched silently.

"They are the souls of dead sailors rising from the sea."

He laughed, but there was something beautiful in the idea, and he turned toward her. She wasn't smiling, and the moon cut out the hint of humor as she stood part silhouette, part shadow, on the bridge.

They turned and walked back as a car rumbled over the bridge and whispered down the road. When they arrived back home, Eulacie had apparently gone to bed, and there was a single light burning on the gallery. The garden perfumed the whole area, and the night was also kinder to the house. In the dark the little imperfections didn't show up, and the lighted gallery gave it a shadowy dignity that ignored the ragged lawn and the scattered bricks.

They entered the house, and Peter noticed that Miss Billy locked none of the doors. They climbed the stairs, saying nothing, for much had been said. When they stopped at the top of the stair, Miss Billy turned to him slightly, self-consciously. "Good night, Peter. I hope you'll be really happy here." She turned toward the end of the hall.

"Miss Billy." She half-turned. "*Who* might not come to another window?"

She frowned for a minute, then laughed. "Oh, I don't know. A bird, perhaps. A butterfly. The garden is full of them. And sometimes, a squirrel—" A clock chimed downstairs. "Good night." And she was gone, leaving him alone before the door.

After exploring the drawers and closets, he undressed in the middle of the room, stepping out of his clothes swiftly and self-consciously, even though he was more alone than he had ever been.

The light from the street came subtly in when he had turned off the light; the outside light felt its way in and lessened the impenetrability of the vast unknown night. Here at last was all the unknown he had feared and never known to fear. He could not know what was on the next street, in the next house.

The few days before when he had left Birmingham, he had watched the familiar frieze of a world he knew fade slowly past the train window—lamp posts, street corners, and drugstores, until they snagged behind on the things which distance would dim and time would obscure. Then, Miss Billy, somehow stranger, somehow not, downstairs speaking of something ephemeral like butterflies or birds outside her window but not really meaning what she said. And here are the lights to sneak in after the inside is turned off, but lights are friendly things. It is the dark that is unfriendly and bumps leaves and shadows along the window-panes to frighten those inside. Some of those inside. Others— well, others—imagine strange things for the shadows and learn to watch for them and wait for them when they don't come.

A boat horn out on the bay sobbed throatily in the stillness, and a distant dog told its troubles to the moon. The house was not asleep but was drowsy, doors seeming to ease shut and glass clinking distantly. Full night whispered finally, where white-limbed and exhausted he slept.

2

DOWNSTAIRS NOISES creaked along the walls and up the stairs bringing breakfast smells and old-house smells. Negro singing sifted with the morning along the polished floors and reflected off the shiny furniture. Peter opened his eyes when someone whispered. "Peter, it's tomorrow. Come along, dear."

Miss Billy looked through the half-opened door, dressed as she had been yesterday in her black silk dress. He rolled over when she opened the door, realizing suddenly that he had kicked the sheet down and was lying nude, but she had closed the door by the time he recovered the sheet. He got up then and tried to stretch away the soreness from the long trip and the long sleep. Morning blew cool from the bay, fluttering the curtains and lifting the crocheted scarf on the dresser.

Early morning was the time for him when his spirits were at lowest ebb. Homesickness came then, homesickness for a place that had scarcely been his home. Anxieties and unguessed troubles came, tumbling into the night-emptied cells of consciousness. It was necessary that he repair before a mirror the damages that the night had done and eat breakfast before he tried to look at the world.

"Mama she say love and time two diseases to eat up your heart. She say get shed of one and there's still the other one. Like Smoky. Got shed of Smoky, of love, but there was time along that river, time you could hear and touch with your finger-tips. Time countin' down on the current, takin' part of your life with it when it turned the bend."

They ate on the gallery again, and morning lay in the back yard and at the edge of the garden. "In Moss Bayou," Miss Billy had said, "nearly everybody eats on the gallery." The back gallery was in reality another room. Most of summer living was done there; sleeping, too, in the smaller houses. The refrigerator stood at the lower end. The unpainted table, flanked by two wooden benches, was old and velvet shiny.

Back of the porch a tremendous magnolia rose, sweeping skyward in graceful arches, spreading its ancient limbs over the back gallery. Then to the left, the garden started past a row of hedges. From where Peter sat, all he could see of the garden was a clump of azalea and a low-growing palmetto.

"And have you seen Smoky again?" he asked, trying to remember if she had told them that the night before.

Eulacie stopped, her fork halfway to her mouth. "Seen him! Lord, honey, seen him won't touch it. It's the don't-seen-him that gets me. You know how you don't see the devil but know he around somewhere. Well, that's Smoky. People tell me—and they always will, given half a chance—there's Sister Fite,

Wonderdean Hughes, and Birdie Tatum—tell me they seen him close as I see you, last month on Squall Street. Yet I don't see him."

"Maybe he will come back."

Eulacie looked out the screen and away, maybe all the way to the river, and said not to them: "Maybe."

Peter thought, sipping his coffee slowly, how much already he knew about Miss Billy and Eulacie, both still unmet this time the day before. Now they had permitted him into certain mysterious and meaningful edges of their lives. And he wondered, after the reference to the window visitor the night before, how much further he would be permitted.

There was a remotely tragic look about Miss Billy, as though she had lost something and wouldn't know when she found it, if she found it. Her eyes were that pale lavender color that made you think of crushed sweet peas. There was neither youth nor extreme age about her face, although she was—and you knew it —old. It was just that time had neglected to make the furrows deep; her gentleness was somehow too soft, perhaps, to remind time. It was an odd sort of gentleness, too, for Miss Billy pried. Yes, and into all sorts of people's business. He found this out from the way she and Eulacie sat in the kitchen smacking over delicacies of village small talk.

Miss Billy would sit on her wide magnolia-shaded gallery and keep time with the coming and going of life about her with her slowly moving fan. Miss Billy could tell you about things —births, deaths, adulteries, and even what people thought about in Moss Bayou. Sometimes she was gone from her afternoon rocker, and then you knew she was either serving tea in the high old parlor and whispering dark secret things to Mrs. Clara Foster, Miss Bubs Whitten, and Miss Alta Holt (for they were always the same), or she was picking her way uptown under an umbrella that had once been red-colored silk.

Uptown (there was no contrasting downtown) she would keep an eye peeled for anything that looked suspiciously different from last time. Finding nothing, she would make her way across the street and enjoy a chat with Miss Essie Banks, the postmistress, who remembered every letter and card sent and received in the last three decades. She could recognize anyone in Moss Bayou by his or her handwriting. She would study it through half-lidded eyes, fat wise old eyes with caked powder on the lids, and in a few minutes she would wheeze: "Yep, that's the little old Phillips girl, got knocked up by that Camp Blanding soldier three years ago come March." Miss Billy would cluck admiringly and say, "Lord, Essie, if you don't beat all!"

But this part of Miss Billy was not significant enough to change the initial impression Peter had had of her. In fact, it took several days for him to understand that she had a life beyond the big house and its garden. And in these days he found that all impressions in Moss Bayou were not sudden things but were gradual, emerging things which even then could not be thought final.

3

ONE AFTERNOON a few weeks after he arrived, Peter lay in a hammock in the back yard under the scuppernong arbor half-heartedly trying to read one of the mildewed volumes from the upstairs bookcase. The old plates were speckled with rusty-looking spots as he leafed through, trying to make up his mind to go to the beach; but he knew the picnickers would be over from the other side of the bay. He was, after the first novelty of arrival had worn off, beginning to admit a little boredom.

The summer dripped around him, into him, and stayed all ambition. Now the nights overlooking the city were far away like the pinpoints of light he had once watched from the window. The bay fascinated him, and he dimly recognized that it would be a part of him forever, just as the now-indistinct vision of the splashing children had always played in his memory.

The drone of bees and grass things snapped the taut string of remembering, and he let the book fall on the grass. At first he was almost unaware of voices coming from the garden beyond the arbor, but when they came closer, he couldn't help listening. Miss Billy's voice he recognized immediately; the other was a child's voice. It was little Miss Emmajean from the servant house at the rear of the yard.

He had often seen Miss Emmajean playing house beneath the chinaberry tree at the side of the house. She was a fat sassy-looking little girl, but she almost never bothered anybody and, besides being mean to her dolls, she might have been a very nice little girl. He often heard her droning away in the morning, scolding the teddy bear for not sitting straight. Sometimes she threw chinaberries at the jays, who screamed "Thief" at her as they flew away.

Miss Billy had more than once expressed an opinion that Miss Emmajean picked her flowers and ate them during her doll dinners, but there was nothing to prove it. As for Peter, Miss Emmajean steered a wide path around him, and so far had never been close to him. ("Wild thing born in the woods, can't expect nothin' but wild. Candy'll tame her, though," Eulacie said every time Miss Emmajean beat a retreat at Peter's approach.)

He couldn't hear what Miss Emmajean was saying, and actually, he remembered, he had never heard her say words. She mumbled in a singsong voice and was in a way another one of the garden noises. Peter could hear the soft sound of weeds being pulled.

"Dear, I suppose you want a story, but the stories I know are all old stories, and you need young stories—stories about birds, and bears, and butterflies."

There was a long silence, while hummingbirds whirred on soft wings about the garden. And then Miss Emmajean's voice moved insistently again into the silence, and Miss Billy's answered.

"Well, honey, I know one story, and then you must run

and play with your dolls. It's a very short story, and I had forgotten I knew it."

Perhaps it was the hedge softening her voice, but it seemed to Peter that an unusual quality had crept into it. As if she were talking to herself. It was a story about a king whose daughter had fallen in love with a poor young man, who used to visit her in the palace garden. Little by little the king came to understand his daughter's behavior, and he spied on them one night and realized that he must do something about it. So he declared war on a peaceful little kingdom to the south and sent the young man away. The young man managed to slip past the guards one last time and see the princess. This night he gave her a golden locket that he had done without food to purchase, and then he left the garden for the last time. Miss Billy stopped and told Miss Emmajean to go play.

There was a pause, and Miss Emmajean's voice rose in a questioning grunt. Peter could certainly see why there should be a question.

"What happened then? Why, nothing. The princess lived happily ever after."

Another mumble high and breathless.

"Who? Oh, the man?" and Miss Billy's voice was as casual as if she were merely remarking on the weather. "Oh, he was killed, of course. His head chopped off. Almost everyone got killed in wars then."

Peter heard Miss Emmajean gasp, and then it sounded as if she had wandered off, talking to herself in bewilderment. He was a little bewildered, too, as he lay listening to Miss Billy snapping off little twigs and humming to herself. He went to sleep after a while, for there was nothing else to do, and he felt a little sad that Miss Billy didn't know any stories but that one.

That night Miss Billy went to a meeting of the Theosophical Society, leaving him to go to a movie, which he sometimes did since the theatre was air-conditioned. After she was gone he sat in the kitchen with Eulacie while she washed the dishes.

"Unh, unh, no more'n get some washed up, other'ns ready."

"Eulacie," he paused, turning his head to the side.

"Well, spit it out, and don't chew it." She broke a cup and cursed.

"I heard Miss Billy tell Miss Emmajean a story today. I wasn't supposed to be listening, and—"

"And it had a man that went off to the war and got killed? Lord, she been tellin' Miss Emmajean that story for four years. Sometimes it's the Revolutionary War, sometimes the Civil War, and just any old war she happen to have handy. I'm goin' to have to beat Miss Emmajean's butt she don't stop pesterin' Miss Billy."

"But why does she always tell the same story? And why does Miss Emmajean ask her, if she knows it will be the same?"

"Honey, you askin' questions Eulacie don't know the half of. That Miss Emmajean just have to be in the way, and she don't care how. Used to make her have fits to hear about that man gettin' his head chopped off. Now the bloodthirsty little bitch, seem like she love to hear it."

"But Miss Billy?"

"Unh, unh. That ain't my business to know—although—" she loitered on a delicious thought with the same look she always had when she and Miss Billy talked about other people. "Although, business or not, I just seems to know in spite of myself."

"Well, what do you know?" Peter had to find out.

"I know lots of things, but I gets paid to keep my nose on my face, black as it is." She swore as she slopped dishwater over the floor.

"Well, I guess I know when I'm getting nowhere." Peter shoved his chair back and started to leave, but Eulacie stopped him.

"Peter, if you value your life, you goin' to your mouth shut. You one of the family, and besides I couldn't let you walk out without tellin' you if my life depended on it." She scratched her behind and sat down opposite him. "I has a good friend in Houstonville up the road who puts conjures on people, and if you ever breathe—I said breathe—what I am on the point of tellin' you, I'll have her put a grisgris on you that would give a whole army liver trouble."

"I promise," he said impatiently.

"Well, it all goes back. Miss Billy was havin' a spell of sickness, some kind of fever, and that was some time ago just after I come back from the Tensaw when I have Miss Emmajean. I used to wait on Miss Billy hand and foot, and some of the time she was in a coma (brought on I don't doubt by some of that poison the doctor feed her at eight dollars the bottle). One day as I was puttin' away some linens in her room she started talkin', and when I realize she wasn't talkin' to me, my kinky hair stand straight as a board. She had someone else right outside the window, and you know her room is on the second floor where the gallery roof juts out over the garden. She was tellin' somethin' to come closer, and if I thought it was a bird or squirrel I was sadly mistaken, since birds don't wear blue sweaters. She kept sayin' somethin' about it bein' warm for that blue sweater. Well, boy, I was by that time anything but warm, and I started callin' her name to pull her out of this trance. But, honey, it wasn't no trance. I seen people all my life go in and out trances—alcohol, pneumonia, dope, and love trances—and this was either a new kind of trance or just a plain old ghost. She answer right up and say, 'Eulacie, tell her to come in so I can ask her about time.' I say, 'Miss Billy, you better lay off that blue medicine for a spell and switch to the pink,' and I shut the window. She look real hurt then and have me open it, but whatever there on the roof done gone. She say in this creepy voice, 'Eulacie, do you reckon she'll come back tomorrow?' I finish peein' in my pants and say I reckon so." Eulacie looked over her shoulder. "Guess I ought to be used to it by now."

"But that was only because she was ill. Anybody might see things."

"Honey, she been seein' this little girl ever since, and funny thing, when I mention it to her the next day, she act like she don't know what I'm talkin' about. So I just keep quiet ever since, but she know I know and I hear her talkin' to her all odd hours of the day. Little girl won't come in but hang around that garden. I make Miss Emmajean play on the other side of the house."

"But what does that have to do with the story about the princess?" Peter tried to look at the whole thing as a silly invention of Eulacie's.

"She say the little girl tell her that story. Least that what Miss Emmajean say. Always Miss Billy tell Miss Emmajean she hear a little girl in a blue sweater say this and that. Miss Emmajean dyin' to meet this little girl to play with, but when she do, I'm just packin' and takin' off for Mama's house on the Tensaw."

"Oh, it's all fantastic. Miss Billy is just teasing Miss Emmajean. Nobody sees ghosts any more."

"Honey, it takes things and conditions to see them. When winter creeps into your life and the wind blows a little somethin' sad, a little somethin' happy. When the shadows lays across your dreams like late afternoon, then there's a lot more than imagination to reckon with. Everything is real and you wish it wasn't. I better go see if Miss Emmajean ain't set the house on fire. And remember, this is my and your and Miss Billy's ghost. I believe sometimes I see it, and you will, too, when you been here awhile. These old houses full of them. I tell Mama they squat on the rafters and gossip about us after dark. Mama she say she wouldn't be surprise."

Eulacie went out like a big tide and left the room empty. It could be true that these old houses harbored ghosts, for it was hard to believe the present owners could fill them as they deserved to be filled, but a little girl in a blue sweater who came on the rooftop and talked to Miss Billy . . . Then the relatives were right; she was funny.

Gravel splattered before his shoes on the road, night phosphorescing parts of things. The moon was late, and the pines were restless, having nothing to silhouette against. Something, not wind, breathed among them, trembling the wisteria which fell like ghost hair from tall trees. Something ran its fingers over the spine of things, sifting unrest in rested things—old houses that had settled long ago, big oaks that had shaded early explorers. Distant thunder rolled barrels across the horizon and struck the edge of the world with a dull rose flash.

No one else moved on the road. No one else was out to destroy the emptiness and silence. Peter glanced at the houses sitting along the bay front waiting for whatever should come, unmoving, imperturbable.

The little movie house was alive, and its life rubbed his pulse awake again. The cheap film he had seen before, but he welcomed it, since the screen faces were more familiar than the people about him, more familiar actually than Miss Billy and Eulacie. He sank gratefully into oblivion for two hours and was sorry when the lights came on at the end and all the people filed out.

Outside, the rain came as only a tropical rain can fall. It lapped at the gutter edge and beat like voodoo tomtoms on the marquee. The late moviegoers huddled under the marquee till they could make a dash for their cars or were picked up. Finally he was left alone, and the rain showed no sign of letting up.

Up the street a café sign swam out of the deluge, and he made his way along store fronts till he reached it.

4

THE CAFÉ was called the Blue Moon, and he noticed that the "n" was upside down. Inside, he was immediately aware that the Blue Moon was like all the rest of Moss Bayou, old, a little sinister, unapologetically shabby. There was a smell of rusty ice water in the place, and a potted palm nodded beneath the old-fashioned four-armed electric fan.

There were very few people in the Blue Moon this time of night—a barefooted old man who sipped a bottled drink with a straw, a thin girl who sat and waved the rain-driven flies from a pastry she was eating, and a few others who had come in to escape the rain.

The proprietress was busy cooking something, scraping with a spatula on the unwholesome-looking grill. She was an enormous, pendulous-bosomed woman with a mouthful of gold teeth and a thin moustache. She wore her rouge on a level with her shaggy eyebrows. Two large silver earrings dangled almost to her shoulders.

"Coffee, honey?" she stopped scraping and came to his booth, staring over her bosom at him.

"Coffee, black."

"Check." She shuffled off. When she returned, she put the coffee before him and some book matches.

"Compliments of the house, sugar. I wrote the poetry."

He glanced at the matches and found the covers bore little verses. One was entitled "Pines at Sunset." She waited while he read it. It was like the place, shabby and vague, not quite belonging with the horn-honking, electric world beyond the Bayou.

"Well, this is a novel idea."

"Well, it ain't novel exactly, but it gets your stuff read. I know it's not poetry; I call it my thinkings. Passes the time. Me and the cleaning man next door exchange our thinkings all the time; don't know how we get our work done. I have another I just finished called 'Black Bayou.' You come in again, and I'll have it on the matches. I'm Venetia Sparrow—Mrs. Sparrow. I run the place." She wiped the table, wiped her nose on the rag and moved off.

Peter sat wonderingly. Here was a scarcely explored world, where café proprietresses published verses on book match covers, old women saw ghost children, and barefoot men sat in cafés. Overhead the fan creaked wobbledly, and the rain dripped down the wall from a leak.

Suddenly he was aware of a feeling, a city feeling, in this middle of the wilderness. He was being stared at, no effort at concealment, no trick of glancing to a calendar or a mirror, just staring. The person was a few booths up and must have come in when Mrs. Sparrow was talking to him. The starer was a blond boy about his own age. He was wearing a black navy raincoat, and his hair was plastered flat from the rain. Mrs. Sparrow moved to bring him coffee.

Peter tried to glace away, at the palm, at the leaky spot that broadened over the ceiling, but his eyes were drawn again and again to the young man. Perhaps it was the out-of-the-night suddenness, perhaps the change from all the people he had seen so far in the town, perhaps a combination of many things that made him decide that the young man was the most beautiful person he had ever seen in his life. He didn't fail to acknowledge the somewhat disturbing implications of this opinion, but nevertheless it was true. The blond boy's face was like the strong, chiseled faces in the mythology books in the Birmingham library.

The face finally shifted its glance and seemed to forget him, but the memory of the deep gray eyes remained as he finished his coffee, paid his check and left. When he went out the door, he was met by a girl, who didn't glance at him but, he noticed, went to join the young man.

Outside, the rain had almost ceased, but the night moved restlessly with the wind that had come with the storm. He walked slowly and for the first time felt the homesickness and loneliness shift to new meanings. When he approached the old house there were lights, and he quickened his step.

5

"What do you think about, Peter, when you see the lights like those out there?"

"Hunh? Oh, I just remember other lights that looked that way in other places." He slowed on the night road and watched the little shrimp boats flicker their lights, dreamily adrift between sea and sky—unknown and unknown. The wharf lights burned steadily, thrusting out into the blackness and then stopping all at once.

"Well, I don't, mainly, I guess, because they're the only lights I ever see. Sometimes they're one thing and sometimes another. Sometimes they're reminders that time is passing, that things are numbered (there are thirty-two lights on the wharf). And sometimes they are points that you have passed in your life —points of pain or pleasure. I like to count things by them. Peter, Peter, tell me something. Do you know, honestly know, what you are looking for?"

Peter caught his breath, for at times Miss Billy could be very vague and bewildering. "Want? I don't think I really want anything. If I do, then I don't know what it is." He wondered abstractedly what the pines were telling each other, for the wind with its searching fingers made more sense than this something he couldn't know.

"Ah, my dear Peter, then there is something, for if you don't know, then you must want something so terribly that you can't admit it." Her voice was soft and a little sad. "Perhaps you, then, someday when summer is heavy on the swamps and meadows, when all conditions are right—oh, not like Miss Claverly says about cause and effect, for she is wrong—you will find what I have not."

"Who is Miss Claverly, and what will I find?"

"Miss Claverly—did I mention her?—oh, yes. She is that strange insect woman who lives on the edge of the gully. You can't have met her yet, but you will, for she is hard to miss. She is strange, strange, with her nets and queer talk. When she walks uptown, traffic practically stops, dogs howl, and babies cry. For, oh dear, I can't really do her justice. She can't be described. She lives all alone with four bloodhounds and does all sorts of weird things. We tried to get her to come to our little teas, but after one appearance it was enough for us and, I'm afraid, for her."

Miss Billy was on safer ground now, for the report of Miss

Claverly savored of the post-office gossip.

"It was at Miss Bubs Whitten's house that Wednesday. And she came right on time, brought one of her bloodhounds—Buster, I think she called it. Came right in with her and terrified us practically to death. Bloodhounds are frightening creatures anyhow, but this one is unbelievable, a great drooling thing that never puts his tongue in. Miss Claverly made herself very much at home; that was one of the things, I think. She rolls her own cigarettes, for instance, and she got tobacco all over the place. Offered all of us one, and after she had licked them, too. And then she got off on sex in the animal kingdom. Seems she did a thesis once on how different types of animals mate. Well, my dear, none of us is narrow-minded, but really. It was too embarrassing. Everyone eventually found something she had forgotten to do at home. The dog wet the carpet—the one poor Bubs got in Philadelphia—and Miss Claverly began to get bored when no one seemed at all interested in how long it takes elephants—oh, but you can't imagine."

Peter could imagine after all the other curious people he had seen and heard about in Moss Bayou. Were people like this elsewhere? he wondered. Maybe they got like this after staying for a while in these strange and desolate swamps, where nights were luminous with stars and phosphorescing things, where days were sun heavy, time heavy, tired of time and weary of sameness.

"I think I should like to know her."

"Oh, you probably will; she is very friendly. She comes over every once in a while to get Eulacie to show her how to cook something. She hardly notices me, but she seems to find Eulacie fascinating—functionally speaking. She has a few cronies, too —persons who speak her language, such as old Mr. Birnham, who does carvings of animals, Kirsten Reaves, who believes in reincarnation (she was once a Druid priestess), and that nice Norwegian couple who have a farm outside town. She has parties for them, and they take her places. I suppose she is just too much of an individual for most of us." Miss Billy stopped to pick a rose that had spilled over a fence.

They turned to walk back, and Peter suddenly realized how

he had come to look forward to these walks. The first few times he had come out of boredom, but now he knew that the first dim signs of acceptance had gradually become something a little more positive.

"Now where do you suppose the Big Dipper is?" Miss Billy had stopped and was looking up. "I all at once missed it."

They looked for a while but couldn't seem to find it, for thin clouds confused the sky. So they walked along home. Summer lightning crinkled the water-edge horizon, and the little shrimp boats had begun to steer toward their moorings. Muted thunder vibrated across vast night distances, and somewhere there was rain which would soon be falling here.

6

A DAY CAME finally when summer hung like a glistening drop of hot liquid metal ready to splash and sear the whole region. Rain had not even threatened for weeks, and time had lost meaning, suffocated in the dreadful dryness. Dust had settled on the trees and had turned the crape myrtles a rusty pink. At low tide the seaweed gave off a sickening medicinal odor, while tar melted on the uptown streets.

On this day Peter left the house and wandered down the cliff, seeking the shade of the cypresses on the beach. Once there, however, he found that there was even more than the usual number of picnickers from across the bay. Fat-hipped women shouted at naked babies, and hairy-chested men fought at gnats and cursed the heat. The tide was out, and children splashed through the black seaweed.

"Kath'ern, if you throw sand on that baby again, I'm goin' to beat your ass."

"He was throwin' it on me."

"Well, you heard me."

On down the beach, some high school kids were throwing soft-drink bottles at each other. The little wharf was swarming with gleaming sunburned bodies—muscular boys conscious of their physiques, overdeveloped girls with wet hair. Neurotic dogs threaded themselves in and out the legs of people, whining when their owners went into the water. Everywhere was the smell of sun-tan oil, perspiration, and watermelon rinds, besides the sun-baked seaweed smell that hung like a plague over everything.

Peter turned and followed the beach road that eventually would run out to a dead end at the north edge of the beach. Little by little he left the cars behind when the road stopped. He followed a path now, which curved under the high bank where the big bay-front houses looked over the pine trees at the water. Between him and the beach was a dense, impenetrable jungle of honeysuckle, brambles, and kudzu. Soon he had left the picnic sounds behind, and there was no sound now but the nervous flicking of birds through the tangle of vines and the twanging sound of marsh frogs. For he was approaching the great marsh which met the curve of the cove between Ecor Rouge and Moss Bayou. The ground became boggy, and the stagnant iron-colored water sucked through the meshed grass at his shoe soles.

Now the vines disappeared and were replaced by the tall green-black grass which silvered in the sun. The path continued, however, but became rough and partially obscured where last year's weeds had met and been trampled. Then he saw lying near the path a boy and girl completely naked and unaware of him; so secure they must have felt in this rhythm of limitlessness of grass and sky. Their bathing suits were dropped carelessly on the flattened grass. The boy and girl were brunet, both deeply tanned except for the parts of their bodies usually covered with swim suits. These white areas moved slowly under the sun.

Peter felt a weakening and overwhelming desire to stay and watch, but he knew that they would see him if he did, so he went on along the path, careful not to make a sound. When he looked back, he could see nothing but the long stretch of grass and beyond that the water. He sighed and walked on.

Eventually the path entered a wooded region, where the tree-tops became thicker and closed out the sun. It was a lovely spot with a slow clear stream. A narrow belt of sand spread along the water edge. He sat under an oak and stretched out, realizing that he must have walked over two miles. But here, at last, was the shade he had started out to find.

He looked at the water and breathed in its muddy and mint-like fragrance. He rolled on his stomach and thought again of the boy and girl by the path, and in response to the thought there was a warm pressure between him and the sand. His mouth was dry and salty, and he felt sticky. He sat up and started to remove his shoes. The cold water would take away for the time being the pressure of the heat and the other pressure as well. He unbuttoned his shirt and dropped his trousers, and it was an almost sensual pleasure to stand naked in the open.

As he waded into the icy water he looked down at his body and wondered what experiences there would be for it—the flat stomach and narrow pelvis with its bony turn of hip, the long slender legs. Tenderly he felt his body with flat hand and cupped hand, and then he dived headfirst into the deep, translucent depths when the sand bottom stopped.

He floated on his back, looking up through the branches of trees where the sun was half obscured. On the shore the oaks dropped their roots over into the water like great silent anglers. Where the marsh grass grew in the shallow edge, dragonflies wheeled on almost invisible wings, darting blue and lavender across the tree-sifted sunbeams. It wouldn't be hard to drown in a place like this, he thought, as he turned over and swam again. He had drifted downstream a little, and before him was an island, not much of an island, completely hidden from the bank he had left. It was covered with reindeer moss and tall grass, and on it were no trees.

He climbed up the bank and stopped, dripping in the flat sunlight. The moss was deliciously soft under his feet. Here on this tiny bit of island one was completely hidden from anyone on the stream's bank, for the tall rushes surrounded the island where it met the water, leaving the center clean and velvet-smooth with the moss. It was the most inviting place he could imagine on a day like this, and with a groan of pleasure he sprawled face down on the moss.

The penetrating warmth encompassed him, bathed away the fatigue and held him suspended between consciousness and oblivion. Away off the stream could be heard rubbing the rushes and slipping over the embedded rocks. He watched, as if from a neighboring grass blade, an ant scurrying on some important mission, but the ant passed out of focus, and Peter lay on his arms and slept.

Later—much later—time uncounted by hours, he rose, startled that he had forgotten time, startled that the sun was now thin and smoke colored. On the only part of the horizon he could see, black clouds were piled like volcanic rocks. Their solid-looking edges were flying in vaporish gray wisps, driven by a wind that was not felt here. He looked at the short stretch of water, now inky and opaque, dreading the fearful shock. It seemed to congeal his blood as he waded in.

The dragonflies were gone now, the rushes left motionless and stolid, their magic somehow gone without the sun shapes and insect shadows. Distant thunder rippled the water, excited the rushes, and extinguished the last of the sun. He swam faster, thinking of the marsh in a storm and after that the vaguely frightening wood.

She was sitting almost on top of his clothes, jackknife position with eye to the ground, unmoving. Her hair hung forward as though she had been drying it in the now-vanished sun, and her arms were bowed, her hands holding something before her eye. Beside her was a straw bag and a litter of things strewn about on the sand.

It was the woman on the bus the first day of his arrival. He had not seen her since, and he had often thought of her. He could tell that she wasn't aware of his presence, so unaware probably that she would never leave. He treaded water, letting himself drift once more a little downstream. Several minutes passed, and he paddled back close to the shore. She hadn't changed position. His arms were tired, and the water was numbing; he didn't know what to do. When he finally brought himself to call to her, his voice was loud and hollow in the vacuum of quietness.

"Lady."

She hadn't heard him.

"Lady." Plaintively.

This time she moved her head, uncertain, but he had to call a third time before she finally looked up to see where the voice came from.

"Here," he said, splashing an arm, white-foamed in the black water.

"Oh, so there was somebody." She peered at him through thick glasses, tossing her hair back. "Tell me, is the water nice?"

"Yes, but I want to come out."

"So, why don't you?"

"Well—you see; I'm not—I don't have any clothes on," he blurted.

"Hmm," she reflected, still not moving. "Then I suppose I must go or not look or something. It really makes no difference. You see, I'm a scientist."

He drifted downstream a little farther, and still she didn't move.

"Oh, all right, then. I'll take my glasses off. Can't see a tree without them." She whipped off her glasses and leaned back. "Well, come on."

He watched her uncertainly as he waded cautiously out, feeling painfully naked. Hunched over he made for his clothes and retreated with them behind a clump of bamboo.

When he emerged, clothing clinging wetly to his body, she was back at the glass, buried once more in the weeds.

"Hmm," she murmured, feeling his presence. "Know anything about wood lice?"

"No," he said, "I don't."

"Not many people do, of course. Never bother to look at nature. Take it for granted. They're too busy trying to make money in their wretched worlds, trying to spend more than they can afford. And all around them are thousands of tiny worlds full of interesting life. Do you think they ever stop to take notice except to spray them with DDT?"

"No," said Peter, "I don't guess I ever really thought about it."

"Oh, my dear, you are probably like the rest. Who are you anyhow? And what are you doing here? I thought I had finally found one place completely remote from everyone. Sometimes I have trouble finding it myself."

"I am Peter Abbott; you probably know my great-aunt, Miss Clarice Billy. I came here because, like you, I wanted to get away from everyone."

"I see." She looked at him with more interest. "Yes, I know Miss Billy. She is very nice even if, if you don't mind my saying so, a little dull and unimaginative."

"Oh, but she's not really. She sees—" He stopped, remembering in time that he couldn't ever tell about Miss Billy and her little ghost girl. Besides, for a scientist it would be even more ridiculous than it had been for him.

"I'm Margaret Claverly."

"Oh, then you're— Miss Billy told me about you." He felt that he should have known that this was Miss Claverly all along.

"Yes, I can imagine. She probably had some interesting observations to make." She squinted forward. Peter thought of going, but she motioned to him suddenly. "You must see this adorable spider. She's dragging a beetle into her hole."

Peter looked through the little hand lens she was holding over the hole. "How do you know it's a she?"

"Oh, with this species, the female does all her own work. She allows the male to stay around until they have mated and then promptly eats him. Actually, it is a female because the female is larger. There is a kindred species in which the male— I'll have to hand it to him—is clever enough not to get eaten.

While they are mating he at the same time is quietly tying the female's legs together; then he makes off as soon as he has enjoyed himself. Almost like some men in our own society."

"You certainly know a lot about them. Did you study biology?"

"Yes, my dear, but mainly it comes from watching things. Remember that. Study doesn't stop with books and papers, but only starts."

"I'd like to hear more about it sometimes. That is, if you wouldn't mind telling me."

"My dear, nothing would give me more pleasure. As a matter of fact, if I didn't have an invitation to tea at old Mrs. Ives' house after a while, I would insist that you come right over now and have tea with me. I have bottles and bottles of things you would love." Miss Claverly's face was almost beautiful now that she had removed the glasses and was showing such enthusiasm. "It is rare to find a disciple these days. Why don't we say Saturday? Are you doing anything Saturday?"

"No, I'd like to come then."

"Good. Four o'clock then."

A crash of thunder crackled the quietness and a strong wind set the branches of trees in motion. A shower of leaves rained down, and a few drops of rain freckled the pool.

"These damned hurricane seasons. We'd better hurry if we don't want to get wet. Although I don't really mind. There's something nice about walking in the rain."

"Yes, there is." Peter liked the way she had of saying things— as if she took it for granted that you agreed.

He helped her get her things together, and they started back, walking slowly and talking. By the time they had reached the beach road they had learned quite a lot about each other. He recalled to her the day on the bus, but she didn't remember.

"My dear, isn't this glorious?" Miss Claverly turned her face upward into the rain.

"I suppose so."

They climbed the long wooden steps at the end of the beach and reached the top of the cliff where the houses started.

"I go this way," Miss Claverly said, and Peter gave her the

straw satchel he was carrying for her.

"Miss Claverly, just one thing." Peter stopped her as she started to walk away, head lowered against the rain. "What do you like in your world best of all?"

She looked puzzled.

"I mean, of all the little lives you study, which do you find most interesting?"

"It's really very difficult to choose, but if you mean which insects I know most about my answer would be butterflies, of course. I would almost like to be one. Well, good-bye, I must go. Mrs. Ives will have the water hot by now." She went on.

Peter stood for a moment and watched her, trying to decide why of all the small life of the fields and woods she would choose butterflies—butterflies which if you rubbed off the fuzz on their wings would be unable to fly and would soon die. She seemed much more at home with the more vital, earthy things, the positive things.

The rain fell without ceasing, and he was glad when he turned in at the gate.

7

Miss Claverly's house lay in a tangle of honeysuckle and kudzu vines on the edge of Rainbow Gully in the eastern part of town. From a little way off, the house seemed to be leaning over the gully, as if the vines were pulling it over the cliff. A ruin of a chimney leaned on the side of the house away from the gully, while a rickety porch hung precariously over the edge. A path led to the house from a dirt road that followed the gully to the bay. Lining this path, which gradually mounted to the house, were all manner of untended plants, plants which required much attention from other people. At the end of the path a somewhat crippled scuppernong arbor tunneled the front steps which led abruptly, minus front porch, to the door.

Inside, the abandon and confusion continued but not enough to disguise a rather comfortable sitting room composed mainly of a heavy couch and several bookcases. Rows of specimen cases were in every corner. The room was a compound of shoddy comfort and gorgeous abandon. On a makeshift window seat, a gigantic hound lay, tongue and legs hanging over the side, watching emptily. Two more lay on a rug, a heap of haunches, paws, and twitching relaxation.

"They're such a pleasure really. Much nicer than people, for people ask questions and expect answers." Miss Claverly fitted a self-rolled cigarette into a long holder and blew smoke luxuriously. She lay on the couch in a faded pink house coat. A tarnished medallion hung on a long chain around her neck, and a bracelet of beaten copper encircled her thin wrist. "I've tried people all my life, and they are always a disappointment. Perhaps I'll tell you about them one day. Meanwhile, what destiny brought you to this end of places?"

"Oh, I doubt if it had anything to do with destiny. My aunt and uncle in Birmingham thought I should come here to go to school in Mobile."

"There is more to destiny than you think, my dear. I could point out some rather overwhelming examples in evolution, but there'll be time for that later. More tea?"

"No, thank you."

"You're a dear, really, to be interested in my wonderful insects. I have such trouble conversationally with most people. They talk about things—radio programs, scandals, babies, and automobiles—I can never know. If I talk about animals they get bored and leave. I discover a new little creeping thing, an insect larva or a little known species of red dragonfly, and I have no one to run and tell it to. I should like to run into the post office and shout: 'Come quick, I have found a mutant beetle,' and I should like everyone to follow me and see it. I should probably be hauled off to a home or something if I tried it. But to me unshared beauty is one of the saddest experiences in life. My researches have taken me all over the world, and I have seen things, unbelievable fantasies and beauties, all alone. It never is the same to tell about them later, for no one understands color, light and form without the real thing before him."

"Would they see them even then?" asked Peter, caught with some of the cynicism, yet the undeniable truth, of the observation.

"I doubt it. You remember that theme running through all poetry—Emerson, Wordsworth, Gray. It's universal, I suppose —like the intangibility of, the immunity to, love, unless it happens to you. Could you describe to anyone the feeling of love, or, more than that, the consummation of love. Beauty is the same way; it is practically instinctive. Even our words for it are weak and repetitive, and any discussion of it must be full of indirection and choked with metaphors. Oh but, my dear, I am sorry; I do get off. Would you like to see some of my specimens? I have some dragonflies the Museum of Natural History would love to get hold of."

She rose from the couch and crossed to a low shelf. Here were ranged a great number of cigar boxes carefully labeled: *Nymphalidae, Lycaenidae, Papilionidae, Hesperiidae*—like names from Greek myths. She took one of the ones marked *Papilionidae* and brought it to him.

Peter had never seen anything so exquisite as the butterfly labeled *Papilio crino*—translucent aqua on duller-textured green. How anything connected with all the messy business of being born and dying could be so absolutely beautiful.

"To think, my dear, it actually was once a caterpillar, so prosaic in comparison. I think that is why I like butterflies so much. Their metamorphosis. Of course, some of the other insects do it, too, but not so completely, so fantastically. Look at that wing edge. Did you believe such colors were possible?"

They went through box after box—moths, beetles, spiders, and insects unrecognizable in their neat mountings.

Then they took the microscope and looked into more intimate worlds and lives. Peter was exhausted with the infinity of things he didn't know, and he marveled at a mind which accepted them almost casually but with worshipful interest at the same time.

It was dark when he left. Miss Claverly accompanied him to the foot of the path, and she insisted that he should come whenever he chose, even if she happened to be out somewhere. The dogs wouldn't bother him, he was assured, for now they knew how he smelled. If they were too friendly, of course, he was at liberty to ignore them. But by all means they must talk some more, for they had scarcely begun. There were many worlds in science—tremendous worlds of space and violence and small worlds where time crawled with insect feet and seconds were days—for him to know.

"And who knows," Miss Claverly mused as she turned to leave, "I may learn much from what you don't know."

8

SUMMER HAD sifted the days like sand along a creek bottom. Summer had gradually fashioned new days from old. Summer had burned into his days and nights with a weary monotony. He saw no one except Miss Billy, Eulacie and Miss Emmajean, and, of course, Miss Claverly. He would see people his age walking and laughing together, but he didn't know what to do to become part of them.

Soon school would begin, and already the prospect of shattering the unhurried drift of days and nights was a welcome and terrifying consideration.

"Peter, you should, really should, get out and meet some young people. They have dances every Saturday night down at the Casino, and pretty soon everyone will be back at school."

"Umm! good-lookin' boy like you have half the gals in Moss Bayou walkin' in they sleep." Eulacie turned an egg over in the skillet, and it sounded like rain blowing against windowpanes.

Here in the early-morning kitchen it was cozy and remote. Rain caught by the wind lashed whiplike against the north side of the house. Out the window, frosted translucent, the nandina bushes gestured wildly and cowered against the side of the kitchen with thumping noises.

"That old hurricane close enough to suit me. Mama say one more like the 1926 one would take the moss out of Moss Bayou." Eulacie shifted her toothpick to the other side of her mouth with her tongue.

"I wonder if there is anything to that six business," Miss Billy pondered, folding her napkin into a flower shape. "They say that years with sixes in them invariably produce bad hurricanes. It is true the 1906, 1916, and 1926 ones were very bad. I believe it skipped in 1936. Didn't it, Eulacie?"

"Depression, honey. You can bet your life them other ones was bad. Floated boats in Gov'ment Street in Mobile and ripped up trees and railroad tracks. Ain't no stoppin' them once they gets started. Miss Emmajean, you don't quit tearin' up that newspaper, I'm goin' to beat your ass."

"Miss Emmajean's all right, Eulacie; there's not much she can do on days like this." Peter held down a hand to her as if he were trying to coax a kitten to come to him.

" 'Cept make a mess." Eulacie brought the food to the table.

"So, I wonder if 1960 through '69 there will be a hurricane every year," Miss Billy still mused.

"If so, honey, I'm takin' off for Chicago. That damn wind give me the weak trembles."

Breakfast over, the four people in the house went their separate ways. Peter went to his room and stood looking out the window, watching the shifting gray veils of clouds lift and hover over the water. The pine trees clawed for a finger-hold on the edge of the cliff, when suddenly the wind would leave them and feel its way into the gullies and woods. Then back again it would send the trees wailing and thrashing.

He undressed and lay in his shorts on the unmade bed, listening to the certainties of uncontrived things. Somewhere, minutes later, he might have been on the edge of sleep, for he was thinking anxiously that perhaps Miss Claverly's house might blow with Miss Claverly and her hounds into Rainbow Gully.

"Peter," softly, still a part of fern-edged sleep. "Peter," a turn to withdraw, understanding perhaps the aloneness of storm days.

"Yes, come in." He pulled the sheet up.

The door opened a little and the lighter gray of the hall window sliced across the bed.

"Oh, were you asleep? I thought perhaps we could talk. I hate days when the flowers are wet and the birds are somewhere to keep dry."

"Yes," said Peter slowly, "I know. Come in." He propped up on the two pillows.

"Pretty soon the hurricane will blow off over Pensacola or somewhere, and it will be even lovelier than before. Then fall will come, and that is the lovely time."

"I hope the causeway will be open tomorrow so I can get over to register for school. The paper said the water has been over it."

"Oh, for the old days when Ferndale was at its peak. The boys from Ferndale College used to come into Mobile. They were so beautiful in their sweaters and caps. Angie and I used to spend hours dressing and then have to watch them from discreet distances, while they went straight from the street cars to St. Anthony Street, where the girls were a little more alive and certainly warmer. I was warm but uncertain."

"How long has Ferndale been there, for goodness sake?"

"My dear, Ferndale is over one hundred years old—even older than I. Moss Bayou was just a stretch of sand and sand spurs and cypresses then. To think you'll be at Ferndale, but somehow you seem too young, or maybe the boys were older then." She looked through the years for several minutes, not aware that they were not out the window but that she herself was the years.

"Peter," she changed suddenly (and the wind changed sharply

and dropped to a new moaning key). "Peter, I am an old woman, and often I am a foolish old woman. I am, really. I once lived with realities until I found they were false, so now I have chosen the fantastics and they are my realities. I mix them occasionally with whimsy and even a little silly village gossip just for the sake of variety, but somewhere—and I know this—there is something that will spell out the reality and spell out the fantasy and which is which. It will tell where dreams go —the ones that disappeared once on a long-ago evening when the moon was up toward Daphne, and the cypresses were silver. There is a something that only I know about that will do this. I know almost where to find it, but it has been a long long time, and I might have forgotten the way."

"What, Miss Billy?"

"The butterfly tree. That's what I call it—the butterfly tree." Her voice caressed the words, giving them a faraway flavor, a bruised fluttering sound like moths bumping wings under a porch light.

"Butterfly tree?"

"Yes. I have meant to tell you all along, for somehow you are supposed to know."

"Why?"

She didn't seem to hear him but was listening to voices beyond the storm. Her eyes were half closed, looking elsewhere, toward the winds of some distant autumn or the grasses of another spring.

"I was waiting for a perfect time, for I have long been aware of years and where they take us, and to think I might have lost the chance. Chances are rare bubble things that drift with color and promise, and as you reach they often break against grass blades or low-hanging limbs of mulberry trees. We must go, you and I, before autumn has been stealthy with us, for summer is the time the butterfly tree blooms in the swamps."

"What is the butterfly tree?"

"Peter, Peter, don't ask what a rose is, for one wonderful writer has told the world in a simple statement that we have all made

cryptic. So I cannot tell you, only show you. It is a magic, a real
live thing that is so perfect that it is non-existent unless you
look for it."

"But how?"

"That will be for another day, for nothing is real but the
suddenness of days. And that day will be sudden, like today, but
a special day, which I shall know, and then we shall go and
look for, perhaps find, the butterfly tree, for time cannot take,
must not take, that, too." She stopped and watched the gray
square of window for another moment, then, "What in heaven's
name am I thinking of? If we do have the Theosophy meeting
tomorrow night I have a paper to read, and I haven't even
started. And I know I'll never find those magazine articles I
intended to plagiarize. Eulacie probably gave them to Miss
Emmajean to cut up."

After she was gone, Peter lay still, wondering why when things
were as simple as the outside and the fierceness of wind, dim
phantoms of halfway things crept on silky wings into the un-
guarded edges. So tenderly told, as if he were part of the
mystical vision, when really he felt like an intruder. This tree,
whatever it was, was her dream, and why must she be telling
it to him? After all, she had not told him about the ghost child.
Eulacie had; so it must be that Eulacie didn't know about the
tree and that really only Miss Billy did. Where, down all
the labyrinths of becoming the one you are and are not, did this
fit in, or could it be one of those purposeless experiences that
make the real things more real? Hurricanes, invisible, after all,
tear trees and drive walls of water across the combined gray of
sea and sky. Real and unreal, magic and unmagic, black and
white, water and sky, they all unite somewhere in bursts of
iridescence and there, maybe only there, stands a—what did
she call it?—but no, it is only the tree beneath which Miss
Emmajean eats striped petunias.

When he awoke it was still gray, neither morning nor afternoon, and the wind was quieter. Somewhere there was light
and there were voices, laughter. He lay still but found it un-

bearable to be out of things, although he knew it was only Eulacie and Miss Billy mulling over the village pregnancies and the prices at the A & P.

He was barefoot and in a sand-colored jersey and dungarees when he came down into the kitchen. Miss Billy was cutting things from an old magazine with a pair of fingernail scissors, and Eulacie, as he had left her, was cooking.

"Like a old tomcat, up, and all he wants is to eat. Better than a wet tail, huh, Tom?" She squawked her cotton-patch chuckle and motioned to a chair. "I was about to holler for you. Goda'mighty, you can sleep."

"Peter, just as I said, I couldn't find the Theosophy articles, but I found these instead. I wish you'd look at these old valentines. Aren't they lovely? They once said more and came from more to say. Love has become very short-winded. Once they swam Hellesponts and built Taj Mahals."

"Now it's a blind date, a hamburger, and into the woods." Eulacie slapped her thigh and dumped a skillet of fried potatoes into a dish. "Y'all goin' to eat or not?"

"Any news about the hurricane?"

"Radio say it tore up Pascagoula and some of Biloxi. Unless it turn around, we goin' to start dryin' out tomorrow."

"And then we can all get back to normal." Miss Billy clipped another valentine and laid down the scissors.

"Normal, huh!" Eulacie served the food, snatched at Miss Emmajean, who was rubbing flour into her hair, and went out back.

They ate, both saying nothing. Miss Billy still turned the valentines over reflectively, sipping her coffee daintily. Peter looked about him at the dark unpainted kitchen and was suddenly a little startled that it had become so familiar. The oil stove which gurgled once every few minutes, the light bulb that hung on a cord from a rafter, the linoleum that had once had color and a pattern—these were part, now, of the everafter.

When they were finished, he stood up. "I believe I shall take a walk."

"Good idea. I'd go with you, but I must think about that

paper. Besides I want to save up, and then we'll take a long long walk to where I was telling you about."

"Where? Oh yes, I remember." He had almost forgotten, for it had been a part of the rain and the morning and somehow not a part of now. "Well, I'll see you a little later."

Outside, the impact of the flat gray of sky and the ruffed surfaces of earth was a little frightening at first, and even the low whine of wind did not break the unearthly silence that seemed to press in on all sides. He took the path that led off from the road and dropped almost perpendicularly to the sand road of the beach. On the beach road the wind was almost a rumble in the interlocked branches of the oaks and pines, and the honeysuckle was atoss where it laced the trees together.

Past the clearing there was the water, magnificent, elegant and overpowering, lifting and dropping, spreading white on gray-green, plunging and rearing. The sound was not in whispered ebbings as usual but constant and wailing like a conch shell held to the ear. And there was no sky but water—white clouds, white caps, whirled together in a common maelstrom. Where once there had been a sand flat with twisted drift-logs was a shallow sea which writhed to fall back with the waste of sky and sea. The bushes dragged their underfoliage in the water and bent their tops against the wind.

There was no longer the narrow strip of sand for a beach, so he walked in the swampy marsh grass toward the point, for there would be a view of the cove and the red cliff up toward Daphne. The hoarse wind voice caught imagined voices and told things of other times and future times—the voices of children running in the surf, the sounds of night-crying birds, the troubling voices of sorrowful times and happy times. White water, green water, undoing vast times of imagination—the times when ancient heroes urged their horses across raging rivers—and imagination confused the senses so that sight and sound were for moments synchronized.

One of the heroes, naked, had slipped from a horse and was tossed in the waves, grasping at the frothy white manes of the sea, but he was laughing, and there was a girl beside him. This rage of sea, this afternoon of infinities, was a proper time for mythologies, and so they weren't lost and forgotten, really, in the dusty upstairs books at Miss Billy's.

They didn't see him, but hair in eyes they were in another time. He might have walked on, but somehow this was the purpose of his walk down the cliff, and he stood behind a group of three sapling pines and watched them in a fantastic ballet with the crashing surf, listening to their laughter which might have been the wind.

They were the boy and girl of the café, but they weren't the same; they were where they belonged, among the infinities, where part of one thing was part of another. Here, they were both beautiful, with a beauty that was sad and wonderful, the white and green sadness of sea deities and the white and green fierceness of the foaming steeds they rode.

The wind dropped sharply, and the manes of the seahorses disappeared for an instant, then were back. The boy seemed to be shouting, and then he stood knee-deep in the water and laughed, his head thrown back. The girl, thrown by a wave, rose and tossed her hair back. Then she pushed the boy down and plunged away, grabbing the foamy mane of another wave.

Their bodies were white and tan like those of the lovers in the marsh, but far more beautiful. They were straight and tall, blond, exquisitely balanced. They twisted and turned, riding the water up and down, chest and hip, breast and hip, arm and thigh sliding muscles down and up.

The eerie hurricane light caught their poses and recalled the image of horses. A leg thrown over one here and a head bending to urge one there. The neighing was the wind, and the surf beat was hoofbeat. They circled the steeds slowly in, falling beside them, walking the waves to shore. The water flattened and fanned ahead of them to disappear completely into the sand, leaving a hem of winking bubbles.

They walked hand in hand back the way Peter had come. Laughing still, they stopped by a pile of logs where they had left their clothes. They dressed slowly, although they each put on just a shirt and trousers. Then they walked on. Peter watched

them out of sight and then, glowing from something spiritually
unfulfilled and physically stirred, he turned and followed the way
they had gone, for it was the only way back.

9

DREAMS WERE sea tossed and sea spent, scudding steeds mounting
and plunging, feeling like human forms between pressing thighs,
slippery in green-white water. Water tearing down the battle-
ments of real, sharp and contoured things, eating away with
time's persistence, picking apart the sculptured and wheel-turned.
Turned, the water, to something monstrous, howling, crashing,
when it had looked so weak before when clouds were white
and golden. Golden flesh naked and foam-flecked splashing in
with the sea, going out with the sea, laughing at sky-gray water-
gray. Gray waste of beach with tortured drift-logs, bent grass
tops, and pounded fragments of things awash in water and time.
Time measured in yesterdays to make naked figures in a storm
mean what they meant, time nurtured imagination to make them
more than figures in a storm. Storm of blinding light and gray-
lifted sea floor, rolled over with water and the drag of wind-
pull. Pull on the steed for the tempest is stronger, hold on the
naked flesh, rolling, in with the sea, out with the sea, in with
the sea, till finally the storm has stopped and the sea is quiet.

10

Down the drive of Ferndale College was one of the most beautiful views Peter had ever seen, something from a medieval print. Giant oaks nearly, but not quite, obscured the old buildings which with graceful Gothic arches stood linked together by cloisters around a quadrangle.

In the corridors echoes kicked up and carried to the upper floors. And the smell of a century lay in the halls—not the smell of boards and chalk of new schools, but the odor of bricks and yellowed pages, polished old furniture and heavy draperies, unmoving air and sun-dancing dust motes.

After he had seen the proper authorities and had registered for entrance he stopped and looked in at the library. Here, at last, was a place to escape everything else, a sanctuary at the end of the oak avenue. Here he could read about all the things Miss Claverly talked about. He could understand and answer her, maybe even bring her a new thing. There were seemingly endless rows of books, and experience could now be as endless.

Before he left he walked down to the lake below the quadrangle. There was no one at the lake, and he followed the path which laced around huge trees, under low willow limbs which floated their finger-tips on the surface, and through meadows of azalea bushes. The clear water was a mirror for the trees, and cloud-shadows moved across beneath him. The waterscape showed him the first almost-imperceptible hint of autumn, and the always magic thrill of this discovery changed things for him. Many times he had made this discovery when the summer was even deeper, when heat would burn as intensely for six weeks longer, but the suddenness of an autumn sense was always the same and always unmistakable.

He looked back at the lake as he walked up the avenue, and already he could imagine its surface floated with leaves. He was impatient to begin school, and the two weeks more seemed a long weary time.

Yet, as the bus left the college gates behind, he felt an impatience to get back to Moss Bayou. He was vaguely surprised at this impatience, for so far he had not thought of Moss Bayou in terms of permanence. But, at the same time, there was a little twist of recognition, of identification, that was suddenly and certainly not to be denied.

The bus got back to downtown Mobile in mid-afternoon. Watching the old houses with their grille-work balconies, Peter knew that at one time ladies probably slept away the hot afternoons behind the shutters or embroidered together in high-ceilinged parlors, gossiping about not-present friends and waiting for their sun-browned husbands to come home from the cotton warehouses.

Royal Street, where he got off the bus, was crowded but somehow didn't appear to be. The people moved slowly, casually, going in and coming out of stores. He remembered that Miss Billy had told him to buy some thread, so he went into the large department store by the bus stop and made the purchase. Afterwards he looked round the store and finally stopped to look at some costume jewelry, thinking that perhaps Eulacie might like some earrings. It would be nice to take all three something.

"May I help you?" The salesgirl stood beside him.

"I'm just looking, thanks."

She turned to walk away as he looked up, but stopped as he uttered an involuntary exclamation.

"Did you find something?" She came back.

"No—no. I'm sorry; I was thinking about something else." He was confused, for something dimly past and strongly present struggled for an instant. The dim past disappeared, but the present remained, for it was the girl on the beach, the girl in the café. He was confused and self-conscious before the plain girl, now in a simple suit and blouse, who had been the beautiful, free creature of the day before, splashing naked in the storm.

"Oh, that's all right. I do that myself. Were you looking for something in particular?"

"No. Wait, what about these?" He pointed to some earrings, gaudy red glass with pendants like a chandelier.

"Those are nice. They're a dollar plus federal tax."

"And do you have a pin or something shaped like a—butterfly?"

"Well, let's see." She looked on the counter and then in a glass case. "I don't believe—no, wait a minute. I remember. There are some in the metalcraft section." She went off.

He watched her go. Her hair was now pulled back and caught with a clasp. The blouse was high necked, and he tried to imagine underneath the slopes and pinnacles of her breasts. And from behind, the belted jacket of her suit flattened across the delicate curve and crevice he knew were there. She came back after five minutes or so.

"Isn't it lovely?" It was an earring she held in her hand, a small silver moth with filigreed wing edges.

"I'll take them."

"Good. I like to sell things I like. No one ever asks for butterflies. Maybe because they don't know where to look for them. These were made locally, too. A couple of ladies across the bay run a metalcraft studio. We buy quite a lot of their work."

Later in a café he sat thinking about the salesclerk. There was something warm and beautiful about her, although she was homely and a little awkward. Curious, too, what she had said about butterflies. That people didn't ask for them, perhaps, because they didn't know where to look for them. It was almost as if she were talking about real butterflies, but there was no reason why she should. At any rate, it was curious how things went together. Miss Billy knew about a whole tree of them; Miss Claverly knew all about them and caught them.

He finished eating and went back to the bus station, after stopping in the ten-cent store to buy Miss Emmajean some candy. It was a nice thought to know that soon and all the days and nights later he would be going to Moss Bayou. It was home, at least, for now.

11

"I TOLD YOU candy would tame her. Now you goin' to have to have to think of somethin' to get shed of her." Eulacie shook her head over the butterbeans she was shelling.

Miss Emmajean was rubbing her nose against the back of Peter's hand, which was hanging over his chair back.

"Two more weeks and I'll be back in school."

"Yes, and you'll probably be walkin' around with your rear end higher than your head after a month or so. Mama she say take away the schools and first thing you know people learn to work again."

"There's probably something to that whether you know it or not."

"Where in the world is Miss Billy? I haven't seen her since breakfast."

"The Lord know where she can disappear. Some mornings she spin around here like the latch on the privy door at the Bascombe Club on Squall Street come Saturday night. Other days she moon around like she lost somethin'. If I didn't think I know what it is I wouldn't worry too much, but you know and I know some things just ain't normal."

"Oh, I don't know. Who can say one thing is normal or is not? What is normal for you may not be for her."

"See, what I tell you. Already actin' like college. Miss Emmajean, you don't get the hell out of here and go play, you know what part of you is goin' to remember. I told you that a hour ago."

"I think I'll go write a letter. I should have a long time ago."

"I bet she think so, too." Eulacie lifted her apron at the corners and carried the butterbean shells over to the garbage can.

Peter brought his writing paper down from upstairs and sat on the side porch. For a long time he just sat, trying to think away the late-growing summer and recover the feeling of winter nights when he and Ann had gone to a late movie and then had coffee in the little café by the park. Ann. Funny how a few weeks could diminish faces, blur things a little, things that had been meant to be eternal when they happened. It was strange that Ann could become dim—but, after all, you gradually come to know a person. Why, then, could one not gradually come not to know a person? There must be an opposite process.

He struggled, finally, through some tight statements about living in Moss Bayou and entering Ferndale. That was all there was to say, since he couldn't describe Miss Billy or Eulacie, much less Miss Claverly. They weren't, couldn't be, a part of a windy street or the nodding street lights. They were of another world, and he knew instinctively not to mix his worlds. Maybe someday when both worlds (plus all the ones he was yet to experience) had become part of one, he could communicate parts of it to other parts.

Miss Billy had to whisper to him a second time before he heard her, so intense was he on trying to think of what he could write so that it might be a part of the something else he had known.

"Peter," her voice was insistent, "it's time."

"Time?" and his thoughts flocked back from one reality to another.

"Time to look for the butterfly tree. It's a part of now." She smiled and looked across the weed-twisted garden.

"How can you tell?" and he knew when he asked that the question didn't mean anything.

"I know by something that summer will be gone after today

—up through the trees and across the swamps. It will take many things with it—the silver on the pine needles, some of the flowers and some of the leaves, and certainly the butterflies. We must hurry."

He got up and folded the letter, placing it between the pages of a book. He turned and looked at Miss Billy, who was already going down the steps.

"Where are we going?"

"Peter," she mused, "I believe I'll plant nasturtiums here next. The larkspurs just didn't do a thing except lie down and have a few other larkspurs and then die. I like nasturtiums; they aren't smug, and besides that the stems make excellent sandwiches. Come on."

He followed her down the walk and out the gate, for he had no other choice apparently. They went down Bayview, which was heat drowsy at high noon, giving no hint that this was the end of summer. Sprinklers threw tiny rainbows against the dark green backgrounds of camellia bushes. A late-summer feeling was sensed, however, from the direction of the bay, where the crowds had suddenly disappeared. The jagged flash of reflection was as dazzling as ever, though, as it struck at them between the trees as they moved along.

They skirted town near the school and crossed Big Head Gully by way of a swinging bridge laced with kudzu vines so that it seemed to be supported by them. Far below, the bottom of the gully was bone-white sand veined with ochre and rust-colored clay.

"What is there about heights that makes you want to jump?" Miss Billy looked down, and for a moment there flashed through Peter's imagination a ridiculous picture of Miss Billy hurtling down through space, her black dress billowing around her.

"I suppose," she answered herself, "it is our instinct that we are indestructible and might really fly instead of falling. I've always wondered how it would be to fly, for I have flown often in my dreams, even my daydreams. On the other hand, think how many magics we would destroy if we could fly."

The road led past the Catton Place, as Miss Billy called a

ghostly old three-storied house, and ended abruptly. A path began through a pine wood, sloping gradually toward a vast dark area of trees and undergrowth.

"Someone once told me a beautiful legend about the butterfly tree. He was the one, of course, who told me, in the first place, about the tree. Shall I tell it to you?"

She told how once among the Indian swamp dwellers the chief's small daughter had strayed from the seven maidens in whose care she had been placed and had become lost in the swamp. The chief sought for her seven days, each day killing one of the maidens and burying her beneath a tree in a clearing in the middle of the swamp. The lovers of the seven maidens were so grief-stricken that the gods turned them into butterflies, huge monarchs. After that, every year the monarchs in a long migration southward halted in the swamp and settled on the death tree, remaining there for a while and then disappearing.

"I have come almost to believe in the legend. After all, what more curious legends than those which we live every day?" She extended her arms above her head and breathed hungrily. "Isn't life wonderful? Isn't it a shame that more people don't live it? Let me see, I believe we should bear to the right. I have never been here before."

"You've never been here before?" Peter asked in surprise.

"No, I've never been in Barnwell Swamp in my life. But last year I looked in the last imaginable reaches of Rainbow Gully—it's endless, you know—and the year before I looked all the way along Bayou Volante from its source to where it goes into the bay. Other years? Well, to tell you the truth, I don't know where all I have looked except to say that Barnwell Swamp is about the only place I haven't."

"You mean it could just be anywhere?"

"Yes, anywhere between the two points that you can see from the municipal pier. He said that this was the only place the butterflies will land."

"He? Who are you talking about?"

"Oh, someone you will never know, but I shall tell you of him one night when we run out of things to talk about. You must know of him, for without knowing of him you cannot know of the butterfly tree."

"Well, won't I see it if we find it?"

"Of course, but you'll simply be seeing it, not finding it. But questions are so difficult to answer sometimes. They can be posed in flicker-instants, while answers take a lifetime. And so often answers are not words, but feelings and quicksilver things that flow out of minds before they are actually thoughts. Peter, Peter," she took his arm, "here is the first spring. They say that no one has counted the number of springs that feed Barnwell Swamp. The earth here is alive with them, and some of them actually flow through the floor of the bay where the swamp comes into it."

Now already, although the day was bright, the swamp began to take on a brooding, evil quality as it deepened. The path ran damp and black across wide tree roots and through stretches of swamp grass to plunge again beneath arches of vine and interlocked tree limbs. Some curious condition of the atmosphere caused the water line in the stagnant marshes to be indefinite, so that the bordering trees seemed suspended between the water and the sky, or again they appeared with their funereal Spanish moss to be under water.

Miss Billy followed the path as though she had been there before, not bothering to look out for cottonmouths. Peter followed more cautiously, for the swamp made him uneasy, as if his senses, like the trees, were suspended. There were troubling suddennesses there, too, frogs and things that flopped into the water or birds that set the underbrush in motion.

They had been walking for nearly an hour since they entered the swamp, and Peter was suddenly anxious, for there was the sort of sameness to everything that causes people to lose their way. He had noticed paths branching and tunneling through other vines and branches, and the seeping springs were all alike.

Now and then they passed through sudden blurs of sunlight

that filtered through the matting overhead, and once in a while they were in the open where the sun was almost blinding after the darkness beyond.

"Miss Billy, does anyone know where we are?"

"Of couse not, silly; we don't even ourselves. Why do you ask?"

"Well, what if we are lost?"

"Well, what if we are? One almost has to get lost to find the butterfly tree. You see, it's that important. I wish I could make you understand. Now that I think about it, perhaps that's why I never found it before. I looked in all the magic places I *knew*, places with pretty names. But this place is more magic than the others. I guess I have saved it unknowingly for that reason, also for the reason that you are with me."

"But you didn't know I would be along in all those other times."

"Peter, how many of us know things till they happen? That's very important, and you must remember it. I really must sit down a minute and rest."

They had come to a clearing in the sunlight which they had noticed ahead through the tunneled trees. Birds were singing there, singing in as many colors as the sunlight. They came into the sun, and the clearing was almost an island, a sandy clearing with vines cascading from treetops and ferns etched against tree trunks. Everywhere there was curious vaporish light; even the shadows had a translucence about them.

Miss Billy seated herself on a great cypress knee that thrust on down into the shallow water beyond. The fan appeared from somewhere.

"These swamps are full of legends, like old books that only beautiful and sensitive children read and are never able to find again after they grow up. I have known, for example, the butterfly legend for a long time, but somehow I wanted to save Barnwell Swamp, for it seemed the final place. Now in practical things like my best china I don't believe in waiting, but I like to save my legends and my magics. Once they have happened they never happen exactly the same way again."

She looked back the way they had come, and she looked through decades of trees and days of pendulous vines. Softly

then, the swamp was the sift and count of years, for he knew
that her look was full of wilderness and eternity, both the same
now.

"Once I was a little girl, a very little girl, and lonely perhaps,
but children seldom know they are lonely. I think I was, for
lonely children, especially on Sunday afternoons, find reality and
dreams hard to distinguish. I accepted dew, sunshine, and animals
as part dream, part truth, things that might not have happened
if I had not been there watching. There were secret hideaways,
where I, even then, built legends for myself—tree-root castles,
tunnels in rose bushes. The cornfield was a gigantic forest full
of grotesque and improbable giants. The bare winter fields
whispered wind secrets; the tall autumn grass leaned in rhythm
with the years and all my dreams. Often then, even then, I
cried on long still summer afternoons that time was passing, for
I didn't want things to change; they were soft, gentle and
melancholy things that would lose their shape with time.

"But one afternoon, a rain-searched afternoon, when the far
fences and horizon-line trees were fables and I was wandering
among the rose trellises and the sweet peas, I came to the
edge of the garden where our fence ran. Miles of meadow
stretched beyond and beyond, and I knew that it stretched on
forever and even then there was no end to it but that it came
around to right where I stood and would be there always.
I was the only mover in that vast stretching. I could turn for
a moment, I knew, and when I should turn back, the meadow
with its acres of fennel and sand spurs would be somehow
different, for moments matter only to things that perceive, not
the things that are perceived.

"I stood there, a very little girl in a blue sweater, and had a
great and terrifying thought. I suppose after that day I began
to grow up, and my Sunday afternoon sadness might have been
then for the little girl who was moving slowly across mythologies
of meadow, itself unchangeable, to all manner of unknowables."

The birds had grown still, and the water, felt around them,
reaching, seeping, into the things they thought about. And words
were water milled, caught, forced to softness. They waited for

something that would bring their horizons back to focus, but the swamp was quiet in spite of its thousand voices. A noise here, then, a noise there, a strange tuning up from moments of silence. A sliding noise keyed a ruffled surface of water; then a circle spread in a clean sweep to an overhanging water-floated vine, which twitched the limb to which it was attached, setting a bird into flight and disturbing legions of whirring things. Leaves sifted to the mirror surface, and other circles spread. The noises grew into voices that laughed and cried, prophesied for their listeners a thousand beauties and pains.

Peter lifted his face to the sun and tried not to listen to the insect, bird and water voices, for they told, told truths and lies, and there was no way to tell which was which. Birds flashed blue and gray through moss-hung arcades, and flute voices sang; frogs green and heavy slipped under the pool edge, and cello sounds swelled; gray trees loomed together cathedral-like, and chorus voices deepened and rolled together. They dropped and whispered of all the things Miss Billy was looking for, and they lifted and asked what in all the world he was looking for. They told, and he half-knew this already, that there was no butterfly tree and that they, he and Miss Billy, were two foolish people lost in a swamp.

Shadows had grown unnoticed beside the trees, and the sun had changed the dimensions of the forest of tendrils and leaves. Miss Billy rose and looked at the path beyond, then back at the one they had come.

"We'd better get on before it gets too late. We're almost there."

"How do you know; how can you know?" He halfway wanted to tell her what the voices had said.

"Oh, you come to know after you have waited for a very long time. You sense things across distances and time. You remember all the magnificent times of looking and know that waiting will have a stop and that you are close to the end of waiting."

"But what happens after the end of waiting?"

"Why, the end of—" she stopped, and the other voices stopped. The swamp hung again suspended upside down in the pools;

the late afternoon filled with soft-moving shadow tones and odors of dusk-opening flowers. Miss Billy stood for a moment, uncertain; ahead lay the believed direction of the butterfly tree. She turned and looked at Peter, and a misty light was on her face as if she saw him clearly for the first time and not as another queer magic that had materialized from the Mobile bus a few weeks before.

"If I close my eyes and forget much between, Peter, it's almost as if you and he are the same. He might have asked that question, and perhaps that's why he never—why, yes, of course. But I do have an answer for you (and perhaps, now that I think about it, for him). No, an end to seeking is not what I almost thought just then; it is a beginning of magics, of all the legends. After finding the butterfly tree I shall know about beauty and life, what everything has meant. She will come in the window, too, in her blue sweater, and I can go back to the long meadow with her, and I shall know at last where it ends." She closed her eyes and smiled.

The swamp stirred leaf by leaf, and perceptibly something changed; coolness filled the half-shadowed corridors. The Spanish moss moved gently, and the water sparkled coldly and darkly.

"We must go back now, Peter; summer is gone, and the butterflies have flown away."

"How do you know?"

"That is one question I cannot answer. I just know, as I have always known before. We were close, so close that a few more yards—"

"But you can't just know all this. It isn't that simple."

"Peter, haven't you ever wanted anything? Really, I mean?"

"Yes, I—"

"Then you must know when you wait for something long enough, you are bound to know certain things about it that no one has to tell you. You learn to recognize signs of its becoming, or of having just missed it. Haven't you?"

He tried to think of Ann and the world that he had left, but neither she nor it seemed to fit in here. Beyond that, he wondered if, after all, Miss Billy might not be right, if really he had ever wanted anything very much. There was so much all at once to experience, to want, to look for.

They went back along the path; they had a long way to go.

The way was different, for it was near-night. The tree frogs and cicadas taunted them now that the other voices had left off; but they didn't lose their way, for by the time darkness was full they emerged once more into the pine wood and were soon following the road back.

As they passed the old Catton Place, now gloomy, its spires rising mistily into the silver-green moonlight, Peter knew, and was vaguely surprised, that he was disappointed that they hadn't found a butterfly tree. Elsewhere, perhaps, where time could be measured by clocks and calendars (and not just knowing), where distances were streets and numbers (and not threads of path through a swamp), a butterfly tree would be hard to conceive. But here, all of a sudden—but had it been sudden?—it was believable.

He knew, too, as they walked wearily up Bayview and toward home that Miss Billy had been right. It was autumn.

Autumn

1

Now THE summer was past, and its passing was part of many things. It was a slow blurring of the old life, which was somewhere at the other end of the long road. It was also part of something new—a near-identification with the landscapes that stretched away and promised unfulfillable things.

Autumn comes to southern towns almost imperceptibly, so that, reds and yellows having appeared gradually among the pines and live oaks, which are forever green, there is one day a sudden awareness of the colors, and it is an unforgettable experience. The Spanish moss lifts along the colored boughs like the beards of old men whispering together that winter will come.

The swamps gave other promises then, so on some of the brisk afternoons after school or mornings of the week-ends Peter walked into the paths of the woods and thought about elsewhere places with their elsewhere people. Sometimes he was frightened by all the whys, the tangled synapses of all the yesterdays, the phantoms who crept through his dreams, and most of all by heaven and hell.

Some days he would go to the cemetery—the peaceful little hill just beyond Top Street. It was a hidden place with upthrusting vines covering the fence and climbing up the fence-row trees. He liked the cemetery for its utter disregard for order or formality. There were no even rows, no formal plots, or imposing ornaments. The graves were placed haphazardly, as if the dead had picked some favorite positions and lain down in them forever. Thick grayish moss had crept over most of the older stones, and short little trees locked limbs over ancient sleeping ladies. He would sit on the flat gravestones and look from the hill on to

part of the town, thinking how quick, how soon and sudden time
is gone and often how time is kind. With what indifference those
moving along Top Street, busy, busy with god knows what,
looked on the gray dusty moss. Few ever came actually, except
to dump another Top Street mover in the ground then move
away to forget (if the years were sudden and soon).

This day the wind was ruffing the clouds up, sending long
gray tongues of cloud out to taste the great expanse of blue. He
was sitting on Mrs. Van Neider's great flat stone, cracking pecans
with a piece of broken flower pot. The cemetery was quiet save
for the sea-saddened wind which sang elegies among all the
stones that had been forgotten or neglected by long-gone singers.
There were dirges in the yew trees, and the leafless pecan trees
dropped handfuls of pecans, scattering them among the dry grass
and the crumbling marble.

He was lost in this dismal wailing chorus of ancient funeral
voices, pitching his mind with the low bassoon moan of the wind,
which sucked along the ravine and was steady rhythm for the
uneven whine of the oboe of the yews and percussion of dead
limbs and falling pecans. It was cold, so he had pulled his coat
around his ears and was bent low against the headstone of Mrs.
Van Neider's grave. He was startled when suddenly a man materialized beside him, clearing his throat apologetically. Peter
hadn't seen him coming, and he was a little bewildered until he
remembered the man had probably come through the fence from
the ravine behind the cemetery.

The man stood there in the thin sunlight smiling, and there
was something about the smile disturbingly confiding. His eyes
were large and luminous, burning in a too-pale face, which was
stark and sharp between a round forehead and a too-prominent
jaw. He was middle aged, yet young in a vaguely unpleasant
sense, something wrong about him, a trespassing quality. His
hands hung at his sides twitching softly against his legs; if Peter
had associated him with an apparition, the hands would have
been the main reason. They were longer than ordinary hands
and seemed to be out of proportion with everything else about

him. In spite of their size, though, they were delicate, sensitive, even artistic.

"I'm sorry," he spoke suddenly, and his voice was not out of place in the vast symphony of wind and silence to which until now Peter had been a solitary listener. "A loved one perhaps?"

"No," Peter's voice broke the silence, accomplishing what the man's voice had not. "I just like to come here." He brushed the pecan shells off the stone, hoping that this man was not one of the Van Neiders.

"Yes, I know. I come here often. It is, after my room, a sort of second home." Peter shuddered suddenly, and it wasn't fully from the cold.

He looked again at the man, whose silky black hair was lifting in the wind. He wore gray trousers and an old black coat, threadbare, shiny as though something once moist had dried on it.

"And, too, I had a lot to do with putting many of these people here. Oh, heavens no, whatever you conclude from the statement is wrong without your telling me. I'm in the funeral business."

"An undertaker?"

"We prefer—mortician." He smiled what passed for a smile. "Now putting the cart back in its normal position behind the horse, my name is Edward Bloodgood. And yours?"

"Peter Abbott."

"Oh, yes, Miss Billy's ward. I do hear a few things, though heaven knows how, since my clientele is singularly uncommunicative. But are you here for long? So far I have not learned, though what one finds out from funeral-goers is amazing."

"I am going to Ferndale College."

"Ferndale. College time. I suppose that is really the best time of all. After that brilliance the world dulls down. I have often wondered if that same brilliance in a youth's eyes—like yours, for example—accounts for a corresponding brilliance in the world he sees. Haven't you? So strange, too, how people when they're twenty or thereabouts are sure they can never never die. That happens then only to people who are old or people who are not beautiful. Yet, only yesterday afternoon—oh, but I mustn't throw a pall over our first meeting, for I consider it important, don't you?"

Peter didn't know to which part of this flow of questions and half-answered questions he should reply, so he nodded.

"My rooms are next to the mortuary, so convenient, really. Perhaps you will come and see me. There is so much to talk about; you wouldn't think so in a tiny limbo like Moss Bayou, but that's where you would be wrong. There are always the universals, and they are so comforting in my business. I wish we could talk longer, but I must get back. I have an appointment, and people are so everlastingly impatient—that is, all except one in this case."

He turned to go, and there was again in his body-profile that boyish quality that Peter had first noticed. Mr. Bloodgood turned back.

"I do hope you will come to see me. I have some books you would probably enjoy and an exquisite little statue from Asia Minor which I love to show to people who will appreciate it. Besides, it will be a long winter, and it's nice to have more than one fireside to visit. Well, good-bye till later." He disappeared out the gate.

Peter got up slowly but something prompted him to leave quickly, for now no longer was this scene as peaceful as it had once been. Suddenly the gravestones were no longer impersonal monoliths, but now a crowning finality to something that went on behind closed doors in that gray building uptown he had casually noticed once or twice. All at once he wanted to hear something vital like Eulacie's chuckle. He walked out the way his new acquaintance had gone and followed the road that led toward the bay and the house.

Across the trees a ruddy sunset etched the black twigs of trees, as flocks of birds, silhouetted, too, settled into them. He wondered briefly what Mr. Bloodgood's room was like, but then he was at his own gate and gratefully went inside.

2

He visited Miss Claverly now more frequently. They, it seemed, discovered more and more in common. They swapped books and then talked about them. They explored curious old monographs on natural history which they found in the Moss Bayou public library. At first Miss Claverly was disturbingly eccentric, but he soon found her eccentricity charming and vital.

Sometimes they went for long walks along the beach. Miss Claverly always carried jars or bottles to bring back water samples from stagnant ponds. Peter came to be familiar with her makeshift equipment, just as he had become familiar with her way of life. Miss Claverly was not practical, but she was inventive. She found it difficult to cope with the ordinary things of everyday life, but in matters with which few people were familiar she could theorize and work solutions with astonishing facility.

Peter found her a wonderful audience for all his ideas, all his expressions of enthusiasm and depression. She listened with her head to one side and wisely said mostly the things he wanted to hear. He had been in Ferndale for a few weeks, and she followed his first impressions with interest, asking him questions for which so far he had not thought to seek answers, causing him to seek them out in the college library. And he was delighted when he could bring her a new idea or a fact discovered in an old book or magazine. He was gratified to see her scurry off for a pencil to make a note somewhere in the reams of research she kept.

They drank tea into the night while the wind cried in Rainbow Gully, and they and the hounds became a cozy community of spirits as the autumn nights sharpened and the leaves were burned with brilliant colors by a subtle and secret alchemy.

"My dear," she would say often, "you are going to be somebody. So many people barely miss it, but there is some little something that prevents it—some chromosome variation, some genetic influence too minute for measurement."

"Or something environmental, maybe?"

"No, no. There is entirely too much of this environmental nonsense. I won't discount training and surroundings, but they effect surface elements; the million-to-one combinations of genes are the real story."

"But natural selection?"

"Purely a matter of protective coloring, a growing of legs or arms or pseudopodia for a purpose, leaving the entity of the plant or animal much the same."

"But," Peter would persist, for he knew Miss Claverly loved this sort of thing, "whole species are created because of environmental demands. Dr. Anson says—"

"My dear, your Dr. Anson is probably a fool—but he can perhaps still teach you a lot, so don't hold that against him. I have a theory that such evolution of species is itself a genetic influence—that is, the potential exists in the animal so that it is prepared to turn out any number of ways according to environmental demands. By *heredity* it adapts to an environment. If this inherent potential for adaptation is not present the species dies out; if present, it adapts. But I suppose I am going off the deep end."

"I think I'll ask him what he thinks about that."

"I wouldn't. He has been straddling the heredito-environmental fence so long he probably can't conceive of anything but a bland fifty-fifty ratio interpretation. Or if he should see any possibilities in the notion he would probably write a book on the subject, thereby stealing my idea and making money on it, as well as a possible ripple in contemporary evolutionary investigation."

"Why don't you write it?"

Sometimes she would haul out a section of her research and read him about the "halfways" as she preferred to call certain tiny animals, which she used as examples to support her theory.

She had them divided into interesting categories such as side-pool animals or mid-stream animals. She had done illustrations of these animals, and they would pore over them long hours, contemplating the freaks and dead ends in nature.

Peter soon became familiar with the contents of the cigar boxes, even to their names, such as *Oeneis melissa semidea, Glaucopsyche xerces,* and scores of names with sibilant and whispering sounds. She told him where she had caught them, their habits, and all the knowns and unknowns about these butterflies. The unknowns were to her the most fascinating, of course. How certain species had got from one continent to another, whether by migration or as stowaways on ships.

"To me," she said one evening as they looked at the stretched and pinned brilliancies, "one of the commonest is the most wonderful of all—the monarch, the *Danaus plexippus,* which migrates hundreds of miles every year. I have never seen a flight of them, but someone I knew once saw them, hundreds of thousands all at once. Imagine!"

"Why do they migrate?"

"That is what we are trying to find out. Where and when they start, what route they travel, whether these migrations are in relation to a certain weather condition or a food supply, dozens of questions. Your question is the real one, though—why they migrate at all. Some have thought it is from overpopulation; others have thought it is from starvation, but the really wise ones say they don't know. It is one of the greatest mysteries of the natural world. I think the greatest."

"But other animals migrate, don't they?"

"Yes, but there is a better reason in almost every case—food, breeding purposes, parasites, overpopulation, climate. The monarchs actually fly a thousand miles to hibernate, and then it isn't really hibernation. Most of all, the climate to which they migrate could support them all year round, but they fly back to where they came from."

"But how do you find these answers?"

"By research, my dear—a looking into the law of cause and effect. There have to be reasons, good ones. Whole legions of butterflies don't just up and migrate for the fun of it. We, the scientists, must piece together fragments of evidence and collect this evidence in a positive direction. For certain persons quite advanced in this research, a wing, a twig of a bush where they have settled, the way the wind was blowing when certain movements were observed, all are vastly important hints."

"But do you simply collect this information? What do you do with it?"

"Indeed not. I send wings, notes, observations off every week. You see, I am not one of the advanced ones. I am simply a field-worker. While I know what I am looking for, I still haven't spent my life at this. There is so much I don't know and so much I know I must know. Science must not be a selfish thing but a concerted effort in a single direction. There are butterfly people all over the world who help the nucleus research along yet are, like me, off on individual aspects."

"Do you have an individual interest, something different that nobody else is doing?"

"As a matter of fact, I do. I'll tell you about it one of these days, but right now I want us to look at some bacteria cultures. They should be just right by now." She arose from the couch and began getting her equipment together—another cigar box of slides and tweezers.

After looking at slides and illustrations for a while longer and a final cup of tea, he had to go, for the hour was late. Miss Claverly lighted him to the road with her flashlight in the company of the dogs, who thrashed around with unaccustomed enthusiasm in the night brush and sniffed at familiar stumps and upthrust roots. The wind had risen from Rainbow Gully and was scurrying hundreds of unseen leaves through its complicated recesses and vine tunnels.

Along the sand road home it was dark, and the trees loomed gigantically lonely on each side of the road, pointing with their topmost leaves to one infinity and with their bottom-most roots to another. For the first time Peter felt not so lonely but hurried with a warmth and understanding that every tomorrow is a new time—beginnings, continuations, and ends for each thing in its element.

Miss Claverly dealt in a different species of magic from that of Miss Billy. She could take hers out and look at it in a hundred brilliant forms, while Miss Billy's was something not of the real but the unreal. Miss Claverly's magic was something that could be measured, and in a way her world was more comfortable.

Yet, as the dilapidated old mansion came into view, Peter quickened his steps and felt a surge of excitement.

3

WHEN HE arrived home from school the next evening (evenings were earlier now, and dark came across the swamps and hammocks suddenly), there were brightness and laughter inside, kitchen noises and the music of the phonograph all together. He shut the door, which always slammed in spite of.

"Peter, is it you?" Miss Billy came from the parlor into the hall. "Of course it is, for who on earth else would it be? Although," she reflected, "people in Moss Bayou never knock. If you aren't home they come in and borrow canned tomatoes and ice cubes. But hurry and get ready; we are having a party."

"Party? But who?" Parties had always been things where people got invitations and planned things.

"Oh, nobody's coming. Just us. That way we don't have to be on our toes." She hesitated. "Is there anyone you would like to ask? Eulacie and I just all of a sudden decided, about an hour or two ago, to have a party. We do often, and now that you're here, we'll have one more person. Now hurry."

Peter went upstairs feeling slightly confused, but then, he remembered, everything in this place was confusing. He went into his room and put his books down, fingering them affectionately: *Harbrace's Handbook of Composition, Survey of English Literature, Introduction to Biology* and *Elements of Greek.* The table with the lamp, the wallpaper from which the design had almost disappeared, the smell of the old house, and the window which looked to the bay, all were his, and he knew that again, after a long time, he belonged somewhere. He thought of the long nights from now when he would know, by the long and patient process of learning, the contents of the books, and they, like the table and the wallpaper and the house, would belong to him. He walked to the door, and a feeling of ineffable content and melancholy enveloped him.

When he came downstairs into the kitchen, there were Japanese lanterns strung from rafter to rafter. Flowers were everywhere, spilling out of bowls and glasses. Miss Emmajean was up to her elbows in a bowl of molasses and was trying to stick together popcorn from another bowl. Miss Billy was making bubbles by dipping a little metal instrument into a jar of liquid and waving it through the air.

"They say that bubbles always revolve from east to west, but I have counted fifteen out of ninety-four that do just the reverse. You just can't believe anybody any more. Oh, that record is finished. Miss Emmajean, honey, go—" she regarded Miss Emmajean's condition, "no, on second thought—Peter, go put on that lovely madrigal record I found in the bargain stack at the Home Department Store."

Eulacie was poking around the stove.

"To hell with fried chicken. Slowest stuff to cook I ever saw. Miss Emmajean, you string that crap on the floor, I'm goin' to personally tear you up."

Peter looked at all the activity and was unaccountably happy. "Can I do anything?"

"Let's see, dear, go get that set of liqueur glasses. We are going to have that bottle of crème de violette that Clara Foster brought me from New Orleans last Mardi Gras. This is the time for it."

He brought the glasses from the china closet and placed them by the plates. "Miss Emmajean, too?"

Eulacie looked up from the stove and snorted. "'That little bastard? I can't leave a can of beer around for five minutes she ain't inhaled it. She don't yet know what a good shot of white magic can do for you when nothin' else will, so as long as she don't know I don't guess it'll hurt her none. Just don't leave the bottle out."

Miss Billy sent up another flight of bubbles, and they drifted softly to the ceiling and disappeared. "Such lovely things, so done and over when they're finished, and where do they get such colors?"

Peter wanted to tell her that Miss Claverly had said they have only one layer of molecules and that there was some business about surface tension, but he thought he wouldn't.

Miss Emmajean had got in such a mess that Peter had to get her cleaned up. Eulacie meanwhile had finished the chicken and biscuits and put everything on the table. Miss Billy filled the room once more with bubbles and came to the table, which was laid out with a linen cloth and favors for everyone.

As they sat down, the phonograph was playing:

> The silver swan, who living had no note,
> When death approached unlocked her silent throat;
> Leaning her breast against the reedy shore,
> Thus sung her first and last, and sung no more:
> Farewell, all joys; O death, come close mine eyes;
> More geese than swans now live, more fools than wise.

"Mercy, how true. Although there are fools and fools. Some kinds are fools because they are wise, and that makes a great deal of difference." Miss Billy blew out a little rolled-up piece of paper, which when unrolled and filled with air had a tiny white feather on the end.

"That's quite an observation, Miss Billy. It quite changes the connotation of fool."

"Oh, this college crap; I know we was done for the day he start." Eulacie popped a lump of sugar into her mouth and tugged at Miss Emmajean's pigtails which were gummed together with molasses.

"But, Peter, dear, how many genuine fools have you known? I think it is a special connotation. Idiot is one thing, moron, imbecile, dolt, but fool is something special. When I think of the word I invariably think of the Order of Myths float in the final Mardi Gras parades—Death chasing Folly around a column but never catching him. Fool, the cheater of Death by a thousand devices. Think of all the sober people who die and die because they haven't found the little green door that opens into the world of toys and make-believes."

"But death. That's it for everybody, fool or not."

"Oh, Peter, when will you see? I don't mean that kind of death. I mean the gray death that must look back at a life which was empty of colored stones, soap bubbles, and—well, parties."

"But what has that to do with wisdom?"

"Oh, my big butt," moaned Eulacie. "College."

"To cheat death—death in life or death after life—one must be wise, for what will individual tragedies matter a few years from now? That's why I want things to matter now." She tried the paper blow-out again.

"Oh, you lose me."

"And you both damn well lose me." Eulacie ate another lump of sugar and shot Miss Emmajean a warning glance, as Miss Emmajean with her tongue in the bottom of her glass rolled her eyes at the bottle.

"Take, for example, two neighbors I used to have. One was a librarian and the other a chiropractor. They were very intelligent, talented, and young. Young, although both were over forty. It was a great pleasure to see them blowing up anthills with fire-crackers early on Sunday mornings or chasing butterflies."

"They was nuttier than a five-cent Hershey bar. Barkin' at dogs and talkin' imitation foreign languages through the fence."

"Eulacie will always hold it against the chiropractor that he wiggled the hose through the grass at her one day, and she chopped it—our only hose—into a million pieces with the grass blade."

"If it's anything will make me go ravin' crazy it's a snake, and that bastard know it. Look around after I finish my choppin' chore, and there they was rollin' and laughin' on the grass with a good fence between me and them."

"Yes, Eulacie, and you would have been lynched anywhere else in the state for what you called them."

"Then, Miss Billy, have you ever known anyone who was really a wise fool?"

She thought for a moment, her head to one side and the paper blow-out held like a cigarette. "Why, yes, rather a good number. But some of them, I'm afraid, just wouldn't take life seriously, and a really wise fool is very serious about life."

"Like them chiropractic son of bitches," Eulacie hmphed.

"But there was one—one wise fool I knew. Oh such a wise fool. So much with the world and out of it. A wind and weather fool, a wise man among books and legends, something of the water, sad and gay. Grim as old German fairy tales but again light as butterflies drifting on air currents. Oh, such a swan among geese." She had clasped her hands, and her eyes were dancing with light, but not the light from the Japanese lanterns.

"Who, Miss Billy? And where now?"

The light went down, and the hands relaxed. An unbecoming sadness came for an instant but was rapidly gone. "Yes, who, and where now? Such unimportant questions at last, for the years have hurried, and because of such wise fools one can make a great deal of the years. Now, Eulacie, let's sing that little Creole song we learned winter before last—a lovely thing, Peter, about a girl who locked her lover out. Listen, and you can sing with us.

> "*To, to, to!*—'*Ça qui là?*'
> —'*C'est moin-mênme lanmou;*
> *Ouvé lapott ba moin!*' "

Their voices blended, Miss Billy's a curious soprano like wind caught on a treble harp string and Eulacie's a cotton-patch contralto. Even Miss Emmajean joined them silently on the "*To, to, to*" part, shaping her pink mouth desperately in an effort to keep up.

> "*To, to, to!*—'*Ça qui là?*'
> —'*C'est moin-mênme lanmou;*
> *Qui ka ba ou khè moin!*'"

Peter started visibly all of a sudden. It was alarming how dim Ann had become, how slowly and gently he was moving in quite another world. Something about time, perhaps, that it, too, obeyed the law of impenetrability which does not allow two things to occupy the same space at the same time. At happy moments like this he seemed to be off on the edge of experience, and it was something to wonder at whether he and Ann had ever really existed. But they had, they had; and he realized that his mind was shouting at itself above the final verse of the song.

> "*To, to, to!*—'*Ça qui là?*'
> —'*C'est moin-mênme lanmou;*
> *Laplie ka mouillé moin!*'"

"Peter, where, where are you. *You* haven't been locked out. Just the girl's unfaithful lover, and he deserved it."

"Damn right. The son of bitch." Eulacie said meaningfully.

"Oh, parties are such fun. We really should have one every week, but," Miss Billy reflected, "if they are planned for they lose something. A party must be sudden, while one is in the mood. Think of all the poor dears who plan so hard for a party that when it gets there, they really had rather be in bed asleep."

"Speakin' of asleep, I think this young'un has drunk herself into oblivious with that lavender stuff."

Indeed Miss Emmajean was looking rather wall-eyed, her canned-beer taste not quite up to the heavier liqueur.

"Well, pile those dishes somewhere, and forget them. Peter and I need to get some air. It is a lovely night, and maybe there will be lots to talk about, and maybe there won't. Maybe we'll even try to count stars."

They watched Eulacie throw Miss Emmajean over her shoul-

der like a sack of flour and go out, then they went out back and
circled by way of the garden toward the road.

The night was gigantic and wonderful, still so that one could
almost imagine that the stars made a noise (like faraway carnival
ferris wheels) swinging in their orbits. Their shoes made a sharp
barking noise in the sand of the road, and even their clothes
whispered loudly as they moved.

"Peter, Peter, you are beginning to want something. You don't
know quite what yet, but you are."

Peter felt unaccountably annoyed.

"What do you mean? I don't want anything."

"But you do. Suddenly at the table your expression changed,
and I knew something had clicked in you somewhere. Some
decision had been made; something had been admitted, perhaps."

"Oh, but that's silly. I don't think I have thought about anything much tonight."

"Yes, but someday you'll look back at tonight and know that
you did think of something and that something did change.
You'll see." Her voice dropped to another plane. "Perhaps someday you'll be, too, a wise fool. Wise fools can change your life."

"Tell me about your wise fool."

"So much to tell; yet," her voice dropped further, "so little."

"Tell me."

"Once there was a wise fool. (Is that the proper place to
start?) No one would have called him particularly wise, and
certainly not a fool; but people will never learn that a person
can be many things together while not any of them separately.
He came along when I was perhaps eighteen, for years mattered
to me then. He was somewhere out ahead in years—but I shall
never know where—perhaps twenty-two or so, maybe a hundred
and twenty-two; for some people have no age. We met at a
gumbo supper at the Normal School at Daphne. He was suddenly there with gray eyes looking at me. I would have been a
little alarmed with such a frank stare had there been anything
positive in the eyes; but since there was sadness and humor and
many other things, I looked back, and to each other we all at

once meant. And had we not meant, I would have been frightened at his first words to me as he stood over beside me.

" 'Did the morning-glories open this morning? I forgot to look.' And this in all seriousness. Before I could answer (for I tried to remember if they had), he said: 'But of course; they always do. They're a lot more dependable than people in that respect. But I remember when I was small I always checked to be sure. Did you come with someone?'

"And there it was; there he was, all of a sudden. I remember that I mumbled something about being with Amelie March, and he said that didn't matter, that there were worlds of time between then and heaven. He then introduced himself to me and Amelie, who just had to see who was talking to me. It was an unusual name—Creston Robert—almost as if his first and last name had been reversed. So we saw him leave down the stairs at the Normal School, and out beneath through the grove of old oaks with their draperies of moss.

"I couldn't in that short time have received enough of a physical impression to become fascinated, but all at once the night took on a different meaning. I saw the fireflies for the first time, how they seemed to flash brightest in the darkest places, and I caught the moon-ruffle on the far-spread stretch of bay. What in so few words could startle into being the sleeping creatures of the imagination? What is there about people that can do this?

"And there was a world of time between then and a still-to-be-discovered heaven. He came again and wondered why the water-edge cypresses turned blue in the fall. He came again, and it was winter when wood smoke curled across stark and sudden landscapes. And we talked of many little-known magics (for he knew all of them—dogs that cried and were lonely, rabbits that danced in the moonlight, and flowers that reproduced by shooting sparks of fire at each other); we saw each season unfold and blossom with its particular type of beauty; we were sad and happy together over what was lovely and lonely (and often they were the same, in spite of their very slight difference in spelling). And we loved, or what passed for love. When people are happy and sad together, see things a great deal alike, and learn to know each other's thoughts a little, they often love.

"And there was, of course, the butterfly tree, which was there for his knowing about it, where for me it hadn't been before. He told me about the colors of the butterfly tree, the shape and size of it, and that I might find it if I knew the where and how of it. These two things were the important things, and there could be no telling of them. I must go in my season and simply find it where it was. That's all I could ever manage to get, yet we talked often about it. He explained many of his magics with it, telling me that the butterfly tree was responsible for them. We never looked together, for it was as though he didn't have to look any more. . . .

"We'd better get back, for it feels late, and it begins to be cold." She shivered and pulled her scarf tighter around her.

"But what happened? What happened to him?"

"Always the conclusions. Oh, Peter. He came once when the pear trees were full of feathery snow blossoms and the sky was a stabbing spring-blue, and when I saw him I knew that was all—forever. He was wearing the old threadbare tweed coat he always wore. I try to remember him without it, and I can't. He was sad but not sad, and this was a farewell that was somehow inevitable. We stood there underneath the pear tree and said good-bye, and I wanted to know what was wrong. He said I must remember what was right, and then he said, 'Try to see the butterfly tree where it is, for it is nowhere else,' and after that he was gone, his kiss warm and sad on my mouth."

They were quiet, and in spite of the dark and chilly night air, Peter was thinking of sunlight and felt that Miss Billy was, too. He turned to her. "But what was he like; what did he look like?"

"He was no one you have ever known, Peter, yet everyone. I can't remember what he looked like, but I should know him again, no matter what the years have done. He had that about him. He was tall, yes, and his face was full of earth and stars; the sun came a certain way on his hair, and the rain made his eyes laugh."

"And has it been forever?" Peter asked softly.

"Many forevers. For it has been impossible to create another world since. Worlds are difficult to create and after that to hold together. I never heard again and didn't try to find him, for I felt that perhaps that was all I was supposed to have."

There was nothing to say after that, so they walked back in silence, night and climate combined in autumnal Hallowmas, leaves winging upward like startled birds. Somewhere below them the water sighed late and alone, flow tide starting to scatter the moonglow.

4

"Watch it, dear; not even a *Papilio marcellus* is worth breaking your neck for." Miss Claverly stood beneath the cliff, squinting up at him. "Oh dear, he got away. Well, never mind. I'm almost glad. It's rather nice to think that he will be free to go fluttering through the woods. On the other hand, he would have looked so magnificent mounted."

Peter scrambled down the cliff and looked back to see the bright butterfly rising, dropping its way up the cliff, quite safely out of reach now.

"Maybe he'll come back again if we wait."

"No, dear, let's not press mortality. Life is such a delicate thing in these quarters that it would seem a pity to have it escape once and then plopped into the cyanide. That's not scientific, I know, but in a way it comes close to cause and effect. The fact that he escaped once triggered my psychological mechanism to react a certain emotional way. That's not to say if he came and sat on this drift-log I wouldn't grab him without a moment's hesitation." Miss Claverly picked up the large straw satchel she usually carried, after lighting a cigarette and putting it into the holder. Today she wore the usual slacks and had added boots, as well. A floppy straw hat bobbed as she moved up the beach, and around her neck was the eternal tarnished necklace.

Peter followed her, wading with rolled-up trousers in the water edge. The beach curved in a long smooth line beneath the bare face of the cliff. Behind them, across the cove, was the municipal pier of Moss Bayou, looking now as if it were made of match sticks. Behind them, too, was the wooded area of beach with the cypresses (and they did look blue, just as Miss Billy's wise fool had said), and closer were some long poles on which were stretched fishing nets.

Tiny seeping springs ran at intervals into the bay, and their icy water changed the temperature of the warmer bay water around his feet.

They walked on until they got to a smooth piece of sand beyond which the beach curved along another cove.

"Here, here is the place. Cypress Point. There is a cove on either side of us, and look at this splendid stream." Miss Claverly sank into the sand and dropped the straw bag.

Here was one of the most beautiful places Peter had ever seen. A triangle of sandy beach pointed into the bay, and on the point of the triangle was one lonely battered cypress tree. Coming out of the underbrush behind and flowing through the roots of the tree was a perfectly clear creek overlaced by limbs trailing garlands of moss and vines. Back the way they had come, the high clay cliff had grown once more into perspective, and the wharves they had passed were diminutive now. Ahead, the land pointed off again, and houses broke but did not disturb the landscape. Their wharves were closer and reflected in the water, wavering across the distance.

"Are you hungry, dear?"

"Why, yes, but what good will it do me?"

In answer Miss Claverly pulled out a much-crushed brown paper bag and held it up. "Lunch. I always bring one; I never know how long I shall be out when I leave home. Today I simply packed enough for two."

They ate on a fallen trunk, and the battered sandwiches, pulverized potato chips, and shattered cookies tasted better than any food Peter could remember. Afterwards they lay on their backs in the warm sand stretching away the fatigue of the long walk, and the sky was an endless falling-away. At such a time it could be below with the observer clinging to an upside-down world, looking into its bottomlessness. Birds careering below in this blue void were detached, and the tops of trees were the final falling-off place into the dizzy nothingness. What was holding him, the trees, and the water secure against this flatness, pressing against him from underneath as he sought to fall, wanted to fall, into its everlastingness?

"So final—this." Miss Claverly, feeling something of his feeling, perhaps, spun the world upright again.

"Yeah." He was distantly sorry to be down again, and the recent height made his voice tremble.

"It makes everything so somehow meaningless—the biological urgencies, the grim certainties of living and dying, the levels of being."

"I was just trying to keep from falling into it, holding on by pressure to our little piece of sand and ready to grab that cypress if I started to go." Peter closed his eyes and tried to recapture the feeling.

"It is close," Miss Claverly said slowly, "to a feeling—a yet unexperienced feeling—I am seeking."

"Feeling?"

"Well, not a feeling exactly." She leaned up on an elbow and fitted a cigarette into her holder, and her hair lifted silkily in the water-borne breeze. "Feelings are determined like everything else. They are what they are because we are what we are. And yet they are the notches by which we gauge our experience and where experience fits us into the scheme of things."

"You make it sound so—well, mechanical."

"My dear, it is mechanical, everything. It was all wound up in the beginning, and it has been working, every minute part of it, toward this moment for me, which is a different moment for you."

"But what happens to purpose—and magic?"

"Well, what? Purpose?" She blew smoke, and it hovered over the sand, flattened and disappeared. "I don't understand."

"Why do you try to find out things about insects? If it is mechanical the problems will eventually be solved or not ever be solved. Isn't that right?"

"Of course, but that's part of the mechanics. Our curious human existences don't change just because things are going to work out such and such a way. I seek to answer problems because that is part of my mechanical destiny. You may write a book or become a criminal or a minister, but that doesn't change what was fitted out in the original machinery. I may discover something, and that is part of the plan (although I use this term with caution, for machinery can't be said to plan; it works a certain way and only relatively can we call a result a plan).

"But magic?"

"What do you mean by magic?"

"It's hard to explain." He thought of Miss Billy and her world of ghost children, toys, and unreal landscapes. "I mean the imagination, I guess, but not quite that. The outskirts of the mind that take the real and painful certainties and make them fanciful. It is the part of us that finds something beautiful or not beautiful."

"My dear, it is again a part of our deterministic make-up. It is the same thing. Beauty is perhaps the most relative of all our human values. It is not intrinsic, although there is a scale of potentialities that says such and such a thing is more likely to be considered beautiful than another thing. Take the matter of artistic taste for one example. No two people feel quite the same way about an object, although they both might agree that it is beautiful. The human senses are curiously delicate precision instruments. They respond to certain colors, forms, and textures more positively than to others. That response plus conditioning and associations of various sorts accounts for esthetic evaluation. And remember, it is a human characteristic. Other animals don't have it."

"What about the brilliant plumage of birds that attract the female?"

"I think that is tremendously overstated. Nature has done some rare and unusual things. Those birds would mate regardless. They would have to. They are far more beautiful (and I am forced to use the term for lack of a better one) to us than to the female bird. And their mating calls are more beautiful to us. They inspire us from time to time to write poetry, yet they merely summon the female bird for biological reasons."

"You spoke of an unexperienced feeling. What did you mean?" Peter watched a small cloud loosen itself and smear smokily near the horizon.

"Yes, there is something special that I am looking for, and I seem to be getting closer and closer. Still there is that wonderful and damnable scientific elusiveness that baffles me. It is here in these swamps, and this time I am almost sure. I first doubted it when I heard of it, but I have learned a great deal about it since. My research requires it as a missing gap to be bridged before I can move on."

"What is it, or would I understand?"

"In a way, perhaps, but then again nobody understands. We spoke of it once, and I think I told you it was one of the imponderables. There is that about it, though, that, once discovered, would lessen the unknown and move investigation forward tremendously."

"But what exactly? We have talked about so much."

"My dear, I believe that somewhere in this area there is a spot to which the monarch butterflies migrate every year. We have known for a long time that they come in this general direction, but—"

"You mean—a butterfly tree?" Peter rose to a sitting position and looked at her incredulously.

"Why, yes, but I didn't say anything about a tree, did I? Or did I before? I don't recall."

"No, it's just that—" He stopped, for he knew he would never be able to tell about his already knowing. Besides, this was a different thing entirely, something positive and scientific.

"Well, it is a tree—or at least we think it is a tree. We have long known about the California migrations, but our research shows us that this area, too, over two thousand miles away, is a stopping place. There does seem to be a preponderance of monarchs here, but so far I have looked in vain."

"You are looking today." It was a statement.

"Yes, I am always looking, although it isn't likely that we'll find them along this beach. More likely they'll be in a pine forest. Evidence is presented that they prefer such a surrounding. Personally I would like it here better if I were a butterfly." She stretched again on her back and breathed deeply.

Peter lay back and tried to fall again into the sky, but it was vacuously blue and hopelessly above him now. The clouds, beginning to boil over the horizon, were gigantic white butterflies, cautiously but inevitably taking over the sky. Why didn't he tell Miss Claverly about Miss Billy's butterfly tree? But it wasn't the same thing at all. Miss Claverly's tree was a thing of footnotes in reports and mildewed appendixes, while Miss Billy's was ephemeral and not quite of the world, heard of from a man—a wise fool, at that—who had run away before he himself was quite real to her. Yet, they were similar, but how, he could not think; something made them alike.

A bird splashed the water edge of the creek and fluttered off with a whirring sound. Peter rose quietly, glancing at Miss Claverly, who seemed to be asleep. He walked along the creek, bending to avoid the chaos of vines and moss hanging to the ground. The water was perfectly clear, and he watched the three levels of life at once—the bottom with its crayfish, the middle with the minnows, and the surface with water spiders—linked together by the undulating moss.

His image lay among the collected worlds somehow incongruously, and he found himself wanting to tell his image many things—things he could not tell Eulacie ("Hell, honey, you don't know what problems is!") or Miss Billy ("We are our own world, Peter, and all problems are our only way of knowing what happiness is by comparison") or Miss Claverly ("Part of the pattern, my dear; you nor anyone else can do anything about it").

He sat beside the stream and all at once found himself crying softly, aware that his reflection cried with him.

"I want to know how to keep from being alone. I want to know someone completely, for now my closest friends are strangers. Do you know what that is like? That's what I want more than anything else. I don't even—no, god, I don't—want to find the butterfly tree."

He cried harder, and then no more. The worlds of the stream which had blurred together moved back once again to their proper levels. Flecks of sunlight slipped through trees, and he was made aware of other worlds that opened around him and above him. He was overwhelmed by bird worlds, tree worlds— multitudes of worlds. And he was a part of all of them, yet having a world of his own.

He got up slowly and went to join Miss Claverly.

5

THE LIGHTS of the midway flashed up at him from behind a row of low buildings—colored lights that whirled and turned to the rollicking slow-motion sound of an electric calliope. The crowd moved like a huge, restless gulf tide, and the sound of their voices rose and fell with a curious rhythm. Beyond this regular rise and fall, there were the steady confused voices of the side-show barkers, sounding, all together, like a strange foreign tongue. Peter moved aimlessly from one booth to another, swept along by the crowd. Everywhere there was the smell of popcorn and candy, sawdust and sweat.

The ferris wheel was like a swarm of fireflies circling around a gaudy pink flower, turning its screaming burden up slowly, down rapidly. Its rocking lights and dizzy riders spilled sound and excitement among the deep distances of the night fields beyond.

The crowd was the kind of crowd that would be at any partially free attraction—women in tight print dresses and sweaters, men clawing at the seat of their pants, some sailors from Barin Field. Kids ran with piercing screams among the crowd, tripping over the lethal-looking electric wires that coiled everywhere.

It was a lonely feeling to be moving through an unknown crowd in an unknown place. The carnival was in Robertsdale, a town about fifteen miles east of Moss Bayou. Here the faces were unfamiliar. Everyone seemed to know someone else; even the sailors traveled in pairs, stepping on girls' heels and making awkward advances.

He stopped by the merry-go-round and leaned against a post, watching some silly little girls bouncing around, screaming, on the horses. The horses went around the circle to some vaguely familiar (but weren't they all vaguely familiar, nostalgic) carnival tune, plunging up, now down, with their gilded mouths open and their eyes wide and staring. One horse, prettier than the others, was yellow with black spots and a long black tail. Peter watched it as it came around again and again. Kids got off and on, and the music ground to a stop, then began all over. The yellow and black horse reared 'way up as though it were trying to get away from the shiny bar that pinned it in place, but it always came down again. Something was remotely disturbing about it, and he was suddenly reminded of Miss Claverly's butterflies fixed in place with shiny pins. He thought of them fluttering black and gold to get away from the pins.

There was a deeper thought, too, that maybe people had invisible pins they tried to squirm loose from or that they, too, went round and round a circle, never being able to get off. But it was a thought for a quieter and saner time. For now the sounds grew more insistent.

"Come in and see. This is only a sample of what's inside. What these young ladies don't have won't ever be missed. Come on in. Hurry! Hurry! Only fifty cents! Show starts in five minutes. Just a few seats left."

Peter stopped by a gambling concession (or a Magic Wheel,

as this carnival was safely referring to it), which seemed to be attracting many onlookers. It consisted of a flat disk with tiny nails around the circumference. A stationary carboard strip flicked across the nails as the wheel was turned, so that whichever number was indicated when the wheel stopped was the winner. A glib operator had a half dozen players lined up with their eyes revolving with the wheel and their quarters.

"Number fifteen! An' here's the lucky winner. What prize you care for? No, the watches is for the winner of five straight games. O.K., a genu-ine French harp with instructions to play in one easy lesson." The disgruntled losers milled around and moved off.

"Who'll be next?"

Peter looked at the prizes, and there was every variety of them. What caught his fancy, however, was an array of dolls dressed like chorus girls. Miss Emmajean desperately needed a new doll, he thought, remembering a headless one and others with assorted mutilations. This would be a good way to get her one for Christmas.

"Step up and see how easy it is to win a fabulous prize— watches, lamps, radios. Nothing to it."

Peter put a quarter before the wheel.

"Ah, here's a good sport. Come on, the wheel is turning. The number bet is twenty-three. Only twenty-five numbers—always a winner." A couple of other quarters were put on the board.

The wheel revolved slowly, catching the lights from the midway rides, spinning out the voices with grim finality, slowing, stopping, then: "Twenty . . . twenty-two—no, three—twenty-three! Here is another winner. Which of these fabulous prizes you wish to have?"

"I'd like a doll," Peter said, feeling ridiculous before the reticent viewers and the smooth operator.

"Sorry, Mac. Dolls is two straight wins. Try again?"

Peter felt cheated and foolish, for they were, he remembered, all like this, promising glittering items, then dragging out flyspecked and dusty consolation prizes. He started to turn.

"O.K., Mac, but twenty-three's been a hot number all day.

Better stick." The wheel was turning, while the man planted a feathered walking-stick before him.

Peter said nothing but placed another quarter down.

"Fifty cents, if you stay now, Mac."

Despising the man and himself, Peter reached for another quarter.

"Twenty-three trying for a double. Ah, we're coming. Slow, slow—twenty . . . one, two . . . th . . . three, oh, four, five— one, two. An' two it is. Sorry, Mac. Can still stay. Three chances on the double.

Peter was disgusted, but now he was angry as well.

"You mean I get the doll if I win this time?"

"Sure, but now it's gonna cost you a dollar."

"No, thanks." He started to turn.

"You already got seventy-five cents in." The man's eyes sneered at him, challenging him.

Peter put a dollar on the square and waited.

"Wheel is going, going. There she goes. Come on, bets down for all these genu-ine prizes."

This time the wheel stopped on fourteen. Desperate, Peter put another dollar on the square, and the man spun again, quick double-talk computing the amount to win now. The wheel stopped on fourteen again. Peter started to leave. There was nobody standing there now, for a fight had started over by the ferris wheel. The operator leaned forward, his green eyes slanted.

"Tell you what. You hit that twenty-three again, you get all your money back plus the doll." Peter looked at him numbly.

"What do you get out of it that way?"

"It's a gamble, Mac. You run outta money before you hit twenty-three, that's tough on you. You hit twenty-three, that's tough on me. O.K.?"

Peter put another dollar down. The wheel turned. In his anger and loathing for having got involved, the motion half-hypnotized him, and another dollar followed. Another.

He saw the futility of this. Twenty-five chances to one that the cardboard strip would stop his nail. The wheel turned, and he felt the two dollars he had left. He had had fifteen when he left home. But he knew now that he would go all the way, for otherwise he would be forever plagued by what might have been with that last dollar. The wheel slowed, and the cardboard ticked around the nails. Again it wasn't his number.

The wheel spun again. He wanted to walk away, but the loathing fascination to see the thing out rooted him there. The calliope music was grotesque and ugly; the smells were suddenly nauseating. He hated himself desperately, because nothing mattered as much as being trapped into something which could have been so easily avoided. The wheel turned, turned in slow motion and slowed and slowed. . . .

The hand was quick. Even the operator was startled. It shot across the wheel, and, with tearing cloth, ripped nails loose. The operator moved then but not before a gadget had been ripped from underneath the counter.

To Peter: "How much did he take you for? You can lie if you like. He won't complain." Peter started to answer and stopped when he saw that it was the blond boy of the Blue Moon Café and the hurricane-swimming afternoon.

"Well, how much?"

"Fourteen dollars," he said in a small voice. One or two persons were stopping.

"Tear up my game, wreck the place—" The man started to vault over the counter, but the boy held a hand on his chest.

"Hold it, friend. Don't think you can get us in a fight and then say to the sheriff you were protecting your racket from a pair of dumb country boys who are bad losers. The sheriff is my uncle. Gambling is illegal in this state; illegal gambling devices are illegal in any state, and I have the evidence in my hand. You'd better just keep quiet. I won't turn you in now, but tomorrow I shall. That will give you a chance to disappear. First, though, let's have the fourteen dollars."

"Fourteen dollars," the man said, subdued. "Couldn't have been over eight."

"Fourteen dollars," the boy repeated, holding out his hand. "Count it," he said, transferring the bills to Peter. He turned and moved his head for Peter to follow, leaving the man glowering and defeated behind his broken wheel.

"Fourteen dollars! You know you're a fool, don't you?"

"Yes," Peter said quietly. Then, "Frequently."

"It always surprises them to find anything close to a clever person among all these gullible country people. I think he believed me about my uncle being sheriff. Would you like some coffee?" His voice was beautiful, too, thoughtful and rather sad.

They went into one of the crude booths and sat at the plank table. Their coffee came in paper cups with spoons that resembled tongue-depressors. Flies rose and fell in swarms. The night became different now, and the fair was somewhat magical again.

"I remember you from somewhere, but that's rather unlikely since there are so few somewheres that would put us both here in this improbable place now." The boy lifted the arm with the torn sleeve and wiped his face.

"N-twenty-seven," came in a bored monotone from the bingo booth adjacent.

"I have been living in Moss Bayou since August. That's probably where." Peter didn't think the boy would recall the night in the Blue Moon Café, even though he knew it was the only time the boy had ever been actively aware of him.

"Oh, then that's where. Perhaps it was in the Blue Moon. I usually go there. I am amused by Venetia Sparrow." The boy laughed easily and genuinely, and Peter noticed briefly that his face was not so attractive when he laughed, for it was a face for other moods.

"I have been there only once. Mrs. Sparrow gave me a poem."

"It would be curious, I guess, anywhere but Moss Bayou to receive a poem with a cup of coffee. But that, too, with lots of other things I have come to accept, almost expect, from Moss Bayou. But who are you?" This, too, casually. "Someone to know, or someone to know for now?"

"Peter Abbott. Miss Clarice Billy is my great-aunt, and I am living with her until I can finish school at Ferndale. She's unusual."

"Really? Well, that is somehow a necessary attribute for residence in the Bayou."

"She sees ghost children." Peter didn't know why he wanted to confide this.

"Well, that is interesting. Everyone there does something unique. I collect psyches like other people collect books and buttons. They are the evanescents, but that is what makes them interesting."

"What do you do with them?"

The carnival whirled remotely now; Peter was so detached from it that it barely impinged on the senses, and even the bingo caller had been absorbed in the complex rhythms of the night.

"Do?" The boy smiled charmingly. "Oh, I can't catalog them or arrange them on shelves. I wouldn't if I could, for such collections gather dust and need attention. I suppose it is not a matter of what I do with them, but what they do with me."

Peter was delighted and dizzy with the idea, any idea this person would communicate.

"What is that?"

"They can change me—several times a day, even. Not my mood or my intelligence simply but the sum of the integers. And change is what we really want, except for the very rare philosopher, these days. Everyone sits around waiting for something or somebody to come in and change things. Or people rush out to their mailboxes, wait for the telephone to ring, go to bars, fortunetellers. Me, I don't wait but go to minds; it's one way to get through life." He smiled pensively. "Let's walk around some more. Perhaps there is, after all, something to see."

They walked aimlessly and detachedly. The curious world of make-believe out front was nothing but an avenue of cardboard and canvas fronts supported in the rear by wooden and metal props. It seemed that if one of the ropes were pulled, it would collapse the entire midway to the ground, strewing its twinkling jewels among the sawdust and spilled popcorn.

The crowd was gathering by a ladder with a tank at the bottom. Soon a man in spangled tights emerged from a nearby tent and began to climb the ladder, slowly and somnambulantly. Peter's new friend made an impatient gesture.

"It is indeed surprising what some people will do for money. Or maybe the basic death wish that operates in all of us causes this. Do you want to stay or go? No use to stay; they always make it. Besides, I think it will storm before long."

As if in answer a long, grumbling roll came above the wheedling, monotonous music, and people began to thin out.

"Let's stay. I have seen this before, but it always seems to renew my sense of identity." The new friend looked at him curiously and with a different kind of interest.

Forked lightning shot a bolt of clouds over the moon, and like tattered draperies they darked out the sky.

The man was atop the tiny platform now, and he seemed to be holding his breath. The wind swayed the ladder, straining the cables which kept it upright. Behind him the clouds, lined with an eerie mother-of-pearl glow, scudded by. His outline was sinister and alone. Peter tried to imagine the loneliness up there—the sure but not quite sure feeling that it would soon be just one more trip down and then a cigarette and bed. A clatter of thunder seemed to unleash the wind again, and the tents billowed, one of them letting go an awning which gestured frantically.

Still the man stood, poised, waiting, and it wasn't indecisiveness, Peter felt, but a posing, perhaps, for an open acknowledgement of approval from the crowd, who should be aware of the risk, the always-present spectre risk, waiting, too. A few catcalls and a sprinkling of applause, and the figure stiffened. Not yet, though. A crackled-glaze lightning silhouetted the black figure, and the outline seemed fissured as the spangles lit up.

A gust that came just then seemed to follow the figure as it dived, down through space and time into the upthrusting reality of metal and wooden spikes and poles, the creased tops of tents, and the ruffed-up tops of trees. Easily he came down, almost suspended between the unmeasured depth of sky above and the shallowness of the tank below. A human body was a delicate thing to hover in this imponderability; it was delicate to have left a reasonably solid footing above; but it was delicate, more than ever, to break itself on the edge of the tank, splashing a sheet of water high into the air to fall with the rain on the hypnotized bystanders.

The rain fell in a sheet. Peter and his friend moved away as the crowd surged forward to peer at the catastrophe. Peter was ill and confused that it should happen here on this night and in this time. He looked imploringly at his friend, who, blond hair plastered flat, gestured, running. Peter followed, the rain sounding a loud, insistent drumbeat around him. He had to run fast, for the other boy dodged dizzily among tents and drowned marshes of colored paper, leaping over stakes and ropes.

An agony tore at his entrails in the imagination of what the moment must have been—the shattering of nerves, muscles, and wildernesses of veins and tissues. The instant shock of pain and finality to the brain; the plunge then into nothing—a dimension greater than the reach between sky and tank.

Other figures leaped around him, soundlessly and quickly gone. He followed still, the lightning off-focusing the large bulk of buildings. Ridiculous tunes riddled through his mind flickeringly, and he wondered if this other, this pulp by the tank, could have, at the very last, heard for a split-second such tunes. Ahead the alien yet intimate, known-now figure dodged, side-hopped gigantic puddles and gushing ditch torrents. Peter didn't know what endless direction they went, but it didn't matter, only that they should run for a long distance.

And now another flash came with a flat crash, and in the light he saw the other boy holding open a car door and shouting something. He couldn't hear but got into the seat, and, reaching across, held open the other door. They were inside with the deluge on the car like a waterfall. They were able to hear now, and they looked at each other.

"I knew it would happen someday," Peter finally said.

"And such an insensitive way to have it happen, but that's what happens when you stand on a peak and defy the thunder. That's what happens to us all." They sat, still, hemmed in by the limits of the limitless rain.

The boy rubbed at the windshield. "I could try to make it, but these ditches are treacherous. Takes a tractor to pull you out once you're in. But think how many other things that applies to, and think how many things even a tractor could not undo." (Peter shuddered as in his mind a sawdust doll fell from Miss Emmajean's tea table and unseamed across a croquet wicket.)

All at once the rain lifted its weight and left a rhythmic falling. Cars around them, like a huddling herd of livestock, moved cautiously apart and sought the highway. Lights searched the night. The boy moved, too, and they were in motion. Now, too, they could see lights in the direction of the ladder, which was detaching itself from the sky, manipulated by unseen hands below. Lights were flashing, and persons were scurrying about mechanically. Perhaps even such a thing as this was more or less anticipated, rehearsed like a fire-drill at school.

The car was on the highway now. They sat not saying anything, for there was a lot not to say. The pines, gargantuan in the night and rain, beyond the headlights dropped their tops into the needle-sprayed sky, while the lower shrubs showed white undersides of their leaves with up-tossing wind.

When they stopped at Miss Billy's sagging gate and Peter got out, the boy leaned over and shook hands, whispering, "By the way, I am Karl Heppler, and we must talk again." And he was gone almost as suddenly as he had appeared.

6

THUNDER ROLLED sleep with rain on the tin roof, slippery tin from which you slipped and fell down and down, dream-saved in time, however. Ladders led upward through night-pointed pines till world was deep below and sky shallow above. Climbing, climbing forever (for what is forever but a string of nows), lifting, lifting soul and body through aeons of sky and slate-toned clouds. Now an oyster-colored moon wading through clouds, now a smoked-glass sun in eclipse. Always rain, though, slanted in sheets, drowning the moon and veiling the sun, rising up the ladder, leaving faded strips of crepe paper laced in the rungs.

Still up, for there has to be a stop; there is no down, for the water is there. Dimly, distantly a top, but wind and rain lash away voices that speed you on ("Step up for genu-ine prizes") and force you to get involved in decisions ("Who'll be next?"). Closer now and four, thr . . . three, two . . . slippery rungs, world spinning one way below, water the other. The top! Pull yourself over; the wheel is turning; watch it, here it comes, it's slowing, slowing, and the winner. . . . Standing on the wheel with the red cardboard flicking across the nails and your feet; will it stop on your feet? No, for there is a gadget (isn't there always a gadget?). But wait, you fool, you don't have to play. Jump (that's one way out) jump; you can't win with wheels, not even with merry-go-rounds (for they have shiny pins sticking the butterfly horses in place). Jump! Through space, now, fall. As far down as up but faster, seeing the ladder with its multitude of carnival-faced climbers fly upward and out of sight. But where now, for there was no time to think about that. Where to land, for there is always that. To break, perhaps, shatter on solid realities of pointed things. Now it must be here; it has to happen, this last. It can't stop . . . but the bee, yes, the bee, has come to this flower and caught it in mid-air, saving its psyche, its bee-tongue reaching in like a fork of lightning and following the storm out of night and out of sight.

7

AUTUMN BURNED slowly and stealthily along vines, the final vulnerable outermost leaves first, then downward to the twining stems, leaving them seared and shriveled with rattling seedcases. Autumn landed ducks in the shallower waters of the bay and defined subtle colors in the strata of the overhanging cliff. Autumn brought into focus all that summer had flattened and diffused.

Peter's days consisted of a definite routine, of which Ferndale was the biggest part. Classes followed a pattern, a manic-depressive continuum between the sometimes monotonous lectures and the crises of examinations and special papers or recitations. He fought out long assignments in the college library, or, finding it deficient, the public library downtown. In a library the hours hurried, even more so because of a constant awareness of all that had been written or said and the little time to know even a fragment of it.

In his room there was his table and lamp and bed, the anchors in a world of shifting tides and motions. About him the old house had unbent, and even its strange creakings and echoes were familiar, as were the trees out the window and the changing perspectives of the bay. This landscape had associations now, for to the south the beach would eventually become involved with Barnwell Swamp and its uncounted springs, and to the north it would finally reach Cypress Point. This cove, then, was the limit of a special world, outside which Ferndale and great thinkers and personalities might move and vary but leave it unchanged.

It had been several weeks since the trip to Robertsdale, and he had not seen Karl Heppler again; and as the days passed the events of that evening became indistinct. The newspaper, of course, carried the report of the disaster, and Miss Billy had made a remark that she was now more than ever convinced that flying should be confined to dreams. Eulacie was openly envious and asked for all sorts of loathsome details, saying that she couldn't get Miss Emmajean to sleep without telling her about it.

Miss Claverly came by on Friday afternoon, just when the sun was giving a final Midas-touch to the sides of the houses and the sides of trees. She had never come before to the house, for their meetings had always been planned in advance, and he usually went to her house, the only place (excepting the woods and swamps, of course) where she was in her proper climate.

"My dear, there is suddenly a great deal to tell you. You must come at once," she said to him at the front door when he went to answer her knock. She was dressed as usual in her whimsical collection of odds and ends, but this time they looked as if they had been thrown on with more abandon than ever. He brought her into where they were finishing supper. Miss Billy was rather flustered by the visit, since so few people just dropped in. Eulacie was openly suspicious, for she had expressed herself once that Miss Claverly gave her the all-overs. "Can't be natural with them baggy clothes and chasin' bugs on her hands and knees."

Miss Billy begged her to sit down and potluck with them, but she said she couldn't and she needed Peter to help her with something. When Miss Billy asked her what, she ignored the question. Peter finished his coffee and shoved his banana ice cream at Miss Emmajean, who immediately devoured it without taking her eyes off Miss Claverly.

As they went out the front door Peter heard Eulacie muttering: "And I whup my arm off beatin' them bananas. Miss Emmajean, get your arm out of them peas."

Miss Claverly said nothing till they were on the road, which dark now echoed their steps and clicked with the pebbles they kicked up.

"My dear," she said at last, "I am going."

"Going?"

"Yes, I didn't know it until a little while ago. I am leaving; it is necessary."

"But why?"

He was sick at the thought of losing her.

"Well, I must. My investigation has ended here, and time matters a great deal. I have had a letter from some friends in New York, and I must be there this week. They are leaving on an important expedition."

"But you can't just leave. You live here. Your dogs. . . . Everything." He wanted to cry that Rainbow Gully would no longer be there for him.

"I've taken care of that. The man who sold me the dogs will take them back. I can ship the rest. Yes, that's the disadvantage of my kind of work. You get started in a certain way of life, and then something starts somewhere else and you have to be in on it. There is so much to see and so little time to see it all. If life were only longer and things in life a little closer together."

"And people not so far apart," Peter added miserably.

They had reached the path to Rainbow Gully. "Well, here we are," said Miss Claverly, as the dogs came squirming up on their stomachs, whining with delight. "Poor darlings, I suppose they'll miss me at first. They've been such a comfort."

The lights were blazing from the little house, and inside was confusion—suitcases and books tumbled together and clothes thrown in heaps across the bed and chairs.

"I'll make us some tea, my dear. If you'll put the books in those boxes, it will be a big help." She rattled some pans in the little kitchen, and Peter caught his breath when he thought that this would be the last time. She was back then while the water was boiling, busying herself with folding up the already-wrinkled clothes and stuffing them into the battered suitcases.

Peter fingered one of the volumes, and it opened to a penciled passage:

> Will they ever come to me, ever again,
> The long long dances,
> On through the dark till the dim stars wane?
> Shall I feel the dew on my throat, and the stream
> Of wind in my hair? Shall our white feet gleam
> In the dim expanses?

It was something he would not have associated with Miss Claverly. It was delicate and unscientific. Yet—

"I'm going to miss you, Miss Claverly."

She got up from the floor and put her arm around him. "And of course I'll miss you, my dear. We have had such a lot of fun together. Everywhere I've been I've had to give up someone, and it's difficult."

"But it's not just someone for me. It's someone very special."

"Real friendship is the noblest of human emotions, even more than love, for there is a more lofty motivation for friendship. Oh, what a mess there is here. Maybe if you'll stack those specimen cases for me." She scratched under an armpit and then fitted another cigarette into the holder.

Peter moved to pile the cigar boxes together—the treasures he would be able to look at no longer, the beetles, the dragon-flies, and the butterflies. He stopped.

"My god, Miss Claverly. Wait, you can't go. You haven't found it yet," he half-shouted.

"Found what, my dear? You startled me."

"The butterfly tree. You came here for that, and you can't just go." Dimly on the edge of his mind flashed the intelligence that he was asking her to stay for something he scarcely imagined to exist.

"But I have looked and followed all the established leads. I have one more set of variables to check, and then I shall know it is final, that it simply was a piece of erroneous information. That's what one gets for listening to unscientific persons. Even supposedly authenticated information is often unreliable enough. But the idea was after all so thinkable, and the source of it was so unusual, so—but we'll never get done if we don't hurry. We'll go, you and I, to look for it tomorrow afternoon before we go to the train."

"But what if we really do find it then?"

"We'll find it, that's all. I wouldn't leave then, of course. I'm used to changing my plans."

"But this way it looks as if you don't expect to find it." He couldn't help but be discouraged by the look of finality that her parceled belongings were taking.

"My dear, scientific investigation is a hydra-head affair. It can be certain and not certain all at once. Investigators must be prepared for all eventualities. This way I shall be ready to leave or not leave depending on the way things turn out. That doesn't lessen my belief that we may discover the butterfly tree. In fact, it's quite likely."

The tea was ready then, and they sat on the bed and talked about some of the things that had brought them together and were, at the same time, taking them apart. The dogs lay on the floor, all the activity making them suspicious and restless. When

Miss Claverly moved they opened an eye apiece and whined affectionately.

"If I go, perhaps you'll go to see them occasionally." She looked at them tenderly, and Peter couldn't help but feel a. distant stir of jealousy at the thought that Miss Claverly would miss them more than she would him.

"I shall. Maybe the man will let me take them to all the places we have been, you and I."

"That would be nice. Oh dear, let's get on with it. Hand me that carton for my manuscripts. If I only would learn not to accumulate things."

They worked for a couple of hours, Peter finding many things they had not got around to talking about—drawings, card files, and photographs. When he came across a snapshot of Miss Claverly with another woman sitting in a boat, it occurred to him all at once how slightly he knew her. She had never mentioned her personal life, and somehow he had never wondered enough to ask, or perhaps there hadn't been room to think about it when they were together. And how much he had told her he could not remember.

Finally he had to go, for it was getting late. She lighted him to the road once more, and told him when to meet her the next day. Night moved shapes over the moon as he looked back to see her with her firefly flashlight swing back up the steep path.

8

"DON'T TRY to outguess nature until you're sure of cause and effect, then be cautious." Miss Claverly looked over her shoulder at the sun and seemed mentally to test the wind.

They were moving eastward out of town away from the bay.

They left the pavement beyond the point where Rainbow Gully was just a muddy ditch under the highway to Robertsdale and followed a dirt road by the Goldsby Place. The sun was about twenty feet from the horizon (Peter wondered how much that was in millions), and the hill up this way had received a glancing blow from its last rays. Tall dry grass filtered some of the glow, and on the top of the hill the pines shafted what was left.

"By cause and effect I have followed a thousand tracks, but something was off—either the cause or the effect or my misreading them. Sometimes so close, too, so that I could almost say which tree in which place."

"And isn't there any other place to look?"

"My dear, the world is enormous beyond the wildest imagination. One square foot of earth is a world; a square mile is a galaxy of worlds. Finding anything must be either according to the deadest reckoning science can evolve or by sheer accident. Accident has been valuable, but its limitations are obvious. As badly as I want to find the butterfly tree, I'd rather not find it by accident. I've studied too hard not to find it by the scientific method."

They cut off the road and went across the matted pine needles deep into the grove. Beneath the needles twigs broke under their steps. The fragrance of the pines was accentuated by the clear cold air, and it was something like the smell of burning leaves and pine straw.

Was there, could there be, after all, a butterfly tree? Now at last would there be, when it mattered that there should be? Would that make it happen? For hadn't Miss Billy said that one must want something badly enough? After all, Miss Claverly's opinions were sound in everything else, so why couldn't there be a butterfly tree? But still there was the fact that she hadn't found it; there was the thought that Miss Billy was looking for something similar. The very idea that Miss Billy knew of a butterfly tree, told to her by a wise fool, seemed to diminish his belief in Miss Claverly's tree.

Yet, in spite of feeling that there was no such tree as a butterfly tree, he knew that he wanted more than anything at this moment to find one. He, too, was starting to try to imagine its shape and color, but an image would not stay clear. He looked at Miss Claverly, who was walking a little ahead, and thought how they would react if they found what they were looking for. They would go back to the little house and unpack again, and there would be water boiling on the stove. She would appear in a faded pink house coat and part of her inexhaustible supply of tarnished jewelry, and perhaps she would tell him about herself finally.

Miss Claverly turned now and then to a new direction, and Peter saw that she was counting her steps and using a compass. He started to say something, but she held up her hand. They walked on a certain line and into a clearing. In the clearing a single pine stood, and a last cone of sunlight measured its length. She stopped and pointed.

"The butterfly tree—complete except for one thing. No butterflies. This is it by all the evidence possible at this time."

It was now that Peter accepted her going as definite. Up till then he had halfway believed she would find something to change her mind. He had halfway believed that they would find so improbable a thing as the butterfly tree, for, after all, she was using something definite to measure a location. Not like Miss Billy, who looked in only the pretty places she would go if she were a butterfly.

"We must hurry, for we don't have too much time to make the bus. It is exciting to be going, but I'm really sorry to be leaving. It would have been so much better to have found the butterfly tree here where it was supposed to be."

Peter rode with her to Mobile, and he couldn't help but remember the day he had first seen her when he came to Moss Bayou. The trip was short, for they talked about what she would do with the expedition (it was really a field trip, she explained, into the upper state, and they had to hurry because of the weather).

When they got to Mobile, there were still a couple of hours till the train, so they went for supper at a dim oyster bar near the station. They sat in a back booth and talked above the blare of the Dixieland jazz recordings. Miss Claverly had a beer and gave Peter some while the proprietor was getting their order.

"So sinister, really. I suppose I should have known, but it was so right in line with certain facts." She licked off a moustache of foam.

"You mean about the butterfly tree?"

"I mean about the way the whole thing came about in the first place."

"Wasn't it a result of investigation?" He couldn't imagine anything else for Miss Claverly.

"Well, not exactly. Someone told me about it. Someone I had never seen before. Isn't that strange. It was all so suddenly convincing that I came here even after many years had passed, and I've stayed five years. Even now, thinking about it I still want to believe it—but I have proved it impossible."

Peter watched the colored lights of the record machine revolve on the beer bottles and wondered how in this world of complex destinies anything could be proven impossible.

"Who could know?" he asked, and even the small quantity of beer made him a little dizzy.

"He had seen it, he said, in these swamps. He described it, and it seemed to check with the California data and the habits of the migrants. It is a curious story, and he was a curious person. The more curious, perhaps, since I so infrequently indulge in curious persons."

"Tell me." And he wondered if maybe at this last he would discover some of her life beyond the books and cigar boxes.

"It is not a story to tell, for it is not really, if you think about it, a story at all. But perhaps it will amuse you in this little bit of time we have left.

"While I was a student a few years ago, I was in the habit of stopping every morning in a little cafeteria by the subway stop on my way to the museum or library. One morning the place was crowded, and a man came and asked if he might sit with me. Of course, I didn't care, so he sat down, and I kept glancing at some notes I kept on three-by-five index cards. I was afraid he would want to talk, and you can't imagine anything more deadly than some of these polite, desultory New York cafeteria conversations. He did speak, though, and I suddenly lost interest in my cards: 'I know where there are some red velvet dragonflies.' My dear, I was at that very moment doing research on dragonflies. I knew he couldn't have seen the cards I was holding, and I couldn't do anything but look at him stupidly. 'Don't be alarmed. How did I know?' Well, a part of me knows cities and rainy streets; a part knows the deep silences of woods and the smooth contours of meadows; a part knows people and what they know, and this was it. Would you like some more tea?' My dear, I had no thought but that he was utterly mad and with an uncanny sense of intuition. New York simply crawls with that sort of thing. But there was something so charming, so believable, about him, that I couldn't decide to get up and run while he was getting the tea. That indecision changed my life.

"He was back, and he began talking about his cities and his woods and meadows. Before he had got very far, I was so lost in his words and ideas that the clock did strange things, and I forgot all about the museum and the library. He talked authoritatively on every subject I was working on, and I had a suddenly fantastic notion that he could have held forth with as much ease had I been working on nuclear energy or translations of Pali manuscripts. I was afraid to let him go, afraid that I wouldn't see him again, but he promised to see me on the following Sunday for dinner.

"He came, and I was frantic that he wouldn't. I had spent the time in between trying to rationalize him. (I knew, of course, that in the general scheme of things there was a good explanation of his knowing, as well as my not knowing how he knew.) We went to dinner and talked again. We got on other subjects, and I tried to explore him, but I'm afraid he learned (or did he already know?) a great deal more about me. I have never met a person with so much perspicacity and genuine learning. He must have experimented in certain fields for years."

"How old was he?" Peter didn't know why he asked this, except that it always served to put people within definable limits.

"That's another thing. I haven't the vaguest notion. At first I thought he was middle aged; especially while we talked he seemed so, I suppose by the sheer total of his experience. Yet when I remember him—even when I had just left him—he seemed young, vital and spontaneous, in some respects a lot like you."

"Was that the last time?"

"Oh, no. We continued to see each other for a couple of months. My work went lacking, but how much I learned. All except about him. That part I don't suppose I'll ever know. We went to all sorts of lovely places I never had seemed to have time for before. I found that I was discovering worlds beyond my world. I came to believe in a number of things I had never given myself a chance to before. I even came to believe I could love such a man, although I took great pains to translate all my feelings for him into non-biological terms."

"What was his name? but I don't guess that is important."

"No, not particularly. It was quite an ordinary name, I suppose: Robert Norman. But let me get on.

"We were at the Cloisters one Sunday at those little outside tables having tea, and the crab apple trees were showering pink petals down every time the breeze moved. He kept looking at the trees, and he turned to me and smiled: 'It's as though they stopped here by mistake and turned into pink flowers.' I asked him what on earth he meant. He almost never dealt in whimsy. 'The butterflies, I mean.' I still looked blank. 'Oh, then you don't know. The butterfly tree.' I said oh, yes, I knew about the California business, but he said no that he knew of a swamp along the Gulf Coast. Then, my dear, my ears pricked up. I knew that he was serious, because a man like that had to be. I had heard too much of him to doubt him. I also knew that if this were true it would be a tremendous contribution to natural history. I pursued it, and he told me that he had seen it, the butterfly tree. He would give me nothing specific, telling me that it was one tree only, and that I must look nowhere else. As if that made sense after his almost footnoted observations on virtually everything else.

"And so, my dear, I have looked for the butterfly tree ever

since. Oh, not here. But I made notes by the ream, for years translating French and German texts on butterflies, getting shreds of information from thousands of sources. I joined an expedition to California to see the migrations for myself. And then after many years I came here, complete with my notes and all the necessary data for finding that one tree. And here we are."

"Will you look still?"

"My dear, when you have spent a very great deal of life in looking for a thing you don't just stop, especially if you believe so very much in a thing."

"Then why are you leaving?"

"I have reason to believe something might have happened to the migratory pattern, some tiny shift in climate or food supply. A degree can mean, you know, many miles difference. I must do some more studying."

"And what—what if you still find it is here?"

"Oh, I'll come back, of course."

"And years will happen to us both," Peter remarked sadly as he picked up his coffee cup. "Miss Claverly, where did he go?"

"I don't know. I wish I did. I should like to tell him what has come of that afternoon at the Cloisters. I should like to ask him what made him so certain of his facts. One day he didn't come when I looked for him, and there was a note. I remember what it said: 'Time collects me. Good-bye, and look hard for the butterfly tree, for it is there—Robert.' I looked for him in the cafeteria, and even one day I went all the way up to the Cloisters, but not even the crab apple trees were in bloom. Soon after that I started to look for the butterfly tree, for I had no other choice." She waited, but Peter had no other questions.

They walked back to the station, and the street was wet from the mist that came from the river. There wasn't much to say while they waited for the train. He looked at her shabby clothes and baggage with tenderness, and he knew that this was perhaps what he would remember long after the other details had faded. Finally the train came and she got on. She stood at the top of the steps, the steam gushing from underneath the platform where she stood.

It was a lonely train with not another soul in sight, the few other passengers having gone to the coaches. The windows were a row of blank staring eyes which had lately looked at the twilight desolation of swamps and winding bayous with Indian names. When at last the train pulled slowly, groaningly away, she stood between the cars and waved.

"Don't forget to write," she called in her deep-throated voice.

"And let me know," his voice was shrill against the turning wheels and gushing steam, "when you find it, for you will—"

She was gone, and the train was gone.

"—won't you?" The wistful urgency of the unanswered and unheard question was like the plaintive sound of late-singing locusts in night trees.

He turned and walked back the way they had come, and far off he heard the train whistle and wondered if Miss Claverly was thinking to miss him. Leaves were burning in gutters, and people were hurrying to get things bought for Christmas in the late-open stores. He would send Miss Claverly something for Christmas, he decided. In a few days fall would be gone.

Miss Claverly and now autumn.

Winter

1

WITH MISS CLAVERLY gone, things changed for him. The leaves continued to fall; the water washed on the long arc of beach with timeless rhythm; and winter came without suddenness, for even the distances between time and time were slow distances. All the enigmas Miss Claverly had left with him plagued him with gentle insistency. Everywhere was a little lonely for him now without her earthy voice sounding at his elbow or threading through his dreams.

("Beauty, my dear, is a biological luxury—a conspiracy against cause and effect, functionless actually. But human beings are so bored without it. Other animals don't seem to care. We have learned beauty, almost developed an uncanny instinct for it. Flowers are beautiful, but do other flowers know it?")

He wandered along the ways they had known, the wooded paths they had known, where sometimes he found an Indian pipe plant ("No chlorophyll, my dear; you see—") or along the beach where a culture of pitcher plants opened their sinister mouths toward the sun ("Most carnivorous, really—would eat a man if they were large enough"). Perhaps she wouldn't find the butterfly tree (if there was a butterfly tree, after all) and would return again to look for it here. If there was a butterfly tree, they had, he felt, almost found it once, but she wouldn't proceed beyond, for her calculations didn't go beyond. He visited the place again, but it was simply a bare pine grove with a carpet of pine needles and a magnificent pine in a clearing, and the clearing was fragrant with tiny swift butterflies that had ambitions no higher than the forest flowers that flanked the grove. And there was overhead a splendid sky, everlasting and all-knowing, knowing where the butterfly tree could be found (if they were right and there was one). Here it was peaceful and he stretched on his back and remembered her solicitude for the tiny unknown world where she really lived.

2

"Did she like the butterflies?" The girl spoke suddenly behind him, and he started. It was the clerk who had sold him the earrings weeks before. She was in a way familiar now, since he could identify her with Karl, his new friend, who had come and gone with the night. He still didn't know what this identification was, and as he looked at her he wondered more. There was simplicity and warmth here, but not the magnificence and nobility Karl should have. There was not beauty.

"Yes, she was very happy with them."

"Now can I help you find something else? Isn't Christmas a problem?" She looked at him with almost searching warmth, seeming to reach for a footing of intimacy.

"It certainly is. I always have a lot of trouble." He was drawn by this reaching.

"Maybe I can help. That's what I'm here for." The way she said this last meant more than the moment, but if so she had kept the meaning from her face.

"Maybe you can."

"You are Peter, aren't you?" She smiled as if she knew he would be surprised, but she asked it casually.

"Yes, but how on earth did you know?"

"Karl told me. He tells me everything. I'm his sister." She smiled again, and he saw that her face was almost pretty when she smiled. This then was the identification, and it was, he knew, the only one that could be.

"But how—?" Peter tried to remember if she had ever looked directly at him before except when he had bought the earrings, and she would have had no way of making the connection.

"I don't really know. But the way Karl describes things and people. And besides there is a very strong feeling between twins. We even sense many things alike."

"Twins?" He couldn't stop the incredulity in his voice.

Her smile faded a little, but it managed to hang on. "Yes, strange as it seems. Odd things happen with twins, the least odd being that they sometimes don't look alike."

Peter was sorry he had let her see the vast distance he recognized between them. "Look," he blurted, "I don't feel like making up my mind about what to buy. Have you had lunch? I haven't."

She looked pleased and touched. "Well, no, I haven't. But are you sure—"

"I don't know where to go. I have eaten only once over here, and—"

"Well, good. I'll get my coat. Wait here, and I'll tell them I am going." She hurried off through a curtained partition.

He stood uneasily looking at the jewelry and vanity cases. Karl's twin! Of course, there couldn't be two persons like Karl, but couldn't one expect even a pale copy? (What was Miss Claverly's observation about beauty? But she had said so much.)

She was back almost too soon, for he had wanted a little more time to think about this new idea. They went out to Royal Street and walked south. The wind was cold and brought tears to their eyes. She took his arm as they crossed Conti Street. The crowd was heavy, and they had to hold together to keep from getting separated.

"I know a place that won't be too crowded," she said, pulling his arm at the corner. They turned and went toward the river, the wind whipping now into their faces, so that they had to turn their heads aside.

Finally they came to a dingy-looking building with plate glass windows fogged from the heat inside, and they entered.

"Not much to look at, but the food is good, and besides I hate to stand in lines worse than anything."

"Me, too," he said as he helped her with her coat. They sat down, and he looked around. The place was completely what it was. There were no embellishments except a few cards refusing credit and a calendar from the state docks. A Negro girl took their order. Her hair was pulled together behind with a red-painted clothespin for a clip.

"So you're Karl's sister," said Peter. "But I can't always call you that."

"Oh, I'm sorry. I am Karen Heppler." She pushed at her hair and smiled. "I always forget that part. Everyone seems to meet Karl first, and I am simply Karl's sister. I don't remember seeing you in Moss Bayou, but then I'm usually here. I would have remembered you from having waited on you in the store, but I wouldn't have known who you were if you hadn't met Karl. That was a terrible thing that happened, wasn't it?"

"Yes." And he even believed he could talk about it with her, because there was nothing morbidly curious in her reference.

"I suppose I would have been along if I hadn't been sick that night. But then," she reflected, "Karl likes to go off by himself now and then. We do have a good time together, though."

Peter hadn't thought of it till that moment, and he started as he remembered again the day he had watched the two of them swimming naked in the hurricane. They had been both excruciatingly beautiful that day at a distance, and it was still hard to think that this person across the table was the graceful dreamlike creature of that other time.

She talked with animation, moving from one subject to another, yet stopping and listening to him seriously when he talked.

"I haven't seen your brother since that night."

She made a gesture. "Oh, Karl's like that. He goes off into long reflective moods. He's writing now, I think. Nobody bothers him; we know better. He hates his job, too, but then I think he would hate any job."

"What does he do?"

"He's with the docks. Public relations or something. You know what I mean—answering letters from people all over the world. Taking officials, consuls and so forth on tours."

"Sounds like a pretty fancy setup."

"Well, it would be for anybody but Karl. He really is so very different from other people. You'll just have to find out for yourself. Which, by the way, reminds me to tell you we are having open house Christmas afternoon. Mom always does. You be sure to come. Say, I have to get back to work. We have almost overstayed. I just plain forget to look at clocks when I'm enjoying myself."

When he took her back to the store, he was able to find several presents, not forgetting Ann (what perfume was it he had always bought her before?). For Miss Claverly there would have to be something special, so he would wait a little while on that. He remembered that he had forgotten to find out where in Moss Bayou the Hepplers lived, so he stopped back by to ask Karen. Her face lighted up, and she gave him the directions.

When he looked back down the aisle just before going out the door, she was standing in the same spot still smiling.

3

"Miss Emmajean, you turn that damn Christmas tree over, I'm goin' to turn you white." Eulacie came huffing in from the kitchen with a dusty box of decorations. "How these thing is held up is past a miracle. Cats knockin' them off, wind turnin' over the whole tree, Miss Emmajean cuttin' her teeth on them." She dumped the box on the parlor table, and Peter wondered how the contents could possibly survive.

"Isn't this the most magnificently beautiful single time of all the year?" Miss Billy in an ancient chartreuse dressing gown did a tiny complete whirl in the middle of the parlor.

"It comes close, honey." Eulacie pulled from the box a long strand of tinsel. "Whoo, this the piece caught on fire that night the flames got too high on the plum puddin'."

"Oh, we can always put that part to the back." Miss Billy started lifting the shell-thin decorations from the box.

"Miss Emmajean," said Peter from the piano bench, "what is Santa Claus going to bring you?"

"He crazy if he bring her anything the way she dug a elephant trap for him under the canna lillies last Christmas. Only thing saved him I fell in it myself. Only the Good Lord kept me from maimin' her for life, but it didn't teach her nothin'. She probably got one dug somewhere else."

"Oh, Peter, I wish you hadn't been across the bay yesterday when they had the town Christmas tree for the children. It is always so lovely. The three of us went, and you should have seen Miss Emmajean."

"Yeah, you should have seen how I have to slap her silly for not watchin' what or who she run into. Went wild when she see that free candy Santa Claus was handin' out."

"Santa Claus is Ted Sorenson, the dentist. Such a nice stomach for it," said Miss Billy behind her hand.

"Some of them kids that turn up for that candy was old enough to be shavin'." Eulacie moved Miss Emmajean out of the way with her knee and threw an arc of tinsel in a wide loop over the top of the tree.

"Peter, don't just sit there. You must help. A Christmas tree has a personality for every person, and every person gives it a personality. No two people do a tree just alike. Here, now." She handed him a rope of tiny hollow glass bells. "Do something with this."

Peter touched the tree gingerly, laying the strand gently on a wide branch.

"Oh, Peter. Not like that; twine it somewhere." Miss Billy bustled by him with a collapsible paper lantern.

"Well, you see, Aunt Martha didn't put up Christmas trees. I haven't had any practice."

Miss Billy stopped, and tears came suddenly to her eyes. "You mean, dear Peter, that never before—oh, Peter. Oh, Peter." She dried her eyes quickly on a piece of cotton snow. "I never knew your father's people, but I always had an idea they were insensitive. Why, that's almost criminal."

"Bastards," muttered Eulacie under her breath, as she bit into a chocolate-covered cherry.

"But I didn't know the difference. What you don't have you don't miss."

"That's why it's criminal. Because you didn't even know to miss one of the greatest pleasures of life. Well, we'll make up for it now. Here, take this and make it mean something. I'll go put on a record. I think I need something stimulating like 'The Twelve Days of Christmas.' "

And they did make up for it. There in the bright room—with the log fire reflecting on the old wood, the tree adding brilliance on brilliance, the voices rising and falling, and in the other room something about a partridge in a pear tree—it was lovely and warm, and all at once there was an understanding of what Christmas was all about, what it was supposed to mean. He tried to think of the barren nights of all the other Christmases, and they didn't matter. There had always been presents, of course, but here it wouldn't matter about presents. This was enough, more than enough.

"Peter, look. I have had this decoration since I was a little girl." Miss Billy showed him a tiny fragile windmill, so old that the colors had faded beyond recognition. "The forests of trees this has hung on, the years of time it has linked." She put it in a spot near the front and stood by looking at it lovingly.

"Y'all move back if you don't want this eggnog all over." Eulacie carried a trayful of mugs and a bowl. "I for one would like a rousin' toast to a damn fine houseful of people, and before it's over I may even cry and tell everybody how much I love them." She poured everyone, Miss Emmajean included, a mug of eggnog and lifted hers, the firelight running the shadow of her lifted arm up the opposite wall.

"And to a wonderfully happy year which had to be this way," said Miss Billy.

"And to everything in our life that brought us to right now," said Peter solemnly.

They looked at Miss Emmajean, who had spilled her mug all over herself. They howled in merriment, and Miss Emmajean, who had dodged out of habit, was so confused she started to cry.

"Come here, you doll," said Eulacie, half-crying herself. "I couldn't hit you if you burned the house down, but I don't promise anything after tonight."

"Eulacie, you must have been at the nog," said Miss Billy.

"What if I have? There comes a time of year when everything you have felt all year, everything you have wanted to say but didn't know how, has got to come out, and there's nothin' like a few drams of old Crawdad or whatever the hell you got around to help you say it."

"Well, run bring the rest of it. I have lots to say, too."

Eulacie started out. "I'll bring it, honey, but you don't need it; you can say them things all year. But not me, unh unh. It has to be a occasion. Miss Emmajean, darlin', I will have to ask you to kindly quit trackin' that stuff."

She came back with the bottle, and they stepped up the mixture. They turned then to open their presents.

"This is the best part, I guess," reflected Miss Billy, "but in a way it is a tiny bit sad. For in a sense Christmas is over. All the part that has been looked forward to is through. Christmas day is an anti-climax."

"Whatever it is, I'm usually flat out. I ain't just hung over. I am dropped over. Then all to do over. The Bascombe Club has this annual Christmas frolic. Whoo!"

"Eulacie, you angel, when did you have time to do these?" Miss Billy held up a pair of hemstitched pillow-slips.

"Humph, took time." She reached for the bottle again, unwrapping a box with her spare hand. "Sweet Lord, oh, honey

Peter. A purple one." She displayed a velvet turban and promptly put it on. Miss Emmajean wordlessly bobbed a spoon up and down in the eggnog. "It is gorgeous. Oh them Squall Street floosies will pure perish." She paraded around the room, moving her arms in a cakewalk rhythm.

"Miss Billy, this watchband wouldn't have lasted another week. It couldn't have. How did you notice?" Miss Billy smiled coyly but was busy with the present from him.

"Oh, I should never have mentioned I wanted one. People just don't forget. It's such a beautiful handbag. They don't make many like this any more. Oh, thank you both. And, oh, Miss Emmajean honey, you aren't supposed to—look, Peter, violet toilet water. I love you all more than you know."

Eulacie had added a silk scarf from Miss Billy to her outfit and was making the room shake with her cakewalk. Miss Emmajean was looking at herself in the mirror of the vanity set Peter had given her and trying to blow the French harp from Miss Billy at the same time.

"You'll be sorry you give her that harp in about three days."

"But look at the wonderful pocketknife she gave me," said Peter, hugging Miss Emmajean. "And, Eulacie, come let me hug you—I won't pinch—for this belt. It looks like something special."

"My cousin does toolin'—leather and otherwise." She chuckled.

"Everything is beautiful, and I think we should sing a carol to say it for us. Which one will it be?" Miss Billy sat at the piano with her hands poised above the keys.

"Let's just have the best and biggest one of all. It's not real Christmas without it," said Eulacie, immediately launching into the contralto for "Silent Night, Holy Night." Miss Billy nodded in agreement, following with the accompaniment.

They sang, their voices filling the high old parlor, going beyond throughout the house, across the garden:

"Sleep in heavenly peace;
Sleep in heavenly peace"

and, Peter felt, into all the lost and undiscovered parts of their lives, so that it was more than a song, more than words and melody. He cried softly within himself, and he knew that he cried not for now but for all times past and times to come.

4

THE OPEN-HOUSE at the Hepplers' had been something of an ordeal from the beginning. The day had been cold, and even the cheerful warmth of the Hepplers and their guests had been just a little stiff and dreary. He had walked across town to their house, which although old, unlike Miss Billy's, was trim and, with characteristic German neatness, a little severe, especially against the background of flying mare's-tail clouds and a lead-streaked sky.

There had been the elder Hepplers, an aunt and uncle, and some younger persons, most of them German, and Karl. Karl had played the piano, and the guests had sung in German. In between, they carried on a desultory conversation, making an attempt to include Peter, but only Karen had come to his rescue in the heavy barren parlor which even the presence of people did nothing to change.

And Karl had been distant, as if Peter were meeting him for the first time. For the other guests there was a forced informal charmingness from which he seemed to be excluding Peter. Still, as he played the piano, Peter had realized all over again with something of a start how extraordinarily beautiful he was. He had looked at the mother and father for perhaps a reason, but there was none there; they were pleasant, hard-working, ordinary-looking people. Much more appropriately Karen's parents, he had noticed, as he came to see her more clearly. Away from the necessarily formal environment of her job she was more than ever plain, wholesome but plain, with the undeniable stamp of generations of peasant ancestors. In the warm room her face was red, and the lights made her blond hair dull and flaxen.

There had been delicious refreshments of German pastries and tiny glasses of schnapps. A few other guests had come, and a few of the early ones had gone.

Karen had left to get some more refreshments, and Peter had been waiting for her to return so that he could leave, when Karl had sat beside him.

"So my sister discovered you. Even then I had to help." He had smiled charmingly when Peter looked confused. "But never mind; you haven't been gambling lately, have you?"

"No, it isn't very likely I will again."

"It's like everything else, I suppose; you have to be aware of things happening not only during but before and after. That way you have protection."

"I guess so, but how do you know?"

"That is the secret, and I'm not sure it can be learned. But, be that as it may, now that you have come back, now that the next distance has been diminished, let's go on Saturday night to a place I know that you'll like—and I know you will because I do."

Karen had re-entered just then, and Karl moved back to the piano, saying as he left:

"I'll pick you up at about seven. See you then."

Peter had gone after that, and while he was telling his hosts good-bye Karl had nodded formally and distantly, not stopping the German Christmas song he was playing.

As Peter walked down the road, he had heard the piano and the voices following him:

> ". . . *Du grünst nicht nur zur Sommerszeit*
> *Nein, auch im Winter, wenn es schneit . . .*"

He had shivered a little, probably because he had been glad it was over and he would soon be back where everyone was familiar.

5

THE LONG main street was deserted except when an occasional car whisked apart the silence and moved the palm arms with its draft. There were dim all-night lights burning in the rear of stores, and the two small hotels burned lights in their lobbies. The street lights were rocking in the wind and moving shadows across the fronts of the weather-beaten stores. The wind was bitter, and the dim deserted street seemed to make it even more bitter.

Peter came out of the movie and walked slowly along the street, not ready to go home in spite of the cold. It was earlier than the street made it appear, for in the pale two blocks there was not a single building open. Even the café was closed, for it closed at ten except on week-ends.

He walked to the corner where the residences started, crossed the street and moved slowly, opposite the movie, up the other side. At the next corner he looked wistfully at the town's only tavern across the street and knew that it would be useless to try to pass for older. He was standing looking in the window of Wintsell's Department Store at some shirts (they all had the appearance of having been cut from figured, livestock feed sacks), thinking that perhaps he would walk down the hill to the head of the municipal pier and then home.

The shadow was there—perhaps had been all the time—before he knew it, and the sibilant voice was a part of the shadow.

"One is never quite certain whether he is buying or being bought. It is difficult to know." Peter started visibly and gave a short exclamation before he saw that it was Mr. Bloodgood, his cemetery acquaintance of several weeks before.

"I didn't mean to unsettle you. I forgot to knock, so to speak; it is so seldom necessary in my profession."

"I'm sorry. I just didn't see anybody anywhere, and you just materialized." Peter's voice was shaking.

"Not materialized. I just this minute came around the corner. This is usually the time of evening I take a walk, after everyone has decided that it is late. And there is nothing more exquisitely beautiful than a night street—especially a winter night street. It is one of the purely man-made things that is excitingly beautiful."

"Yes, I feel a little that way about it, too." Peter had the feeling of being glad to see Mr. Bloodgood, for at least he was saying things that seemed to matter.

"It is a really magnificent night. The wind is snatching dark secrets from the night trees. What do you suppose they are telling? But you have never come to see me, and I have half-expected you, for I remember the day in the cemetery and have wondered about you—so different from the others around here."

"I guess I have been too busy with school."

"Oh, yes, Ferndale. I remember college, too, but such a long time ago—when leaves were yellower than now and the days full of more exquisite beauty and sadness without being forced. But I have a cup of tea waiting for you at my place, which is just around the next corner. Why don't you tell me about it there, about Ferndale, and perhaps there the wind won't hear you?"

"Well, really I should be going," and Peter knew that he would not go home.

"Should you? Well, if you must."

"But—" Peter hesitated.

"Oh, good, then come along, for you will like my place."

They walked down the dim deserted street, and all at once it was lonelier than before.

6

"This is my place, my room. I don't really know what goes on outside here (and downstairs, of course), except when I walk in the cemetery or the night street."

Mr. Bloodgood indicated a chair for Peter and then proceeded to take off his coat and put on a faded kimono, a woman's kimono, tying it with a snagged yellow sash.

He took a cigarette from a lucite box by the vase of wilted roses. "Grave flowers," he said, indicating them. "I like them because they've had such purpose. Part of the tradition, you know. Yet more than that, they are symbolic of the truth few of us admit. They are always dying from the moment they become full-blown flowers, and now they are dead, as if their life was inhaled, too, into the grave. They prove that beauty like death, is inevitable, and they bring the two very close together. Beauty is one achievement, death another. Something about a beautiful child is always ineffably sad, because that beauty is the result and beginning of death."

He turned toward Peter. "Do I frighten you?"

"No," said Peter. Fear was the furthest thing from his imagination. Here he felt a curious detachment, an utter departure from all that had come to be meaningful. Here, at last, he felt close to the mystery of the ultimate and absolute magics of life and death. "But tell," he was saying, and his voice, too, was detached and came from far away like a distant surf, "tell me about death and tell me about beauty."

Mr. Bloodgood looked at him for a long time then moved across the room. He turned and looked again at Peter.

"I shall begin, but there is much to tell and much to learn. We may never stop learning about them, for they are the alpha and omega of all things. So we shall talk of them now, yet again when the wind has moved across the bay and perhaps when time has moved a little and altered our destinies. But first I shall make us tea."

He stepped into an adjoining room, and Peter could hear running water. He looked at the room now, for he had not been able to see it before. It was a room of many worlds, each remote and a little frightening. By the draped windows was a long table on which were a bronze Buddha and an unpainted box with Japanese letters painted on the front. A modernistic lamp stood on a lacquered round table and was surrounded by delicate East Indian ceramics and charms. Above this table hung two East Indian prints matted and framed in black. A bookcase with glass doors was against an alcove wall, and Peter wondered what esoteric titles were housed there. A handsome high-fidelity record machine with wrought-iron legs stood beside the bookcase.

A grandfather clock occupied the other wall of the alcove across the archway which led to the other rooms. Against the intersecting wall of the room itself was an ingeniously carved liquor cabinet. Besides this furniture there were odds and ends of low tables and shelves cluttered with relics of old and new civilizations. Two chiseled stone lions flanked the sides of the wicker couch by the entrance. A *Samurai* sword leaned by the door. Posters of old vaudeville stars, advertisements for string quartets, and faded watercolor landscapes clamored for attention, yet all blended together in a confused and bewildering harmony.

Mr. Bloodgood came back into the room. "It won't take long. How do you like my room?"

"It's very interesting." Peter didn't know what else to say.

"Yes, it is that, at least. It is very hard to get bored here, for these things suggest something else, and each of them is a special adventure and a special person or time. It is a familiar, consequently comfortable, world, and I am never quite at ease away from it. There are stories here that I shall tell you someday, but they are stories that will have to be chosen for the right days—some rainy, some hot and sultry, some indeterminate, some cold and unfriendly." He smiled, holding his head to one side. His face was long and narrow, undeniably handsome but in a sinister way. It was a face that would always have shadows even in the brightest lights. The eyes were deep and burning, and the lips were thin and long across the face, always slightly smiling with an archaic, almost oriental, smile. Even the hairline was carved with a rough chisel, thinning away from the temples which were strongly defined.

"Our personalities are described perhaps by rooms like these. I can't help but wonder about the vacant tidy minds of some of my clients' families—rooms with no books, no records, no toys, no reminders of lost and lovely times, nothing to take out and look over to see what distance has done for it. Rooms are personalities, and a vacant room is a vacant personality. Maybe you'll tell me about your room someday. Meanwhile I think I hear the water boiling."

While he was gone, Peter pondered on rooms and personalities. He remembered his own room and how vacant and colorless it was at first. There had been nothing added but a few textbooks, but it was now a warm room and had taken on color and was gradually assuming a personality. But then, come to think of it, there were the shells, the pieces of driftwood, and one or two mounted butterflies Miss Claverly had given him. There was neatness in the room, for much was stored in the closets. If things were stored in closets, did that mean that perhaps people stored things in their personalities which they were very careful not to show?

Mr. Bloodgood came back into the room with a black and gold teapot. He went to the long table and took the unpainted box, slipping up the front, which was a little door. It turned out to be a little tea-set, neatly placed on shelves. He took out the cups and poured tea.

"Lapsang souchong. I hope you like it." He handed a cup to Peter. It looked almost clear. When Peter tasted it, he found that it was like no other tea he had ever tasted. It was like a delicate smoke; yet it was tea, tea as foreign and as ancient as the curios and carved idols. It was taste, but taste with the other senses subtly involved. It was not a matter of liking it; rather it was a matter of experiencing it.

"And now I almost hesitate to return to our discussion. It is a difficult discussion, for there is no really good place to begin. Beauty and death," and his voice took on feeling, "are each something of the other, so I'll have to speak of them together. Perhaps, perhaps if the days follow as days should follow (but can we be entirely certain they will?), we'll speak of them separately, for there is something to be said for them as they exist separately." His voice was ambient and with the tea penetrated like smoke the distances, the undiscovered distances, of the limits and infinities of the mind.

"Once," he began, shifting words like sand over lost sea bottoms—"once there was only beauty. Bits of ribbon and flowered things, things that told a story in their silence. For a child like me there was the unfathomable beauty of the secret places of old big houses—deep window seats, staircases, and cellars. We lived in such a place. 116 Cathedral Street. I was spellbound by the slow drift of life, beautiful life, in a big family. I was the youngest of the four boys and older than the three girls. I suppose, with my sensitiveness, I might have been a sort of transition, since I shared a lot with both." He extracted a Japanese fan from the sleeve of his robe and fluttered it while he talked. "Then, this tranquil idyll came to an end when one spring morning—May, I believe it was—my father died. I was seven when it happened, and I remember the awe of the ceremony of the funeral, the gasping sobs behind closed doors, the muffled tread of feet walking across the downstairs halls and porches. I remember the starched white and whispering black of the funeral clothes, the bleak-eyed staring of my brothers and bewildered whimpering of my little sisters. I fled from all this and wandered through legions of gaunt low-voiced relatives to seek out my shadows and my dark places, so that I could cry out by myself, all by myself, the tremendous guilt of grief.

"Now the shadows took on a greater meaning, and now they

were inhabited by my father, the cold, tobacco-scented presence that lingered beyond the sunlight. This then was the first step toward bringing death and beauty together. I could not accept a simple orgy of grief as the final tribute; there was more. Death deserved, those dead deserved, some sort of shrine—spiritual perhaps, but that couldn't be all."

He looked at Peter, his head held to one side. "Won't you have some more tea, my friend? I've barely started." He rose and went to a marble-topped table, fluttering the fan in the gray room where the grave roses hung with broken heads.

Peter nodded and watched the wavering reflection cast high on the wall by a goldfish bowl. There was coming to be in this account a something he didn't comprehend, where it had started so simply. First, there had been simply death and night and beauty (but were they so simple?). Now they were complicated by a groping personality bemused with ribbons and bits of colored paper, now translated to fluttering fans, grave flowers, and goldfish reflections.

"When I was sixteen, I attended a funeral for the daughter of one of my mother's friends. The girl had been in a car wreck and had been mutilated. As I looked at the dead girl's face, I was shocked to see a long pearly scar beginning at the hairline and ending in the corner of her mouth. My sense of perfection was violated, and I longed to lean and model the scar, to touch the lips and smooth out the lumpy smile.

"After that I began to think about death; and if I tried not to think about it, I found myself thinking about it even more. Death came to be very important, for at one moment it represents the sums of all the years added up, the final evidence of all the failures or successes of a life in purely physical terms, for consciousness has gone. Here at one moment in eternity is a suspended entity balanced between the finite and the infinite. From the miracle of organization of a series of human rational systems it will become another miracle of re-absorption into essences, perfumes, vapors, chemicals. Death is the passing point and deserves more than a hasty attention. The ancients were aware of this, as we know from reading of their funeral customs.

"So it was I began hanging around the mortuary, offering to run errands and such. Little by little I was permitted to do other things, and eventually I became an assistant. I had trouble keeping away from the final work, for I felt an instinct for this. One of the morticians took a special interest in me and insisted that I attend morticians' school as soon as I got through high school. I did this, and after many assignments as assistant in this and that place I came here; and now time has strangely flown, and it is hard to remember being anywhere but this room."

"How did you happen to come here?" Peter was startled to hear his voice sound unfamiliar after the long monologue.

"I heard about it from someone many years ago, while I was a student in restorative art in Chicago. It was curious how when the job was advertised in the trade journal I simply came, having no knowledge of the place. Yet, it was all he told me it would be." Mr. Bloodgood smiled a slow smile and poured himself another cup of tea. "It is strange how we imagine places and then see them so really different. This one was not like that. I knew how it looked, sounded, and smelled before I came, and it was exactly that way. It depends, perhaps, on whose eyes you first see it through."

"I believe I'd better go. They don't know where I am at home. Miss Billy worries about me when I'm out late." Peter rose.

"Of course. There are always people to worry, aren't there? Most persons would not be happy if there wasn't someone to worry after them. I haven't that problem, and sometimes—just sometimes—I almost wish I could know the feeling, but then—" He paused, smiling at some faraway memory.

Peter extended his hand. "I have enjoyed this, and I hope I may come again."

"Really? Well, I am pleased. But we barely got started. I have many curious effects to show you, but they lose with too sudden a showing or too many at once. Please come any time you will." Mr. Bloodgood opened the door.

Peter turned in the door at the head of the outside stairs. "I want to hear more about death and beauty. I want to hear about—" and he stopped, uncertain suddenly what he really did want to hear about. "Good night, Mr. Bloodgood." The wind came up the steps and lifted his coat around his legs. It would be a cold walk home.

"Good night, my friend," Mr. Bloodgood said and closed the door.

7

THE ROAD was night crowded, and distance came close on all sides. Night arched with close-packed stars to lost horizons. The car lights swatched a path ahead, and they moved steadily toward a distant somewhere. Occasionally Peter glanced over at Karl, who had been so far like the silences on all sides. He wanted to say something, but he knew it would be shallow. Reticence in other persons always brought out a fumbling and overly cautious quality in his conversation.

They crossed a wooden bridge, a long bridge that seemed to be floating on the river which ran blackly under the lights from fishing shanties beside the bridge.

"This is Poison River," Karl finally spoke for the first time in ten miles. "Really Poisson, but the natives call everything by the most obvious pronunciation—like Pass aux Huitres across the bay which they call Pass Sweet."

"Does this bridge really float or did it just feel like it sank into the water as we crossed?"

"It really floats. It is built on some sort of pontoon affair. They occasionally float out a section of it to let boats through. I guess it is the last one around these parts."

After that they didn't say anything until they turned off the road onto an intersecting farm-to-market road. Here the night was deeper, with no passing cars, and there was about it with its wind-swept fields and lonely pines an ineffably tragic quality. This was a feeling Peter had learned to identify with these southern winter nights which stretched out beyond the final houses across uncultivated fields and marshes where even frogs no longer sang. Where was this road going? Something cold and remote in the arcana of his mind reaffirmed that Moss Bayou was the end for roads, and that all the roads that went beyond the Bayou were dream roads that led to carnivals where grim and unreal things happened, or, tonight, to unreal places known about by unreal people (for was Karl, beautiful and star-cold Karl, real?).

"This is it. Bayou Honorine." Karl wheeled the car around a curve, wheel ruts cut deep in the white sand, and stopped before a green-painted shack overhanging the water of the bayou. A crude sign was over the door: "Felice's—Gumbo." Karl got out and circled the car as Peter opened the door.

The inside like the outside was shabby. Naked low-watt bulbs dangled from the ceiling over unpainted tables and cane-bottomed chairs. Only two or three other couples were there, and the room looked very large and bare. Karl nodded toward a table which looked out over the bayou, and they sat down. Outside, dim winking lights coursed along the night-lost inlets of the bayou, and beneath them Peter could see the winter-cold water swirling as with a swift current under the rectangle of light thrown by the window.

Soon a Negro woman approached, slender and graceful. She laid her hand softly on Karl's shoulder. "So nice to see you, Mr. Karl. It has been some time." She stood there with her hand still on his shoulder and smiled at Peter.

"I know it has, Felice, but it is a long way. Peter, this is Felice. She is only a tradition until you get to know her. Somehow after that she becomes necessary."

"That's probably because so many have become necessary to me. The usual, then, I suppose?" She smiled her brilliant smile and walked away, her pale yellow skin like a delicate undiscovered metal.

"Why, she's the most beautiful woman I think I have ever seen." Peter had been able only to stare.

"Yes, I guess she is. She has a somewhat unusual story, too. Well, not really in these parts. But she is all but descended from the bayou itself. At least, I like to think that she is."

Felice came back then with a bottle and put it before Karl. "Here is your rare and delicious wine you are always talking about. It's scuppernong wine I make myself," she said to Peter and moved away.

The wine was like the spun gold of Felice's features. It was warm and full bodied, and its bouquet was exotic and indefinable like the secrets of the swamps and bayous around them.

Felice entered again with two steaming bowls and placed them before them. "I wish I could sit and talk with you as usual, Mr. Karl, but I am all alone here tonight. I am certainly tired this evening. Anyhow, do tell me, are you reading anything particularly interesting?"

"No, just some contemporary British novels. Nothing important, but do try Ronald Firbank."

"I have," she said, "and he is enchanting. But right now I am doing Kafka. The most terrifying symbolism. He takes a little effort, but what doesn't that is really worth while? But do eat your gumbo before it gets cold." She hurried off.

"Who did she say she is reading?"

"Kafka. Haven't you read any of him?"

"No, but am I supposed to?"

"Well, he is one of the most important of the twentieth century novelists."

"But what is she doing reading him?"

"Why not? She is a graduate of Radcliffe, and even if she weren't she would be one of the most brilliant women I know or have ever known." Karl smiled, vastly amused at Peter's bewilderment.

"But what is she doing here—this miles away from everything?"

"But what else? She is a Negro here, and what could she do but teach, perhaps, across the bay. She has a good business here, and she is really quite happy. You see, she happens to love it here."

"But with her mind she should be doing something."

"Well, she is. She writes articles for all sorts of quarterlies, and I think she is working on a longer thing on the Imagist School. Peter, these bayous harbor strange secrets. The world outside would never guess, not only at those who have always been here but at the ones who have turned in here for refuge and peace. There are tempests here, too, but they have elements of genuine drama about them, not the pathos of mediocrity. How do you like the gumbo?"

"Like everything else, it is unbelievable."

The other food came a dish at a time—oysters, shrimp, stuffed crab, and fried fish. Each new dish was exquisitely prepared, incongruous with the casual and informal serving and the shabby surroundings. Yet, the scuppernong wine, the water which seemed to transfer its motion to the shanty, and the magnificent food had altered the interior so that it wouldn't have been right otherwise. It began to be another dream room, more dreamlike than ever when one felt the miles outside to somewhere else. And night was the necessary element to lend it further remoteness and undistinguished elegance.

They were then served strong black coffee, the kind with a hint of chicory. Even the coffee had been transformed to something else. They sat and sipped the coffee slowly, watching Bayou Honorine move around the lights. Peter felt a deep peace he could not define. There was no restlessness to be somewhere else. He glanced at Karl, whose face was still the inscrutably beautiful mask to god knew what world beyond.

"There really should be fireflies, but there is something better about the winter. It is lonelier."

"Karl." Peter hesitated, but the unaccustomed wine prompted at least one question toward the so far unknown. Karl looked at him, waiting. "Why are you so sad?"

"Am I?" Karl laughed his almost-disagreeable laugh. "How?"

"I don't know, but you are. There is that about you. I knew it before I knew you. Why?—and you with everything everybody in the world wants and looks for." Peter already felt ridiculous for asking.

"Everything? No, it isn't that simple. You never have it, all of it. There is always another thing to want, to look for, to be in need of. Contentment is the hardest bought commodity in all the worlds and all the times. For one moment of it we will labor through eternities of darkness and grief. But, god, Peter, that one moment."

"But don't we all have those moments fairly often?"

"No, we don't. I don't mean this illusory happiness we get from acquiring things, people, or ideas. It is almost a metaphysical thing, a sudden seeing of oneself without the mirrors and without the lies one has started telling himself from birth. Certain people may have this insight more often than others, some may never have it. But try to imagine a view of yourself completely stripped of your conflicts, your conceits; a moment in time where you can see backward and forward in the same instant while still completely in touch with the present."

"Maybe I can't imagine. Can you?" Peter leaned forward, his chin in his hand.

"Yes, it happened once, and this is how I have come to know about it. But do you want to hear about it really? You may think afterwards it wasn't such an experience, after all, for it is difficult to tell about. But I know it was." Karl lighted a cigarette and blew smoke through his nostrils.

"I must hear." Peter already knew that he would believe, for he was a little dizzy with the idea of such a moment.

"Well, then. I have to start a little before to give it the proper circumference. When I was a senior at Ferndale—"

"You went to Ferndale?" asked Peter, surprised. "You never told me."

"You never asked me," Karl said a little impatiently. "When I was a senior at Ferndale, I was recommended by the faculty to be interviewed for a scholarship by a representative from one of the big foundations. The day of the interview I was ill, and the man's questions were smooth and treacherous. I sat and wished it were over and I could start forgetting that I had let one of the best scholarships in the country get away. The man was sympathetic, and after we had finished he gave me a conciliatory pat on the shoulder and left.

"I did forget and went ahead and applied for a teaching fellowship at the state university. This I got, and after I graduated from Ferndale I put all my effort toward getting prepared for the university.

"One night Karen, Ulrich Nelsen, and I were playing pinochle at the kitchen table. We were barefoot, and it was one of those evenings when everything is somehow right. The phone rang. It was long distance from New York telling me I had received the foundation scholarship to study English literature at any university I should choose. When they asked me if I had given this any thought, I said almost hypnotically, 'Yes—Harvard.' They told me I should have to apply and be accepted, so I spent several weeks filling out forms, getting vaccinated, and getting letters of reference.

"Then after I had been accepted, my conflicts began to close in. I was being presumptuous. Some twist of circumstances had made the representative select me, and he had been wrong. I couldn't do it; I wasn't ready. I looked back at my rather sketchy academic background, spotted with gaps and stretched thinly across whole centuries of literature. I was terrified. I walked uptown to get the mail, to try to get away from these miserable thoughts. On the way back, all at once my insecurities avalanched over me, and I walked a few steps till I was under a live oak that stretched a gigantic branch over the path. I stood under this branch and looked up. The branch could fall and crush me to a pulp, but at the same time I knew it wouldn't. It would be there after I had finished Harvard. I laughed and defied it to fall on me. I knew, even as I knew it wouldn't fall, that I could go to Harvard and beyond to anything. I felt suddenly very powerful. There was the proud knowledge that I was a sort of apex of several generations of my family, none of whom had ever gone to college. There was the overpowering awareness that I was young, beautiful, brilliant, and possessed of every excellence. And the limb would not fall, no matter how long I stood there. If heaven could grant this certainty in this moment, heaven could grant a great deal more, and I was no longer afraid.

"I didn't want to leave the tree, for I knew that this would not come again. I walked on, and my uncertainties started again, but they were diminuendo. I had had the moment I needed for many times and worlds to come.

"I have often gone back to the tree, but in the weary ebb and flow of mediocre experience and the random run-on of days and nights and individuals, no such revelation is necessary. The tree and the moment were for a great and significant experience. The tragedy—or maybe I should say pathos—of our lives is that we so seldom need the tree."

Karl turned his glass sideways so that it caught the light in its amber fluid. "Disappointed?"

Peter was almost surprised that it was through, but he was not disappointed. It was an experience he could almost imagine, and he knew in the same instant that he had never had such a moment. "Was it so very wonderful?"

"Yes, so wonderful that nothing matters so much that it happen again." Karl's face was indescribably beautiful as he looked into the amber glass—an angel head in its blondness, but a demon head in its brooding mysteriousness. "I must be told this again; I must have something said positively, even if I don't want particularly to hear it. I can't stand the broad flat glare of nothingness; even a definite failure, provided it is a powerful failure, is better than this."

Peter said nothing but looked at Karl's face once more and then out at the black and silver monotony of the water, attempting to put this time and these words in his memory.

Felice came back to the table and told them good-bye.

"I hope you will come back soon. We'll have more time then perhaps."

"Peter will learn if he stays here very long that he can't stay away. Felice is the only real unreality I know."

"I'll have to take that home and analyze it. I may be able to use it somewhere." She laughed and watched them go. They were the last ones out, and she closed the door softly after them.

"I don't want to leave," Peter said, not sure what he meant.

"Yes, I know. It has that effect."

The car wheeled once more around the same curves, but the late-rising moon had softened the curves and had made the ancient oaks with their moss a silvery-green luminescence. They followed the farm road, and once more the night with its distances seemed to bring on a companion distance between them. Karl was quiet, but it was a more intimate quietness this time. Peter reflected that they might even be thinking of the same things as they rumbled across Poison River, mixing dark echoes with the silver moonlight.

8

"IT WOULD be so easy to be negative in my practice, seeing myself one day stretched like all the others. But it is really not like that at all. One starts with that assumption instead of ending with it. My own real anxiety and regret come when I think that I won't get to apply my talent and experience to myself, that I shall fall into awkward hands. Some of these rural morticians are dreadful; their funerals are travesties."

The room was more familiar this time. With the room you had to start with a certain assumption, also. You had to remember that its occupant was more familiar with solitude and death than anything else, that death colored all his tastes, and that even those things he considered beautiful were equated with death in one of its expressions.

Most of all the room was oriental in feeling, even if the accumulations of objects gave it a Victorian heaviness. There was a suspended quality here, though, and the Buddha with its imperturbable smile gave the feelings of suspension, death, and beauty a curiously blended effect. Death was not horrible here but was a peace and an emptiness, a re-embodiment in lovely fragile things.

"And now would you like to see some of my treasures—books, prints, photographs, scarabs? But photographs are usually nice to start with, don't you think? I'll get my albums." Mr. Bloodgood crossed the room, the yellow-sashed kimono flowing out behind him. Peter leaned back and closed his eyes for a moment, listening to a Mozart concerto.

"I have more, of course, but photographs very easily bore one; some of these, however, are far from boring." He sat beside Peter on the couch and opened one of the books. "We'll go rapidly by the family ones; families attempt to guarantee immortality by smiling into cameras at every opportunity. Ah, here is one you should enjoy as an experience. It is a photograph of one of the Pompeiian murals few tourists ever manage to see. I haven't been there, but I found this in an obscure shop in Chicago that deals in pornographia."

Peter looked at the photograph and was a little surprised that it didn't shock him. The two dimensional perspective made the action in the scene a little unimaginative and naïve.

There were others similar, such as details from a temple in India depicting all known perversions. About some of these he was genuinely curious, for he had never imagined certain of them. And to think they had assumed enough importance among the races of man to be monumentalized.

"Have you ever seen such treasures, my friend?" asked Mr. Bloodgood.

"No, I don't suppose I have."

"Perhaps some of these would seem a little crude, but they represent part of the unknown record of history. Who can know how the destinies of empires might have been affected by bestiality, pedophilia, or sodomy? Those things don't ordinarily get communicated by historians," he said as he turned a page.

Here was a remarkable enlarged picture of a man standing on a beach. He was naked, but there was no detail, for the picture had seemingly been made either late in the afternoon or with the sun at the wrong angle. Even the face was blurred, almost silhouetted. Mr. Bloodgood started to turn on.

"Who is that?" Peter asked. Somehow there was a feeling of familiarity about the picture. It was impossible that he could know the person, but he had to be told about it for some reason. The scene was a lonely one; it was hard to think that someone else had had to be along to snap the picture. The vague water stretching to the horizon and the stark elemental man seemed to hint bleakly at the start of things—man naked and alone against the background of a cold and impersonal universe.

"Oh, someone before you were born, I guess. His name was Norman Stephen (Stephen, not Stephens)—a rare and unforgettable individual. This is the only picture I have of him, and that's unusual, for of all the persons I have known I should have had more of him. And this one is—well, you can see—the same as not having one."

"But it is beautiful." Peter's voice was thoughtful.

Mr. Bloodgood gave him a quick look. "Strange that you should feel that way. You know, it hasn't occurred to me all the time I have known you, but you very closely resemble Norman. I wish the picture were clearer so that you could see how much. He was also beautiful." Mr. Bloodgood's voice was gentle. "There was beauty and death about him. I suppose that's why he fascinated me more than anyone I ever knew."

"How beauty and death? Did he die?"

"I never knew anyone else he knew, but he must have died for everyone he ever knew. When I was with him there was always the knowledge that it might be the last time forever. Consequently there was always a delicacy to our relationship—never anger or violence—for somehow he seemed to be aware of this, too."

"So there was a last time finally?"

"Isn't there always, my friend? What matters whether it is seeing someone walk down a rainy street and watching the misty distance close behind him forever or whether it is shoveling dirt on a coffin lid. There is little difference. A last time is a last time, even if the person should be clumsy enough to stumble back into your life again all disguised with years and happened things."

"Has that happened?" Peter knew that it was very necessary that it hadn't.

"No," said Mr. Bloodgood slowly. "Norman knew about death and beauty as few persons could ever know them. He was an elegant paradox. He was sudden as a bird springing from the underbrush, but the few things about which he was constant he was eternal." Mr. Bloodgood traced his fingers across the photograph tenderly.

"Eternal?" Peter looked again at the picture, which was itself a kind of eternity in shadows and dimly disturbed memory.

"Yes," said Mr. Bloodgood slowly, "there was one thing. He believed in immortality—not a conventional concept—as a metamorphosis. He used to mention frequently the oriental symbol of immortality—the butterfly—and he said the subtle oriental mind meant death as well. Something must die in one place before it can be resurrected in another. Beauty—human beauty or butterfly beauty—comes from the dark and twisted wetness and sliminess of uterus or cocoon and knows always that to find its way again out of a world and into a world it must return through such a door."

Peter leaned forward. "Butterfly?"

"Yes, my friend, butterfly. Can you think of anything more exquisitely beautiful, so eternal, yet so brief? Norman was almost like that himself—free, drifting (and even if one knew that to drift for him was life, one would still try to capture him), gorgeous, and always a little out of reach." Mr. Bloodgood sighed and reached for a licorice lozenge in the bowl on the coffee table. "I don't know why he should be here with Pompeii and Herculaneum, unless some whim caused me once to put him here when I considered, perhaps, that for me he could be thought to be that remote and final. But, my friend, there are more pictures than this one."

"No, I must go, for it is getting dark, and I must get to work on a paper I have to do. Sundays are difficult anyhow and compulsions make them worse."

"Yes, that is true. Long ago I gave up fighting Sundays, and in the bargain I gave up anything positive I wanted to accomplish on Sunday. It is a day for lying with closed blinds reading Saltus or Hearn, a day for drinking a slow pot of tea or sipping a brandy, or a day for exploring old civilizations with new friends. Please come again soon, for there will be many more Sundays, and there is a great deal we haven't said."

As Peter walked past the cemetery home he thought of the gray-shadowed Norman, and the feeling of association persisted. Perhaps it was because Norman had talked of butterflies. Birds were black notches along the blue-cast winter limbs and telegraph wires. Peter smiled to think what Norman would think of Miss Billy's tree full of magic and Miss Claverly's cause and effect. It was somehow nicer to think that Norman would conceive of a tree full of immortality.

9

THE BISQUE was a muddy brown, but the taste was green liquid depths of bayous where mint and water cress grew, where Spanish moss blotted out the sun and silver minnows darted. It was the taste of rusty winter sunsets through marsh grass and silhouettes of skeletal swamp trees. It was the taste of the Deep South.

"It is the first I have ever had, and therefore it will always be the best, no matter."

"Wonderful." Karen looked at him appreciatively. "You are a little like Karl. I guess that's why I feel close to you, even though I don't know you at all."

"Like Karl?" Peter was surprised and pleased.

"Yes, but so different, really. You are handsome, but not in the same way, for you are earth-handsome. You are very intelligent; one just senses this in a person. The difference is that you will do something with your intelligence. One senses this also. Such people are so rare that they stand out anywhere."

Peter stumbled words together in an effort to say something.

"You have no idea what you will do, what you want, but you'll know one of these days, and then you'll have everything necessary to acquire it."

"But Karl— Karen, why is Karl always so sad?"

"Karl is a very unusual person. He is extremely brilliant, and he has not just a good personality but the kind that people never in their lives forget. He is handsome and talented. In every way he is superior to most people, so his unhappiness would have to be superior, too, and it would be unfair to say that he has everything and so nothing to be sad about. Maybe he is sad for something outside himself." She lighted a cigarette.

"No, it's something definite and not outside himself." Peter watched the smoke curl in spirals up the candlelight.

Karen looked at him a slow moment. "Why do you say that?"

"I just know. It is a hurt something about him, something that has happened or is happening. I don't know why I know this."

"I don't either. No one knows Karl better than I do, and I wouldn't say that. Oh, but we're almost arguing, and I'm really not very good at that."

They finished their coffee and left the restaurant. Outside, the rain had not stopped, and the wind slapped the sides of buildings with sheets of water.

"There's nothing like these winter storms," said Karen, shivering into the car. "We can just make it."

They drove again through the flooding streets. Peter watched the gigantic limbs of the live oaks lashing in the wind, dashing the car with water. They went out the street on which he had come into downtown Mobile from school. The houses were dim now, slitting dim lights through shutters, and it was incongruous to think of radios and telephones behind the ancient façades.

They turned left off this street eventually and came to the auditorium, where hundreds of cars were parked, and people hurried from them with umbrellas.

"Looks as if we shall have to run for it," said Peter.

They half-ran through puddles that splashed water over shoe-tops and were thoroughly wet when they got to the building. They were only minutes ahead of the start of the program, and as soon as they had sat down the conductor came out.

There was something about the way darkness closed down in the concert hall, giving the light and brilliance of the music the only light—narrow threads of light along bows, molten spots of light on brasses and the buttons of woodwinds, white light on shirt fronts and black light on polished shoes. The first music trickled up from underneath, seeping out from first one instrument then another, joining, and finally becoming a torrent of sound, drowning the senses in a silver flood.

"It is a river," whispered Karen, "starting in the mountains in tiny bubbling springs, getting stronger and finally moving across the valley."

Peter was pleased that this had been his feeling about the music. He saw it now—a broad river (the Moldau, the program said) coursing through a fertile valley with peasants following beside it with carts and animals. The sun lay golden and pale green over the whole scene, for it was a picture of sun and light, exquisitely mellow light bringing distances together.

It was a short piece, and he was sorry when it was finished. Another piece followed, but he couldn't make a picture this time, for it was a less obvious composition, with melodies threading suddenly out of melodies and into others. But he was fascinated with the mechanics of it, the way all the violin bows rose and fell at precisely the same moment. He watched the conductor's hands in outline, which looked as if they were pulling notes out of the instruments, balancing them, dashing them on the floor.

The selection ended abruptly, and they went out for the intermission. They leaned against a wall, and Karen smoked a cigarette. Her face was rapt as if distantly she were still hearing the music.

"Isn't it lovely? Music is the one thing that really means to me. My German background, I guess. I can conceive of no happier family life than one in which everyone plays an instrument, sawing away at cellos and violas before a fireplace. I don't know why I don't play something; it just gets by some of us. Maybe we don't want to badly enough." She reflected a minute, letting smoke drift out gradually. "Or like Karl, who plays adequately just about anything he wants to, he is as far as he really wants to go. I've heard people say that such and such a person could have been a brilliant pianist if he had kept on. Not really, for if he had had what it took to be a brilliant pianist in the first place he would have been one. You've seen great pianists, I suppose. Well, there is something that grips them as they play. They can't help but be great. They have in many cases done no more than thousands of others toward being great. They just are."

The lights blinked, and they went back inside.

"This is really what I came for—Mendelssohn's Violin Concerto in E minor. Listen to the andante and tell me if you have ever heard anything so perfect."

The music was again translatable into associations. This time, though, the pictures were recent ones, able to be identified with feelings as close as the rainy street outside.

"This is it," whispered Karen. She took his hand and held it tightly. Peter stopped the pictures and let the delicate arc of melody become its own picture, incomparably lovely through its indefinableness. He knew all at once what the music was. It was the music of the butterfly tree. It could be nothing else, for it was music that could have no one picture, but was as various as all the ideas about such an unreality as the butterfly tree. Each time the theme was repeated the butterflies changed. They were at one time Miss Claverly's butterflies, *Danaus plexippus,* hovering around a lonely pine tree in the day's final shaft of sunlight. Look again, and they were Miss Billy's—translucent magic butterflies on a swamp cypress reflected in bottomless pools to infinity. Again they were Norman Stephen's butterflies, a symbol of immortality, blending in and out cocoons. They were mounted brilliants, blue and lavender, stretched and pinned. And finally, they lay on layers of glass counters, metalcraft butterflies with hinged wings, incapable of flight.

Long after the music had gone to another movement, the butterflies still fluttered restlessly, and he sat dimly wondering if perhaps they all really went together and somewhere beyond the music and the swamps there was a key to all of it. But what really was there to explain? He shifted and looked sideways at Karen, who still held his hand. She leaned a little forward as if seeing the music as well as hearing it. She gradually became aware that he was looking at her and turned to him. This time there was not a smile but something else there in the reflected light. It was a look of searching to see what was being said without sound, or rather through the combining sound of the music outside and inside both of them.

Her hand relaxed, and they didn't applaud with the others.

Later, while they were getting into the car, Karen said, "Maybe some people consider it sentimental; maybe it is. Maybe I like things sentimental. But it says so terribly many things, all of them alike and yet different."

"Yes, I felt that, too. I don't think I would hear the same things exactly again, because—"

"Because they would have flown away."

He looked at her, startled, but they had reached a point this night where distantly he was afraid to ask her what she meant. The moment had been too close, and perhaps it was something for another time.

10

THE ROOM was becoming familiar now like all the other rooms of his life. It was a room only he knew about. He had never told Miss Billy about the room, nor had he mentioned it to Karen Heppler when he met her for coffee or a movie. This room was a world he somehow knew he had to keep secret, for it would be a hard world for other people to understand, especially if they should try hard to understand.

Its Buddha continued to smile him into acceptance of the enigmas Edward Bloodgood chose to produce for his inspection. The oriental flavor of the hangings stretched his imagination so that it focused on nothing in particular, and the smoky fragrance of the tea was an opiate. This room became a sanctum for him, a dreamworld where nothing itself became important. A movie or a walk on the wharf ended ultimately in this room, with its shadows, polished surfaces, and tumbled centuries. It became his instruction in many things he would never learn at Ferndale. It was a glimpse into the inscrutable where one learned part of the reason for the Buddha's smile, part of the delicious peace of emptiness.

Edward Bloodgood was a master at uncoiling the imagination, and even if sometimes his world seemed strewn with the wreckage of all the evils time had evolved, he managed to capture the outer edges of Peter's compulsion to know. Peter had come to accept him along with the other trappings of the room as if he, too, were a product of some ruined civilization.

Peter looked up from a book he had opened, for there again was the name of Norman Stephen inscribed on the flyleaf. Mr. Bloodgood looked up, too, for he was sensitive to a shift in attention.

"Norman left a lot of fingerprints, didn't he? Somewhere in everything he keeps coming to the attention, as if he weren't content to be left dead."

"How perceptive you are, my friend. That's exactly how it happens, you see. For Norman, who believed in metamorphosis, this is his metamorphosis for me. He has been translated to a part of all the things that matter to me; we still share them that way. Even you, who look like him. At this moment I have with me the centuries, the death of centuries, Norman who is dead and not dead, the night, and you, who are in this instant a focal point of all of them."

"But Norman. Where did he come from for you?"

"Out of the centuries, my friend, and into the centuries. Each person does this for every other person he knows, particularly those that matter. And out of beauty—beauty as an idea."

"And he was this?" Peter looked at the name written on the page, fascinated again by the twist of recognition.

"Not exactly." Mr. Bloodgood sighed deeply. "Yet, most entirely. How can it be answered, for he was part of the idea, part of the fulfillment. But then so are you; so is all this," and he gestured at the room. "As for persons as they contribute to this fulfillment, I always preferred those with beautiful faces or beautiful bodies—to make up part of this idea and maybe a little to make up for what I was not. To have about me always the beautiful, since I couldn't be. And those not beautiful I saw as something I could make beautiful. A touch here and there where nature had been clumsy or time cruel. There at last could I bring them together, death and beauty."

Mr. Bloodgood tossed the fan to the table and poured a final cup of tea, for the leaves came and sifted to the bottom of the cup. He smiled. "But you, my beautiful boy, should not be puzzling about night and death, for you are a daylight thing. A gorgeous thing that is wasted in the darkness, for you must be seen to have meaning. Yes, you are like something that comes to these swamps, that exists in the swamps without meaning, yet all meaning."

"What do you mean? I don't want to go (for I must go) without knowing."

"You are like the butterfly tree."

"The butterfly tree!" Peter gasped, but then he realized that he should have known it would be here, too, in this room with the other unknowables. Mr. Bloodgood looked at him curiously.

"What surprises you?"

"But the butterfly tree. How?"

"How? You must know about it a while before you can think about it. It is something I have never seen, but I shall."

"Tell me how you came to know." Peter's bewilderment was

smiled out of being by the smug statues. He leaned forward and put his head between his hands, watching a moth flutter around the light.

"I first heard about the butterfly tree one frozen night in Chicago. It was such a night as this and such a person as you."

"Norman?" Peter somehow knew this before Mr. Bloodgood started.

"Yes, Norman. It was shortly before he died for me—so that the butterfly tree is at once death, beauty, night, and all their components. He told me—for we were discussing physical beauty —that my eyes were as deep and as remote as the butterfly tree, for he had, he said, seen it. I asked him to describe it, but he wouldn't, and all I ever learned really was that the butterfly tree, then, when I was young, was as deep as my eyes. He told me that this was where all the hushed unknown, the un-penetrated and elusive beauties of which he was made up came from. Then he died—for me he died.

"The butterfly tree never came clear for me; I suppose I still regard it through his eyes—a night tree with butterflies like liquid fire, luminescent and flowing skyward. He said once it was like the souls of dead mariners rising out of the sea, search-ing the more impenetrable ocean of the sky." Peter's memory sprang away in a desperate effort to remember where he had heard this before, but he couldn't quite decide. "I didn't believe in the butterfly tree for a long time, fully believe in such a tree —as a reality, I mean. It was, I thought, knowing Norman's delight in the abstract, a kind of trance, a hypnagogic manifesta-tion that came between beauty and death, beauty and night."

Mr. Bloodgood had taken from his kimono pocket a pendant, a blood-red glass droplet on a chain. He began to swing it back and forth as he talked, looking at Peter meanwhile. Peter had a chilly sensation that Mr. Bloodgood was no longer talking to him but to someone else, someone from another time. He tried not to watch the swinging motion, but he couldn't help it. His eyes followed it, and his mind joined his eyes. Music came from a hidden place, tracing the contours of the room with slow mournfulness, causing the black drapes to waft faintly back and forth.

"We can never know—ever—what destinies the winds prepare for us, can we?" Mr. Bloodgood's hand caressed Peter's head thoughtfully, casually as if it were a tapestry or a vase. The motion was almost hypnotic, and Peter knew that he didn't want it to stop. "For no matter how much we want to change what we are, what we were born to, what we have done or committed, the wind will search to tell us that these things we cannot change. Perhaps that is what the wind is telling among the gravestones, that not even death has undone the unchangeables. Perhaps it tells me that I may or may not find the butterfly tree, for it tells the all, the final, too. . . ."

When Peter opened his eyes, the room was full of soft light, and music came from somewhere. He didn't know what had awakened him or really whether or not he had slept. The shades were drawn, though, and there was no willow nodding outside, where one, a dark skeletal willow, had nodded earlier. His mind was empty and relaxed, but there was consciousness of something's having happened—a still sea bottom with crashing waves overhead. His body was limp, too, with the leaden pressure of slumber.

Mr. Bloodgood smiled at him from the bed. "Did you have a pleasant nap, my friend? I felt I was boring you." His smile was slow, serene, fluttering briefly like the sticks of the unfolded fan.

"No, I'm sorry; I must have been tired, and it's so pleasant here." Peter lifted himself erect and stood up.

"Then I must be flattered that you find my companionship so calming and comfortable that we can choose to ignore the taxing concessions of the more formal relationships. We shall continue another time, taking up where you—ah—drooped off to sleep." He smiled again, and suddenly Peter knew that the smile was one of absolute evil. The smile was one of amusement. Perhaps it was because he had gone to sleep, but he wasn't sure it was this.

"When you slept you were more beautiful than the dead, but sadder, my friend, for you have awakened to grow old and unlovely. You won't come back again, of course, for a long time. But another time will come. You will know when. Now I fear you must go, for there are those who will worry about you. Be happy that there are those who will care. Now run and leave me here with the music that is playing the dirge of all the dying days of the year." He turned toward the wall.

Peter crept to the door and down the stairs. Outside, the wind continued the dirge which he had left upstairs, and the dry leaves scurried in front of him like frightened birds.

11

SOMETHING OUT of sleep—dimly remembered sleep—tugged at an ancient memory, maybe a dream, crumbled years before under a mind-barrier. Hurry, for the wind races across the barren fields of the soul, seaching for something it can corrupt, some final purity it can shatter with a blast.

Shake with a troubling chill, trying to shake off the primitive dream. Edward Bloodgood, fearfully unknown, fearfully created to frighten like carnival masks springing from dark doorways at night. What of him? What of the music, the fan, the room above the funeral parlor? What could you hide from him, for he was like the searching wind that came even now raking its fingers under the windowpanes and fidgeting with the shingles. Dead vines moving on the house like long witches' hair, shadows of night-flying birds drifting drifting across the thresholds of sleep to vex from peaceful dreams. Everything—everything is predatory, ready to grasp and snag the soul, to cast it toward the sharp, ever-present peaks that loom up from the narrow cliff where we walk, oh so carefully, talking about beauty, death, and knowledge. Know, know only that everyone is destined by the great wheeling condor birds and the tormented wind to crash splash with everybody's fans, everybody's silk kimonos, everybody's dreams. Ah yes, the dream comes back—the young white bodies riding surf-horses, white breasts and buttocks, white limbs and blond hair. White and like the rest will lie on one of Mr. Bloodgood's slabs and become whiter, more beautiful—the most beautiful of us, the youngest of us, the most afraid, the unafraid. Crash, and the sea will roll in with all its majesty and sullenness to draw us away to unreturnable shores.

12

MORNING LAY in the corners of the room when he awoke, sunlight springing from all reflecting things. A moss-covered limb threw its shadow on the opposite wall, and flicking bird shadows came and went. Peter stretched out on the bed on his back, staring at the ceiling. He was aware that something had changed, that he had crossed a certain threshold ("But, my friend, wouldn't *uncertain* be a better term for intangibles," he could hear Mr. Bloodgood say), that something had found expression. Last night came dimly like remembered thunder. Something beyond words had happened. ("But, my friend, something beyond words was necessary.") He had asked about the night and death, and there had been darkness and broken splendor in the room, musty scenes from other worlds and other times.

Eventually, he knew, he would have to get up and go to school, but now he felt incapable of moving from the delicious sprawl of half-sleep. There had been a sort of release the night before, something vaguely disturbing but still unknown. He tried to think back, but it was useless. ("Do I frighten you, my friend; if so I mustn't for you must realize that everything is relative and actually there is hardly such a thing as responsibility.") He threw off the cover and sat up suddenly to stop the voice. ("Well, of course, my beauty, if you insist—") And then it was gone by the time he got downstairs to breakfast.

"Where were you last evening, Peter; I almost worried." Miss Billy didn't look as though she cared whether he answered or not, preoccupied as she was with pouring the coffee. Eulacie was in Mobile and wouldn't be back till afternoon.

"To a movie." He honestly couldn't explain why he lied.

"Oh, that's good. You know, movies just aren't what they used to be. So simple and lovely once. Now they murder and steal and do all sorts of things. Even when they murdered before, they did it so very gracefully. I almost always fell for the criminals; they were always so melancholy and beautiful."

"Yes, they probably were," he said slowly.

"Peter," she asked suddenly, serious and anxious, "are you happy here—I mean now that you have slipped into place?"

"Why, of course. I have always been."

"Well, I worried at first. There wasn't much for you to do here. You didn't make any friends your age before the Hepplers, who are awfully nice. Just Miss Claverly, who, pardon me for saying so, was just a little odd."

"But she wasn't really. She just lived in another world. Now she is gone and so is her world." He thought wistfully how already he had forgotten the names of some of the specimens she had given him. Now there was nobody to tell him about them.

"Well, I'm glad you found the Hepplers. The girl is so sweet you can, after a while, forget that she isn't pretty. And the boy is tragically handsome."

"Why do you say tragic?" Peter lifted his coffee cup.

"Oh, I don't know. But he is like something out of Bulfinch's *Age of Fable*—and weren't they always tragic? It is unbelievable that they are twins, but then I suppose there is more to being twins than just looks. Creston used to say (but he said so much) that twins were lucky, that they were able to serve two reincarnations at once."

"What a fantastic idea." Peter tried to imagine what Dr. Anson or Miss Claverly would have to say about that.

"Well, Creston was fantastic. I don't remember that he ever said anything ordinary. I used to wonder if he thought ordinary thoughts. I can't believe he did. Still, I suppose everyone must have to think about hunger, laundry, and getting up in the morning. This can reduce even the most sublime imaginations to a common denominator. But I hate people who say that everyone is human, don't you? They try to explain everything away that way. But they can't. That is the deadliest truism of them all. As for my part, I'd just as soon forget that Elizabeth Barrett Browning might have had a bathroom problem or that Shakespeare was a— Good heavens, Peter, look at that clock!"

Peter jumped up. "That's what I get for being fascinated with what people say. I'm going to have to run to get the bus. By the way, we are doing the metaphysical poets today; we'll have to take a walk and talk about them tonight. 'Bye."

And he was gone out the door and through the ragged winter garden.

13

WINTER CONTINUED dreamily—wind blowing leaves across the cloud-thatched sky. The days were as swift as the wind and drifted like the leaves. Weeks had happened since he had last seen Edward Bloodgood, and more and more the evenings spent with him took on the significance of a dream. The soft magnetic voice had lost reality and came now remote but dimly troubling. He didn't go back to the room, for somehow he felt no need to go. He hardly ever went to the cemetery, for the dead spoke with more immediate voices than they had before.

One afternoon in late winter he walked down to the water, where the wind raced down from the rivers, whipping the white-caps along and singing a fierce falsetto song. He listened and was afraid, for he knew that somehow he was involved in the song, just as he was involved in a place and with people and their dreams.

Then he saw a figure standing far out on a neck of sand. It was familiar, something out of recency, something out of past, a sil-houette against the sea of water and sky, and the wind and waves seemed to give it flight. Something about this scene of man against the sky was lonely and forbidding like old steel engravings in the mildewed books. Peter kept on along the beach till he had come close to the man.

When the figure turned it was, as he knew it would be, Edward Bloodgood. He smiled sideways at Peter without quite turning from the water.

"If you'll look closely, my friend, you will see that there is no real line between the water and the sky; each keeps going. The sky is washing in at my feet, while the water laps on shores of infinity."

"I have not been back. You said I wouldn't."

"Did I? Well, it is hard to be responsible for what we say."

"Why did you think I wouldn't come back?" Peter was picking out the thin strip of beach that fretted its way along under the bluff toward Ecor Rouge, or the big red cliff, that lay watching over the bay.

"Think, my friend? It wasn't so important really. Besides, we are speaking out of time. This isn't the time of my room or the place of my room. You must have known people who didn't really exist away from certain places or circumstances. I must be that way for you. There I could answer your questions. Here, you must listen to the deeper, more universal, voices—the ones that know about you and me and everything we know. They belong to no room or to no person. They flow into all the cavities of time and search out hidden things."

"But why are you here?" Now Peter had stretched the beach between the two points and turned again to face Mr. Bloodgood.

"Sometimes, sometimes I feel that the butterfly tree may be where I least expect it, that perhaps I am looking in all the wrong places. It could be here in the timelessness of wind, the everlastingness of sky, the infinity of water. It may be a recurring thing that goes and comes like the comets."

"But if a comet and you missed it, you would never see it in a whole lifetime."

"Exactly. But who can describe the dimensions of lifetime or deathtime? Perhaps like that space out there where sky doesn't end and water doesn't end, our lifetime doesn't stop with what we know of you and me. In that case we could go on searching to the end of the stars."

"But we can't be sure."

Mr. Bloodgood grew silent, turning again toward the horizon. His voice came in with the wind and the sea. "No, never. That is why, my beautiful boy, I watch dead faces and try to see where they are looking, since they are not looking at me. That is why nothing matters except that I see the butterfly tree now, on this side of the door, before it trips me sprawling into final and uncertain dreams." He turned and tenderly laid the back of his hand against Peter's cheek.

"Please forgive me if I sound dissociated. There was a body today, a farm boy, electrocuted by defective wiring. There was something of Norman about him, something of everybody—even of you. I almost wept at my art, for sometimes our art is too much of us, and we lose track of why a gift has been given us. We may go to the extreme of epitomizing ourselves too completely in a work of art. This art, this dead face, was suddenly too much of my past, the present, and the future. All at once I had achieved these three stages of myself in a moment of time. I had spelled into the unknowing face knowledge, the unseeing face vision, the unbeautiful face beauty. I had cheated the face of all its more commonplace mortal dreams. What could it have done with knowledge, vision, or beauty, for it never possessed them? We are become what we have always been. I had to erase these qualities and combine the more mediocre ingredients of its life —its shorter horizons of field edges, its abbreviated dimensions of physical love and beer-drinking Saturday nights, its glamored guiltiness of straying from a homely moral code. All this I had to expunge from what I had created, and nothing in art is more difficult."

He turned and started to walk away. Peter and the wind followed him. They went up the long steps, the way everyone came, and stood at the top of the cliff looking off across the bay.

"It is curious that no poet, painter, or writer has ever done justice to a sunset. Brahms has done some rather lovely sunsets for me, but to other persons they probably aren't sunsets at all. Good-bye, Peter. Soon you will come to my room again, for it will be time." He turned and walked away and was part of the winter sunset.

14

February 1
New York City

Peter, my dear:

It seems so far from here—farther than the Far East. Have you come to feel that way about Moss Bayou, too? It is a place to me from which I felt far away even while I was there. Now it seems remote, even to the point that I'm not altogether certain it would be there if I came back. (Perhaps this is truer than I think, for it wouldn't be there actually as it was. Our chemistry changes; our cells change so that only a curious and complex system of cells in one area of our brain can manage the necessary associations, while the remainder of us thinks it believes.)

New York is cold and impersonal. There are still a few weeks till we can be sure of the weather and leave on our trip. Meanwhile I must content myself with long hours of research in the library and museum. . . .

And, my dear, I hope you aren't looking for the butterfly tree. I have all sorts of evidence now that my lead was absolutely fictitious. That's what you get for believing persons instead of facts. Anyone would have believed Robert, though. All his other facts checked. I can't understand his being so entirely wrong. I should like to see him again and tell him how wrong he was— or maybe it is just as well I don't. We don't always like to have our beliefs shattered, and besides it has been a very long time.

Well, my dear, I must get back to my work. I do hope to hear from you. Have you been to see my dogs? Walk our stretch of beach again and find something lovely the tide has washed in.

Sincerely,
MARGARET CLAVERLY

15

THE NIGHT street to Mr. Bloodgood's was like a street he had never walked before—one of those familiar experiences that had become so final, so immediate, that when looked at closely was new. He wanted to walk back, but the wind came from the far cliffs and drove him on, and the leaves urged him on by flying against him from behind.

The mortuary gloomed suddenly like an ancient castle, and he was pressing the little bell by the door. A light, a step, and

Mr. Bloodgood was at the door, smiling his archaic smile, his arms folded into the kimono.

"You said I would come back." Peter shuddered, and the wind shuddered once and went away to poke about in the gullies and meddle with dead trees.

"Come in, then. There will be tea."

Again the room where dreams were dreamed and time could cease with a gesture. A chair, a curtained window, death smiling with a painted mask.

"Soon it will be the time to look again, for it will be the time he left, never to return. I always think of 'Ulalume'—you know, 'The leaves they were crisped and sere.' Each time I have gone to look I find only the dark and the shadows of forever. You will come with me?" The acceptance was implied.

"Yes, but when?"

"I shall know soon, and I shall let you know, for we walk in the same places, stretch our imaginations along the same unexplored shores. And perhaps you will come back to my room as you have tonight. I shall always be waiting as I have awaited beauty all my life. Beauty is a floating thing that unravels from the bottom of a swamp and drifts to the light. Usually it trails its ugly roots in the mud; but no one knows that, for everything stops at the brilliance of its surface. It floats there with no beginning, and when beauty goes it goes swiftly, suddenly, with no trace. Once—" and the hands of the clock snagged on the slow, hypnotic voice and the little red-glass teardrop that had appeared and was swinging, cascading consciousness to the root-bottom of hidden garden pools, where light floated enchantingly far off through the translucent depths, that world of water that Miss Claverly knew about but could communicate to only a few. Here it was, and he could tell her that the spirogyra was budding and the desmids were spinning their vacuoles. He could tell her now, for he knew the whole world was spinning beneath the water, and it was like the nebula-spinning sky. And infinity moved again in two directions, and he could not guess at the difference, for none was apparent.

16

THEY LAY on the warm brown pine needles and looked upward at the sun-spun green needles overhead. The picnic things were strewn beside them, and down a little hill the water of a creek winked in the sun glare.

It was still a little cold, and they had worn coats. Peter had taken his off, though, soon after they had arrived, for the clearing in the pines was sheltered from the wind. Now he had taken off his shirt, too, and was lying watching an ant crawl in frantic exploration across his stomach.

"All this," said Karen, gesturing, "dwarfs the music. It is the same music that filled the auditorium the other night. There it was trying to get out. Here, I suppose, it is back with the things out of which it was imagined." She leaned to wind the victrola again.

"Here it doesn't sound so much like water, for there is real water down there. In the auditorium it was almost more real than this water." Peter brushed the ant away and turned over on his stomach.

"It shows the power of imagination in a way. How things can be suggested to it, how it can create what it wants to believe. It is fortunate that most people have an intelligence that imposes limits on imagination."

"And that society has erected institutions for those who don't have these limits, if they can be discovered. I wonder if the authorities have looked as closely at Moss Bayou as they should."

Karen laughed. "Yes, there are a lot of funny people there, but a too vivid imagination can be charming and delightful. You haven't really seen Moss Bayou at its best. Wait till you've been here a few years and gone to a few civic affairs and dabbled in the culture."

"How does Karl feel about it?"

There was a long silence, and Peter turned his head to see Karen, her eyes open, lying motionless. She caught his movement.

"Oh, Karl? He hates it, says he does, fights it and raves about it. That only proves that he really worships it. He must hate it because he loves it so much. He goes away for a few months and desperately returns. For weeks he is pathetic, hurrying around trying to revive the things that from other times have died, or trying to change the eternal things which he has in his absence remembered slightly different. Then he subsides and starts talking about the trap he is in. But Karl is bayou-caught, chained in a sort of lotus land, tortured by the beat of surf on other shores."

Karen made a motion, and suddenly he felt her lips in the palm of his outstretched hand. He didn't move. She laid her face on his hand and murmured, "Let's not talk about Karl now; he requires too much effort." He could feel her breath on his hand, and also he was conscious of the warmth of her body very near but not touching. Her nearness was natural, and he was stirred. Still he didn't move, and he almost held his breath.

Overhead, the wind now moved the whole tops of the pines against each other, bruising their fragrance from them and shattering the glassy sunlight on their needles. In the silence even the creek made a distant dripping sound.

Then they lay against each other. He thought, on the edge of the suspended time, that this was where the music and the rainy streets had to come. There was always another person, either real or imagined. Here with the lisping pines, the sibilant water, and the undetermined reaches of the sky, he wasn't altogether certain which Karen was, but he didn't care.

He leaned on an elbow and kissed her.

17

It TURNED bitterly cold again. Waiting for the bus between Ferndale and downtown Mobile and between downtown and Moss Bayou was a miserable experience, for along with the cold came rain and wind. The bus trip across the causeway from Mobile was depressing, for in the river delta brown water was chopped by the unchecked wind into whitecaps, and the sere marsh grass thrashed and flattened. It was warm on the bus, but the riders seemed to hover over their evening papers and nobody had much to talk about. They would get off at little sand-road stops and with coats whipping about them would huddle off toward their hidden houses.

Back in Moss Bayou, on the walk from the bus station home he didn't hesitate as he sometimes did to look for seedpods or curiosities but hurried past the cemetery and across the gully. The houses along Baycliff looked forbidding and most of all did Miss Billy's for the loose shutters and scattered shingles gave it a denuded appearance.

But inside it was different. Its very disorderliness made it seem cozier. Miss Billy was melting wax and making candles, and Eulacie, Miss Emmajean pulling at her apron, was cooking. The familiarity of the scene was lovely, and Peter knew again his acceptance was secure each time Eulacie shouted for him to wipe his feet.

He tickled Miss Emmajean in the stomach and flipped Eulacie on the behind all in one gesture and dropped into a chair beside Miss Billy. "What are you doing?"

"I read somewhere in an old book how to do this, and I have

been dying to try." She poured the liquid wax into a soup can.

"Mama got a friend in Houstonville can use wax to much better advantage. Has quite a distinguished clientele—even a few white people calls on her for special jobs now and then. But she say the hoodoo racket ain't what it once was." Eulacie poured the hissing contents of a pan into a pot from which a delicious vapor arose.

"You don't really believe all that stuff, do you?" Peter turned to her, hanging over the back of his chair.

"Believe it won't cut it," said Eulacie, staring at him with wide-open eyes. "I seen too many folks with the wastin' disease to go foolin' around. You don't know what I mean, but in this part of the country you just watch your step about hoodoo."

"How can anybody be safe, then. What if somebody gets it in for you and you don't know it?"

"Keep a black frizzly chicken peckin' around your yard, and he will eat the conjure ball. Don't hurt neither to keep a little asafetida tied in a bag around your neck." She flipped out a gummy amulet on a dirty cord around her neck. "Whatever you believe or don't believe in these swamps, you just play it safe, boy. Miss Emmajean got one, too."

Miss Emmajean grinned up at them a wide missing-tooth grin and went on chewing the wax she had picked up off the floor.

"Eulacie is right," said Miss Billy, dangling a piece of string into the center of the liquid wax mess. "It is just as well to play it safe. Think of all the little superstitions we observe like mirrors, black cats, ladders. I don't believe I really would get upset if I violated one, but still it is just a little disquieting to go against one. So if we walk around ladders and throw salt over our shoulder, why shouldn't we take it further and think that people can work charms?"

"Charms, my eye. Hoodoo ain't superstitious; it's the real stuff. I won't go into any of the details, but I guarantee I could have either one of you in bed in less than a week if I said the wrong thing to the right people."

"Well, don't, dear. With Mardi Gras coming up soon, it wouldn't quite be the thing to do."

"I just said I *could*. Now if you'll kindly get that crap off the table I might get supper fixed. Miss Emmajean, you don't get that stuff out of your mouth, your eyes goin' to bug out bigger'n they already are."

Miss Billy sighed and moved the can and wax to the shelf by the refrigerator. "Voodoo is fascinating, but all the people who really know about it won't talk. I suppose that's where their power lies—the mystery. If there was a formula I guess anybody could do it."

"Well, not hardly," huffed Eulacie, bumping platters and bowls onto the table. "You got to have what it takes. Take for example I couldn't be a toe-dancer just simply because I wanted to." She whirled a couple of times and rocked the entire kitchen. "Mama had a cousin born with a caul over her head. She had the evil eye and could stop it from rainin' or make it thunder."

"We could have used her around here during the hurricane," said Peter.

"Matter of fact, I think it was the 1926 hurricane took her off," chuckled Eulacie. "I don't guess even hoodoo has any power against a good old Gulf hurricane. Y'all goin' to eat or fool around all night?" She flopped into a chair and snatched Miss Emmajean into place beside her, at the same time prying a great gray piece of wax out of her mouth and aiming it toward the garbage can.

They ate with talk of the town happenings, the weather. Miss Billy had always a new batch of rumors from Essie Banks, the postmistress, and Eulacie gave the Squall Street viewpoint. Peter contributed anything of general interest that had occurred over the bay, such as wrecks on the causeway or department store sales.

After they were through, they sat around over coffee and talked further until Eulacie heaved herself up and started washing the dishes. Miss Billy went off to work on the *Press-Register* contest that she was certain she would win, and Peter went upstairs to his room to study.

At his desk he tried to concentrate on the pluperfect tense of the Greek verbs they had taken up that day, but he wandered off into the last half of the English literature text. He found the play, *King Lear,* which he had never read. He opened to a passage near the end, and he was surprised that it was remotely familiar:

> No, no, no, no! Come, let's away to prison;
> We two alone will sing like birds i' the cage:
> When thou dost ask me blessing, I'll kneel down,
> And ask of thee forgiveness: so we'll live,
> And pray, and sing, and tell old tales, and laugh
> At gilded butterflies. . . .

Here again were the mysterious butterflies that came more and more into his world. They had begun to flutter into his dreams. Miss Billy hadn't mentioned the butterfly tree again, but she always included him in her look when she mentioned something that they could associate with the tree. Miss Claverly mentioned it each time she wrote, but she didn't write very often.

He thought then of Mr. Bloodgood, who had somehow put the two—Miss Claverly's tree and Miss Billy's tree—together, making them part real, part imagination. Yet, his was the most unknown tree of them all. Peter shut his eyes and tried to distinguish the three trees. For him Miss Billy's butterfly tree was something of the noonday, fired with orange and white and moving with barely fluttering wings. Miss Claverly's was, on the other hand, a late-afternoon tree, passively colorful like unfallen autumn leaves, caught in a saffron and violet sunset. Mr. Bloodgood's was—but then there was nothing left it could be except a night tree. But what could be the nature of a night tree, except something gigantic, shapeless?

All at once he knew that he must walk in the cold wind, for the walls were pressing on him, and the books were full of things it would take a lifetime ever to know.

It seemed like nights of time later that the moon rode across the pinetops, ducking through clouds which were reeled out by the winter wind. The clear cold bit into his face and sent unseen fingers into the hidden parts of his body. He took Baycliff and followed its slow curve to the beach, where the wind hurled the water against the snaggle-toothed pilings and the narrow beach. He thought fleetingly of the phantom children who had once run in the shallow water, but here in the cold was no place for the delicate and empty memory.

The wharf appeared in the darkness and was wet with the spray and cold moonlight. He walked there on the wharf, huddling against the wind and aware of something about to happen. The moon was a cold eye looking into his deepest consciousness, and he shivered from something more than cold.

When he reached the end, he stood stark and alone on the edge of the void where the storm of heaven met the timeless storm and unrest of the sea. Great constellations swam coldly and dizzily in the everlastingness of night, and he thought how the sky was like a great butterfly tree, exploding a thousand lights and colors.

Then between him and the shore lights slowly grew a figure, a hazy halftone, moving with flapping coat, leaning into the wind. Peter remembered to wonder: How did he know to come; had he maybe bridged the distance between people and places, places and things, minds and minds. But he came toward him, and night took on another aspect, for some time thing was happening, some gap was being closed between knowing and not knowing, and it was closing without sound and without light. Now he approached, and the moonlight hung between them like a spectral sheet, limp and unbillowed in spite of a wind that raced with grieving.

"You're here, I see, but of course you had to be." He smiled the evil transfiguring smile and fingered a nostril.

"Yes, but why did I have to be?" Peter shivered as the wind trembled the pilings.

"Simply for lack of alternatives, my friend. That's the only reason we ever *have* to do anything."

"But there were alternatives—"

"And the fact that you chose this one means that they weren't really alternatives but merely suggestions. Oh, they come easily. But come, we are wasting time."

"And it's cold."

"Oh? I hadn't noticed." He moved aside to let Peter go ahead. "Careful, my friend, I wouldn't care to have you slip."

Two ghost figures, they moved along the high wharf, and the water lashed suicidally against the posts, lamenting the dying of years and the declining of things counted by years.

They left the pier and moved along the south shore, and the gray wind growled along the weed tops and struggled with the cypress limbs.

It was the swamp toward which they were going. Peter knew without asking. He knew it had to be night when they came. But butterflies were day things that thrived on sunlight. A shadow came over the moon, and he felt a threatening quality to everything about him. Mr. Bloodgood walked silently.

They turned after a while and followed the path which entered the swamp, but it was a different path from the one he and Miss Billy had taken, for it ran parallel to the bay.

The swamp at night was like a great force asleep, folding many ancient arms and extending many hands—some of them for grasping and caressing, others for menacing things. The path was solid, and clear as a ribbon where it entered the swamp. Water glowed dully on each side of them, but the glow made it seem almost darker. And the swamp was full of more ancient voices than the frogs and tree insects of the previous trip. Moonlight spangled through leaf gaps and was bluish where it met the blackness. There would be an end, even if the swamp kept going (which it did, Miss Billy had said, till it got to Florida). Suddenly the moon was gone, and there was little but sound to guide them. Then little lights began to glow, the lights that swamps make at night, shiny little water things and the eyes of night prowlers. If you watched long enough, they seemed to develop into a pattern, a spiral that curled slowly toward you until you seemed to be at the vortex with a streak of light winding out into darkness.

He had unconsciously taken hold of Mr. Bloodgood's arm, for he couldn't see him. Mr. Bloodgood seemed to know the path and never paused.

They came to a clearing and found that the moon was out

again, feeling its way to them through a layer of flying clouds and a tangle of vines and gigantic trees. Mr. Bloodgood hesitated, stopped, turned.

"Now the way is confused again." He passed a hand over his face.

"How?" Peter shivered so that he could hardly talk.

"By allowing myself to think, I suppose, that it wouldn't be here."

"But maybe it is here." Peter knew as he had known before that it was not here, but he knew he must pass again through the entire experience. What could the butterfly tree be for him, anyhow, who had not heard of it from a stranger and who had not built a pattern of dreams around it?

"No, it is not. Know this, my friend. It is spontaneous and eternal like seasons. We don't slip up on it; it slips up on us. We must, however, put ourselves in its way so that it can find us." He turned, and the moon caught the deeply sculptured face, beautiful and horrible in the cold, dead-white light, like a tomb carving. "Is it the evil we do or think, the good we imagine or suggest, the admission of neither, that keeps us from the butterfly tree? Peter, you could, perhaps, if you wanted to badly enough, find it, for you are none and all. Again like Norman—Norman, who saw a butterfly tree and became no more for me. I let myself think once that Norman would be no more, and as if thinking wouldn't be enough, I suggested that he would not.

"He told me that he had begun to love someone else—a girl. So I shouted and the walls echoed all the way across the years to these swamps which still throw back their mocking tree-frog voices, their locust laughter, and they know our secret. For I threatened to tell her, the one he was starting to love, what we had been to each other. I remember that he struck me and ran sobbing through the corridor and into the misty street. He still runs, on nights like this, through a tangle of vines and all our dreams.

"Now you know, you and the swamp. There are many ways to kill a person. And when you have done so, you may look for his ghost in a thousand places and till the ends of time."

"Why have you told me, and why have you brought me?" Peter shook so that he wanted to hold on to a tree.

"Because, my friend, you are one of the thousand ghosts, who will after a brief time (for isn't all our time brief?) go, too. Ghosts are more permanent than the person who died to create them, but ghosts are restless and become many things. They peer out of unexpected places and wouldn't think of coming near an expected place. They appear in people who resemble their once-self. They are books, pictures, music, and eventually fever-dreams. They are a little of the sea and sky, and all the good and evil a person can become.

"Or, they can even become something like the butterfly tree, a seeming final unfindable. It is perhaps best that we thus dispose of ghosts, for they are not where we look for them. Yet, the pity of our life becomes this not-finding. The end of all our searching, like the resignation at the end of the wind. But how must the tree be conjured up, discovered, happened on? Walking in deep night into a swamp with a companion, who reminds —a companion who listens, but how much does he, can he, comprehend? If I were sure then I should see the butterfly tree, the unfindable, and death. He and I, Norman and I, would be together again with souls like liquid fire, burning together."

He turned and walked back the way they had come, and Peter followed him, wondering if there could be some objective way to think about the butterfly tree, trying to fit this story together so that it rhymed with the lonely picture in the album. Even these thoughts were vague and grew in distance as they moved back to where the surf swept in, the wind wept in. He was conscious only of the spectre shadow that moved before him, the merciless twisting knife of winter, and the thought that spring would never come.

Spring

1

AN ARC OF color whirled through the air and separated into bits of brilliant paper. The rip tide of people moved in several directions erupting color, smiling with colored masks which had been garish during the day but which were somber and mysterious now. The square was a grotesque garden of dim lights and winding serpentine.

Down the Mobile street the Order of Myths parade floats swayed under the leaping, cavorting figures, who threw candy into the forest of outstretched hands. The torches caused tree shadows to chase each other across the square, and from the square the street-edge people, against the torches, were heads and arms cut from black paper.

The bands together were like a chorus of goblins led by the booming monotony of a bass drum. By the sight and sound and smell of the sea of people all the senses were dissolved into a single sensory perception.

Peter leaned against one of the oaks in the square and watched the miracle of the floats drifting above the writhing heads of the spectators. One was passing, labeled "Perseus and Andromeda." A papier-mâché dragon with eyes flashing off and on leered at a masker lashed to a rock with a gilded chain. Above the rock another masker, seemingly suspended in air, dangled a very convincing Gorgon head. The inscrutable masks alone would have made it difficult to tell who was being rescued, who was about to be devoured, who was the man and who was the woman. The spirit of Mardi Gras was somehow epitomized when the doomed Andromeda threw a handful of candy kisses into the crowd and skipped rope with one of the chains.

"Say, honey, you got a light?" The woman at his side grinned broadly at him as she leaned to light a cigarette from the match he held. In the light he was startled by her brilliantly tinted hair that looked nearly orange.

"Whew! these shoes are killing me, not to speak of all the other things a woman has to fasten herself into. Here, honey, mind if I hold on while I just ease out of one of them for a sec?" She breathed a profound sigh of relief.

"It's wonderful, isn't it?" Peter said because he didn't know what else to say.

"What's wonderful, honey?"

"Why, all this." Peter gestured at the parade.

She looked about uncertainly. "Oh, you mean Mardi Graw? I guess so. Not what it used to be, though, just before the war. Then we had the Mardi Graw. Honey, this town was really kicky then. Know what I mean?"

"It looks pretty much alive now," said Peter, watching the confetti rain into an azalea bush.

"This is alive? Why, honey it was so wild the last year before the war (no Mardi Graw during the war) it wasn't hardly safe for us girls to be out on the street. The place was full of servicemen, and everybody was after them—the whores, the queens, the U.S.O., and the merchants. And fights, migod, four or five a night. Honey, I miss the war days. I hate to say it, but I do. Everybody on the move and making money. Even I got myself a job in the shipyards."

"What do you do now?" Peter asked.

"What do I— Oh, honey." She threw back her head and laughed, leaning against the tree. "Say, you're all right, honey. But surely you can't mean— Oh, baby." She laughed again, so that people stared from the sidewalk.

"What's so funny?" he asked, blushing.

"Say, kid, why don't you let me buy you a drink? That is the reverse of the usual, but I thought I had lived long enough to see everything."

"I'm sorry, I'm not quite old enough to drink."

She peered at him. "Well, you sure fooled me. You look older.

But I don't guess you are. Maybe we can bluff it. I sure need to sit down."

"I don't think I'd better. I have to start back over the bay."

"O.K., honey, but I sure want to be around when you live a little longer. You are an experience. Hey, Mac," she yelled at a passing sailor.

The sailor stopped and, smiling, came over, his face falling when he got closer.

"Hey, Mac," she said, "you need a drink, don't you, or is your mizzen still riding out the storm?" She leaned at him with another cigarette. He shrugged and gave her a light.

"It's all the same to me."

"Well, I know a swell joint just down the street. I was just telling my friend here we needed a drink."

The sailor looked Peter up and down suspiciously and then looked back at the woman. "I ain't got much money. I thought—"

She laughed. "Aw, Mac, whatever you're thinking, he don't work for me. Who said anything about money? I think we can make it." She turned to Peter. "Come on, kid."

"No, I can't. I have to get back."

"Aw, look," said the sailor, "I didn't mean nothing. Let's all go. I'd just as soon."

"Sure, the more the merrier. The carnival just comes once a year." She lifted an imaginary glass and toasted.

"Yeah, come on, fellow," said the sailor almost imploringly.

"All right," said Peter, "but if they throw me out, don't say I didn't warn you.

They left the square and followed the street to the next block, turning at the corner and following the long street leading back to the tunnel. Blaring music came from the doors of the bars they passed, ugly music jagged with loud laughter and the shatter of glasses. At length they came to the loudest bar of all, a place called The Gangplank.

"We're here, you guys. Come on." She plunged into the crowd and the cigarette smoke. Peter and the sailor followed her. "There probably ain't no booths, but maybe we can horn in at the bar," she shouted above the din.

They made for the bar, sidestepping the hypnotized dancing couples and the press of people lining the table aisles.

"Hey, Brenda." A blonde gestured violently from a booth. "Come over here; there's room."

Brenda made an impatient gesture and angled toward the booth, since there was no place else to sit. "Hi, Babe. What goes?" she asked, indicating Babe's companion, who was out.

"I always get one like this." She looked at Peter and the sailor. "Migod, honey, what are you using in your net these days?"

"Oh, they're just friends. I decided to enjoy myself for the rest of Mardi Graw."

"I'll bet. Well, good night, sit down." She bumped the drunk air corpsman over, making room for Peter, while Brenda and the sailor sat down opposite. The air corpsman roused up and muttered something about a low ceiling and drooled back to oblivion.

"He's really very sweet, and I hate like hell to just leave him here, but I can't manage him. I wouldn't care how much he passed out if he had waited till we got home. Well, boys," she said brightly at Peter and the sailor, "how goes it?"

The sailor grinned and grunted; Peter self-consciously smiled and said nothing.

"Say, Babe, this kid here—" she stopped when Peter looked at her imploringly—"is all right." He knew now what she was so amused about, and he didn't want her to tell the others.

"Sure enough? I'll bet."

The waitress came up, and Brenda ordered four whiskey-and-sodas. The place became noisier, and Peter missed most of what everybody said. Strips of serpentine shot to the ceiling and spiraled to the floor. The blare and shuffle of the band gave a nightmarish quality to the dark damp room.

Then Peter felt Babe's hand stroking his thigh. He gave her a quick surprised look, but she hadn't paused in her conversation with Brenda. He tried to move his leg, but the hand followed insistently. He felt hemmed in and a little panicky, but at the same time a remote part of him didn't want the hand to move. His involuntary physical response to the stroking hand made him more panicky, and he was considering bolting for the door, when the waitress came back with the drinks.

The hand left for a while. Peter and the sailor reached to pay, but Brenda stopped them. "These are on me, boys," she said grandly, while Babe stared in disbelief. "Well, cheers," Brenda said, lifting her glass.

The talk resumed, and again the room swam in fantastic shadows and noises. The SP's and MP's made periodic trips through, and each time they came in, Babe would jolt the corporal awake. He would stare blankly at Brenda's orange hair until they left, then he would collapse again.

An ancient whore stumbled drunkenly against the table and hesitated, to sway close in Peter's face. "You been done recently, dearie?"

"Take a walk, Lucille," said Babe menacingly.

"Going, going," muttered Lucille vacantly and moved slowly away.

"Migod, she was working the area when I was playing hopscotch on St. Anthony Street," said Brenda. "Old prostitutes never die, they just—what?"

The sailor got talkative after his drink, and ordered again for everybody. He told a joke, and Brenda slapped him on the chest with the back of her hand. Peter felt the hand come back, this time bolder. He fought against a response, and all at once he knew he had to leave.

"Excuse me a minute," he said, getting up.

"Over there," Brenda pointed helpfully.

He started toward the men's room, colliding with bodies, slipping through openings, feeling bodies with all parts of his body. He went into the men's room, an evil-smelling place with rusted utilities and scrawled walls. He would go through on the opposite side of the bar and get away unnoticed.

The door opened, and the sailor stood beside him. "You not sick, are you?"

"No," said Peter, realizing that he couldn't sneak away now.

"Well, what do you think?"

"Think? I don't know."

"A lay's a lay. I don't know what's up. There's that corporal. Maybe we should both go with Brenda, or whatever her name is. Might be fun for a change. Hey?"

"I don't know," said Peter, feeling desperate.

"Or, if you want to, we can go try our luck somewhere else. I'm for the three of us, though. Don't care as long as it is something, though. Well, let's get back."

They went back through the crowd, and the place seemed darker after the light in the men's room.

"Thought maybe you guys got picked up. It's hardly safe around here any more."

"What say we get out of this rattrap," said the sailor, sitting back down.

"Well, one more drink first, hey, honey," said Brenda, "if we can get that waitress."

Peter didn't want another drink, because he was feeling a little dizzy, and he needed to think what he was going to do. Besides, the hand was back now trying to get inside his clothes.

"Are you about ready to go, Peter?" The familiar voice was out of place in this dark mad world, and his mind reeled in surprise.

"I'm sorry, my friends," said Karl, "but I must get my brother home before you-all get in trouble. He is under age, you see. Ready, Peter?" Peter got to his feet, conscious of the startled faces of the two women and the sailor, conscious, too, of a slight feeling of resentment but a resentment swallowed up in relief.

"If you don't want to go, pal, brother or no brother—" the sailor began.

"Sorry, friend, but I say he is going. The SP's over there would be only too happy to assist me. Come on, Peter."

Peter said good night hastily and apologetically to the booth at large and followed Karl.

"Of all the nerve," he heard Brenda say.

"Don't look like brothers to me," said the sailor.

"I'll bet," said Babe loudly.

Outside, the night seemed oppressively quiet after the shattering noise of the bar. Karl walked beside him, saying nothing. He didn't say anything either, for there was nothing to say. They walked toward the tunnel and turned at the corner. Government Street was long and silent, the noise of the carnival in another part of town. Down the street toward the river there was a light mist faintly blurring the street lights.

"The car is over here," said Karl, starting across the street.

"Look, Karl, thanks," said Peter, as they got into the car.

"Nothing to thank me for. Perhaps I interfered, but I had been watching you for quite a while. I suppose I have come to know you better than I thought, for I could tell you wanted to be somewhere else. You were right in wanting to be. Those two prostitutes are pretty notorious. I see them all the time."

"Do you go there often?"

"No, not often." They swung around and into the tunnel. "It is just well to watch yourself in Mobile—or anywhere. But how did you happen to get involved? You don't have to tell me, of course, for I know how those things happen. Dear god, yes, I know."

Peter told him, though, as the city across the river reeled its strung-jewel lights away from them, blinking their colors between Peter and the things he had not the courage, or perhaps was not ready, to have.

2

THE BAY after the rain lay flat and gray-green with an underlying silver sheen. Heaving, as if uncertain whether to ebb or flow, it seemed to breathe in long deep breaths. The horizon was drawing in the clouds, and the afternoon was being taken over again by the sun.

The beach was pitted by the rain, and the woods were mingling their green somber fragrances with the smell of the sand and water. Peter walked along by a clump of bamboo which grew almost to the water edge. Beyond was a clear-running spring, bubbling from beneath an ancient drift-log. He looked into the water at the brilliantly colored stones on the bottom and the drifting, dragging moss-hair.

The blond hair floated in the breeze, loose and free, and a couple of decades seemed to disappear. She wasn't running, and there were no other children with her. No, he was here, of course, and perhaps the other child could be Karl.

He walked toward her, hesitating to draw the illusion to a reality, for he knew it would be Karen. She stood on a sand bar that ran a long arm into the shallow water that rippled over a sand-ridged bottom, rolling broken shells and pebbles. She turned as he came closer, but she didn't move.

"We were running," he said slowly as he came up behind her, "you, Karl, and I, running along the beach, and it was a long time ago."

"Perhaps." She took his hand and smiled out into the falling sun. "Perhaps." She pointed. "Look, Peter. That doesn't happen often."

On the horizon the silhouette of a ship was moving almost imperceptibly across the orange disk of the sun. It was a breath-taking coincidence of time, space, and motion. They watched, hand in hand, till the ship glided off the disk, which at the same time dropped behind the purple-gray haze of the other shore.

"And if we were running, Peter, we had to run here, way out on this point of sand. That is the important thing. We are here."

"But don't you remember. You and Karl came to where my mother and father and I had a tent. She wore knickers and a sun helmet. You and Karl came and played with me, and we ran down the beach. We ran and ran till she came and called me back. She scolded you for taking me off, and you never came again. Never. And now it is years, and you have come back."

Karen watched him, her head to one side, smiling a wistful

smile. She shook her head gently.

"It might have happened, for so much is possible in a lifetime. We forget more than we remember. And if it happened, why should you remember and I not remember? Isn't it strange that something important to one person is not important to another. But it might have happened."

Peter wanted it to be important to her also, but she didn't seem to be impressed that he had remembered something so long ago. She had turned away to look at the sunset, which was spreading a wash of pastel tints over the water, highlighting the sand bars and wooden pilings. The sky had not quite lost the slightly storm-tossed quality, and the pearly gray clouds were tipped with salmon-pink and coral. The flat surface of the bay mirrored the sky colors which were as far in the water as they were in the sky.

They walked hand in hand along the twig-drifted beach, jumping over the springs and balancing on the long, sea-serpent drift-logs, relics of long-ago hurricanes. Peter wanted to talk about the children running along the beach, but Karen seemed to have forgotten about them.

But this was now the answer to part of the vaguely recalled past, which explained the starts of recognition he experienced when he looked at the shore-line cypresses and the flash of beach disappearing around the bend. It explained a little of what he had felt the day he watched Karen and Karl swim in the hurricane.

They took the road that wound at the base of the cliff through the woods. There was somewhere the scent of burning pine, and the woods were full of activity—whirring birds and rasping insects. Vines floated unattached from treetops above tiny springs that dribbled invisibly beneath the undergrowth. They reached the long wooden steps finally and climbed to the top, stopping to look back over the seascape that became oriental with distance.

"Peter, we must, you and I, come swimming on the first really warm day. Then, even if we weren't the right children, we can be this time."

3

"AND WHAT kind of soul does Moss Bayou have?"

"Moss Bayou? That is a hard one, for it has many souls. One of them is an old mariner with smiles in his wrinkles and a catch in his throat. He sits on the wharf and watches the waves run in parallels to the shore, and he sends out boats on these waves to imaginary harbors, knowing that the boats will all return to Moss Bayou. Another soul is a child who walks along the beach, aware that the crystal springs have clinky sounds like green bottles. Still another soul is a beautiful woman in outdated clothes who sits watching the rain through a screen door, listening to the drum-drum of rain, of years, on the magnolia leaves."

Karl lay on his stomach drawing pictures in the sand with a stick. Peter watched the sand crabs edge out of their holes, their long eye-stems alert to the slightest movement. He would lift a hand, and they would disappear as if by magic. They were the same color as the sand, and their holes were cunningly disguised by flimsy masonry of sand.

Then he turned on his stomach and through the crook of his arm looked at Karl. Karl without clothes was even more perfect than with clothes, even up close where his skin, still slightly tanned from the summer before perhaps, was stretched perfectly over the delicate muscles of his back and shoulders. There were no freckles or blemishes; instead, the sun showed tiny rainbow colors on the smooth surfaces.

Karl turned suddenly toward him. "Peter, for a long time I was wrong—frightfully wrong—about you. You're all right. I was the one who was not all right, for I'm afraid I have become, in spite of my not admitting it before, something of a snob."

"What are you talking about?" Peter sat upright and stared at Karl.

"That's just what I mean. You didn't even notice it. Your simplicity will be your salvation the rest of your life." Karl smiled.

"But what *are* you talking about?"

"I don't know really, except that I took a certain pleasure in introducing you to experiences to watch your reactions, thinking they would amuse me. But it turned out they were so honest and genuine that they made my first reactions to the same things a little shoddy and cheap. I remember many times affecting boredom at a new experience simply to impress someone with my sophistication." Karl shrugged a shoulder.

"But why, Karl, why? There is so much we can never never know. We have to—"

"Yes, we do. And your enthusiasm for things, your face as you have a new sensation or hear an idea that impresses you, has reawakened in me something that responds, too. I have tasted the scuppernong wine with your taste, seen the Bayou and bay with your eyes, and heard music with your ears. I have come to feel cheated that I didn't see them that way when it was really the first time for me."

"And, Karl, I was doing the same thing where you were concerned. Tasting things in the way I thought you had, trying to imagine how you had experienced them. You have made a big difference in things for me." Peter lay back down but continued to look at Karl. "But why did you want to be amused? There was a reason."

"Yes," said Karl slowly, "there was a reason. I don't know exactly how to say it, however." He lay back on his elbows and looked at the water for a long time. There was the same sadness Peter had come to associate with him. Finally he spoke. "For a long time every time I thought I had discovered someone with whom I could share my toys, my dreams, and my thoughts, I found that they were waiting for a chance to snatch them while my back was turned and gild them with their colors and so change them that I could never claim them again." He looked at Peter. "That doesn't answer it, does it?"

Peter looked back at him, then followed his eyes out to the overpowering indifference of water and distance. "Karl, what has hurt you?"

"Hurt me?" He laughed the troublingly unpleasant laugh.

"Something has. Somebody?"

"Hurt, hurt, goddamn it, we are all, at some time or another, hurt—some of us even born hurt. Most of us forget about this hurt and go our way, afraid of suddennesses or silences that might recall the source of our hurt. Some of us, though, remember and are not able to live without remembering. We have a gigantic house of mirrors—mirrors that reflect our hurt a thousand times a day in a thousand ways, small mirrors even for the details, the minutest fragments of the hurt."

"But hurt can't be something so completely abstract. You said source. Isn't there a source?"

"Yes, Peter," he said softly. "Now when it is spring, and love is coming alive, moving along plant stems, no love is coming alive for me. Everything I have been prepared for is a useless waste."

"But why, why, Karl, can't you love?" Peter looked at him, thinking that of all the people he had ever seen in his life Karl was the handsomest, strongest, most capable of love.

"There is a reason—the only reason, and I don't want to tell it to you. Let answers come without questions, for people ask the wrong questions and get the right answers to them. Let's look at the water, and later we'll go look for shells. I wish it were warm enough to swim, but soon it will be, and then we will come back. Meanwhile, talk about the water to me, for I want to see it again as you see it." He lay back and closed his eyes.

4

I<small>T WAS REALLY</small> spring, and the green fuzzed along the limbs and made everything hazy, as if a pale green veil had been dropped over the world. The pear trees bloomed into daydreams; the air was heady with blue and gold, and the world reflected the warmth and fragrance of emerging things. Even the rain was green, so full of the trees it was, as it fell gently and with melancholy along the asphalt streets where the oaks leaned together in ancient conspiracies.

This day he walked around the lake at Ferndale, and he reviewed the past year, still trying to see it more clearly now, with a little more distance.

He had come to Moss Bayou, a not-quite-remembered place, where the reality of roads as he had known them ran out, and with his coming his other worlds had paled out and were, as Moss Bayou collected in memory, themselves not quite remembered.

First, there was Miss Billy, who knew legends and through them sought magics. Miss Claverly looked to remove legends with evidence as irrefutable as natural laws. Mr. Bloodgood sought to recapture memory of a physical past in almost supernatural associations, putting a ghost into all the shadowy recesses of his experience. Miss Billy had a ghost, too, but it seemed almost not a ghost, for it was a daylight ghost. In fact, it seemed that the ghost did not haunt Miss Billy but rather that she haunted it.

And the butterfly tree.

It wasn't quite the same for each of them, yet they called it by the same name. At the same time there was enough alike about the three butterfly trees to make them part of a single impression. A different person had told them about the trees and all in the same location. Then the persons—the wise fool, the naturalist, and Norman who believed in metamorphosis—had disappeared, and Miss Billy, Miss Claverly, and Mr. Bloodgood had started to look for the butterfly tree. Looking for the tree had caused their lives to change shape; finding the tree—but here was where the real differences were. This was where he had to stop, and it was likely that the answer lay in this direction, for the ultimate thing they were looking for as a result of finding the butterfly tree would, of course, determine the kind of tree they looked for and the circumstances under which they looked. But it was really a little ridiculous after so long a time, and on such unreliable evidence in the first place, to continue searching. On the other hand, maybe it gave them a false sort of purpose, which, for lack of another purpose, was vital.

But now it was more important to believe in the blue of sky and its matching blue of water; it made more sense that the trees should have tiny soft green leaves instead of butterflies. He felt inadequate to produce a mood or feeling to go with the day and its importance of being now and forever all at once.

He sighed and started to turn up the long tree-arched drive, on which, during the fall, leaves had tumbled in thin-blown lines but which was now a soft feathery tunnel of vines, ferns, and creepers. By one of the gateposts Karl sat, leaning against the column, his knees drawn up. He looked at Peter and smiled, for Peter had started.

"I get lonesome for Ferndale every now and then. I decided I was sick, at work, and left. Being lonesome for something is as good a kind of sick as any. Well, aren't you glad to see me?"

"Of course," said Peter. "I just didn't expect to see you sitting there like that."

"Oh, I'm a ghost of a sort. Why don't we drive back over the bay. There is something I haven't seen in a long time I would like to show you."

"O.K.," said Peter. "I'm through anyhow. I guess the library will be here tomorrow."

They walked up the avenue of oaks to Karl's car, and the day suddenly had quite another meaning.

5

HERE WAS another stretch of beach, but it was unlike the shore line to the south. It was remote, for there were no houses and no cliff. It stretched back from the bay and became a forest of dead cypresses with scraggly draperies of moss. The sand of the beach was almost solid with driftwood bleached a pearly blond by the sun. The beach curved in both directions around points made by the woods coming out to the water edge. The water looked deep and its color was dark even in the bright afternoon sun. The wind, a hot wind with heavy odors of swamp and seaweed, blew from the bay. There was something unspeakably desolate and sinister about this cove, and Peter didn't like it. Yet he knew that of all the places he had been he would remember this place longest.

They walked along the beach, stepping over the barnacled drift-logs. There was a skeleton of a fish among the logs, looking in this desolate waste like something prehistoric. They stopped where a spring, its bottom rust-colored and spongy, emptied the stagnant marsh into the bay. On the fetid water floated a species of water lily, pinched and sallow. On the low islands among the crowding grass grew an abundance of pitcher plants.

They sat on a large log which it was hard to imagine had ever been a tree. It thrust stiff skeletal roots into the brackish stream, while what had been limbs it arched into the bay. Karl touched Peter's arm and pointed across the stream. On another log a huge cottonmouth lay in the sun. Peter looked at it in horror and fascination. He had never seen one so close, for they were timid snakes and usually were scurrying out of sight before he came close enough really to see.

Karl threw a short piece of driftwood, and the snake plopped into the water and disappeared. "Beautiful things, snakes."

"Beautiful? They're very poisonous, aren't they?" Peter looked at the empty log and shuddered.

"Yes, beautiful. They're such independent and lonely creatures. They inhabit the lost stretches of these swamps; the swamps are their kingdom. Isn't this a wonderful place, Peter?"

"It has a very strange feeling about it, as if something were watching you from behind, no matter which way you turn."

Karl laughed, and his laugh was in place here. "Something probably is, but isn't something usually watching us no matter where we are—somebody or we ourselves—making judgments about us, telling us things we don't want to believe and letting us find later how true they really were?" Karl looked back at the water and sighed painfully. "Something might have told me once, for example, in those vague shifting years among the complicated shocks and starts of learning, among the chalk dust and paste smells, the acrid smell of children in long schoolrooms, among the wistful illustrations—the Lang fairy books and the Elson basic readers—floor polish, and the sun-gold smell of spring outside, that I was different. Angel in face, in bright enthusiasm for every new word of meaning in the books, the pictures, I was the favorite, the impeccable, the ideal. The other children hadn't learned to be jealous yet, and the teacher couldn't resist lavishing affection on one who was more beautiful, more perfect, than the rest. But angel in spirit? I have to laugh. My sunny disposition, innocent blond handsomeness, was belied when I lured little after-school girls into bushes and probed at them with insatiable curiosity. Apparently they never told, for I was never revealed as anything but angel. Angels have license, I suppose. It's all in the face—the breaks in life, the ups instead of the downs, the choice particles of experience.

"I might have guessed, too, in the autumn days when youthful energy sent boys and kites flying, leaning on the wind, with ball games in vacant lots, dogs and children in a tangle of running, sprawling, laughing, crying unawareness of winter, the far legend. For here again I was not of them— Outdoors, yes; I wandered to grasp at the troubling mysteries of leaves and trees, clouds and sky, things, but people I left alone unless, drawn by my angel self, they intruded. But more often, while kites ripped clouds apart, while rain scurried the children home, I stayed indoors alone reading the dust-gathering books beyond my years, before my time, or drawing pictures which imagination-yawned chasms forced me to.

"The universality of me—for I could do everything the others could, and better—gave me this option, and I accepted it."

Peter had to ask, to break this flow of the long-dammed stream: "What of Karen all this time?"

For a moment the smooth elegant angel face clouded; the perfect brows knitted and the perfect fingers tightened around a small piece of driftwood.

"Karen was one of the rompers, the laughing scrambling knot of legs and arms that filled the vacant lot and made indoors a little lonely and more wonderful. As for my underbrush activities, she attended and watched unjudgingly from the sidelines, often keeping watch for me. I came to expect her to be there and had no heart for the performance if she wasn't. She accepted it as she has always accepted everything else about me.

"Years drifted up their toll of dead leaves, withered stalks, and dark ticking moments of our life. She was there always beside me, a shadow self that beat the alternate rhythms of my life, unmasking the angel, completing beauty with truth (for her plainness is a greater truth than my beauty, since it gives what it promises—perhaps more). We would sit by the fire, and I would read to her from the exquisite poetry the rainy afternoons had taught me. She would listen wistfully, many times uncomprehendingly, and there would be a wall, yet a closeness, between us that I have never managed with another soul.

" 'Karl,' she said once when the afternoon was silvered on the wet sycamores along the street to the bay, 'What are you that you can know and you can be what I am not?' Since this question showed an insight I had never associated with her before, I stopped, put down my copy of *Leaves of Grass,* and looked at her long long and knew that I could not answer, since there was no answer, since an answer would have to tell her something more than she asked. Instead I said, 'Come, baby, let's go and see if it's really spring yet.' So we ran along the empty street hand in hand till we discovered a meadow of thrusting yellow flowers. 'It is, it is,' she cried, and I supposed she had forgotten, but then: 'Unless,' and she faltered, 'unless they, too, know of another meadow where the flowers have not bloomed and won't be golden.' She cried, and I took her in my arms. 'Don't, baby, every day isn't spring, and we must live in and for this one. Soon, you know, they will be wilting stalks, for even the most golden lose their beauty when the seasons go.'

"That afternoon was somehow prophetic, for soon after I discovered something about myself that I should have known sooner since angels—even angels—can't be perfect.

"The changes—the subtle changes—that began to tell the untruth of bedtime stories came to others of my age, and they entered the stage, rather disgusting stage, where beards appear and voices change. But not I; I was left with the looks of an angel, like some legendary youth chained to a rock who never grows old. I become more beautiful as I grew taller and older, but the other things did not happen. I have remained a child except in appearance and have sacrificed function for beauty. I am a statue with a fig leaf, a mute thing that cannot give voice to its song, a stream without a current. Now, Peter, you know."

Peter breathed deeply. Something had shattered like a rifle shot down the corridors of his imagination, crumbling the statues, ripping petals from the flowers, and scattering the sunsets. Someone had betrayed beauty. Or was it rather a sort of confirmation of Miss Claverly's observation about beauty. Here at last was pure beauty, without function, the evolutionary end of beauty, the death of beauty.

"Not at all?" he asked quietly, not looking at Karl.

"Not at all." Karl broke the stick and threw the pieces in the water.

They walked back to the car along the marsh, the path that curved around the water with silent circles spreading. The cypress grove was silent, for no birds came here. The bay was motionless and edged with a steamy haze where the sun was dropping. Slow smoke hung without wind on the horizon.

A further moment of silence, and the tree frogs began.

6

ANOTHER DAY, time suspended motionless like buzzards hanging on extended wings above pine trees, they lay on a sunny hillside in the tall grass where they had walked. The fecund pressure of overproducing life pulsed in the earth, and Peter, flattened on his stomach, felt an answering pulse which he could not deny—an upthrusting physical quality which troubled the senses and lapped over the edges of unconsciousness.

Karl lay peaceful and serene on his back watching the pregnant fulness of white clouds tumbled together and unmoving. His fingers lay relaxed along the bent grass, which excited Peter with its spermy smell. There was a chasm of silence between them, for there was nothing to say in the openness and unendingness of earth. Insects whirred drowsily, and the sweetish smell of little ground vines breathed on the air and the silence.

"I wonder," Peter finally spoke, "why there are no butterflies."

Karl turned suddenly toward him in a quick motion.

"Why butterflies?"

"No reason. Why?" Peter again didn't feel like bringing up his relationship with Miss Claverly, Mr. Bloodgood, or Miss Billy.

"You had a reason, didn't you, for saying butterflies, when you might have said bumblebees or something else?" Karl turned back to look at the sky, sighing deeply. "But then you might have heard—no but that's impossible—unless Karen—"

"Karen what?"

"Nothing," Karl said, breathing the word to the earth.

The grass crackled with tiny sounds. The sky pierced them, the flattened figures, focused them, with bottomless blue. So here, even here, it was, too, and had been all the time.

"Karl, is there really a butterfly tree?"

"Then you do know," said Karl, sitting up. "But then, of course, Karen told you."

"No—no, she didn't—I—" and Peter was on the point of telling him about the others, but Karl interrupted him.

"Of course, she did; there was no other way. We agreed not to tell. It is important that no one else know. I don't suppose you matter, however, for all of a sudden you seem almost a part of us. You certainly know just about everything there is to know about us."

"What will you find when you find the tree? It will just be butterflies on a tree, won't it?"

Karl looked at him incredulously.

"Peter, is that all that it means?—everything, I mean. Doesn't the curve of the beach in a mist, the path of moonlight on the bay, the thin rain of street-reflected cities mean more than what they appear? Then the butterfly tree will for me—for Karen and me—mean many times more than that. We do not have to look for the mist, the rainy streets, or the moon; they are there. But surely something we have looked for and waited for will be all these, many times over."

"No, I don't mean that. Of course, all these things make a difference. You know that. I mean after you have let it be what it will be—what, then, more than a lovely memory?"

"Oh, you don't understand. It won't be finding a lovely memory. It won't be passive and an end. It will be a beginning." He lay back, looking into the sky. "Perhaps it will be this way: one morning I shall say to Karen (and she will know what I am going to say before I say it), 'Come, baby, it's there in the marsh meadow.'

And we shall run lightly through the honeysuckled woods and into the sun along by the stretch of beach where the driftwood piles up like bleached sea serpents. Then through the loose sand and wire grass, through the meadow—where flowers will have been both opened and closed by the sun. There are little trees there, and all together they close out the larger trees nearer the gully. Here on one of these trees there will be butterflies, and we shall know that morning which one.

"As you know by now, she and I are two incomplete parts of a perfect something. So together, and it must be together, we shall become complete, each of us. Oh, not exactly a miracle, but suddenly we shall know how. For me the tree will be a beauty so startling, so perfect, that it will reduce my beauty to human beauty, and along with this the other human attributes will return. At the same time, like a magnet it will take the earthiness of Karen and lift it to something a little closer to heaven. It will be a power, a synthesizer, an anodyne to restore what we gave up so entirely to each other before we knew what we were giving up."

"Karl," Peter stopped him, "Karl, I think now I should like to happen on the butterfly tree. For I guess I have come to believe in it also."

Karl reached over and gripped Peter's hand till it hurt. "You don't happen on the butterfly tree; you don't guess that you believe in it. It is necessary to look—maybe for a lifetime. And you don't guess; you know."

"But isn't it really something like religious faith or a philosophy —a Golden Fleece or a Holy Grail?"

"Oh, if you care to make it casually symbolic, we can carry it further. I suppose everyone is looking for some kind of butterfly tree—people who scurry along the bypaths of glory, people who drink late in bars, people who lie down in dark rooms with strangers. They all expect a revelation someday, something that will come in and change things. Otherwise they have no reason for being. For some their kind of butterfly tree will give a meaning to the waste of past years; for some it will point out a future; for some it will stab the present with bright light where there was only grayness before."

"But your tree?"

"Oh, it is different. It is real; a particular kind of butterfly tree. I even know what kind of butterflies—monarchs. Most of all, unlike the others, I shall know when I have found it."

"How?" Peter stretched again, feeling warmth course along his body, warmth beyond the sun's warmth, fitting his nerve ends to the nerve ends of the earth and carrying him in the slow roll of things entire.

Karl smiled and held Peter's hand suspended between them. "That is impossible to communicate. How can you know about the moment before birth, and how could you possibly tell about the moment after death? It will be something like that, a sudden tripping of all the mechanisms that have chained us to one identity and have walled us off from another. A moment of darkness and of light, a moment of superb silence and golden-throated roar of earth and heaven. It will be the revelation of the great secret where we shall discover the identity of the face that has looked at us from mirrors, the voice that has troubled our dreams, the statue in whose form we have been a prisoner. Everything will be release, freedom, uproaring, non-stopping like the wind in all the springs of our life, the sun in all our summers." He stopped breathlessly and released Peter's hand, letting it fall back into the grass. "Yes, I shall know, but afterwards how shall I—and this is somehow unimportant—how shall I know myself?"

7

"PETER, WHO was the Roman goddess of toys?" Miss Billy touched her tongue to the pencil point.

Peter looked up from the newspaper. "Are you working another double acrostic? You really shouldn't because you get upset when it doesn't come out the quotation you want."

"I know. I've started out with some very splendid quotations—much better than the ones I ended up with. Once I simply left it like I wanted it."

"You mean yours really fitted?"

"Oh, not exactly. I had to black out a few spaces and add a few, but it was a lovely thing." She squinted again at the magazine.

The room, open now to the spring, its windows having become doors since they reached to the floor, was full of space and night. Night grew right up to the edge of the circles of light from the two floor lamps. Outside was deep and warm, rubbed softly by crickets and scraped by cicadas, scent-heavy with four-o'clocks, petunias, and honeysuckles. From farther away a tantalizing magnolia fuscata scent came in with the distant call of a whippoorwill, and the sound and fragrance were a part of one perception.

"Where have the others gone, I wonder?" Miss Billy spoke so quietly that Peter thought she was talking to herself about a word that wouldn't fit in the squares. When he glanced up, she had put the magazine down and was looking at him and past him out the window into the night garden.

"Who?" he asked, a little confused by her change in mood.

"Not who. No, these nights. Where have the others gone? It's so short, Peter. All of it. I looked at you just now, and it was almost another time, a night like this when spring tumbled into all the rooms and spaces of my life, for you are so like him. The light falls a certain way on some people, and it fell just now like that on you. You were like him, and I was like me, and both in another night. Then I looked down at my magazine and a wrinkled hand was holding it. Then I remembered whose it was. Oh, Peter, hold these nights, hold all of them, for the seasons are sudden and over."

"Yes, but they are all new every time. You said that before."

"I know, I know. It just slips up on us every once in a while. Time is the most terrifying thing of all, mostly because we aren't aware of it except when it slips up like this. You don't know what I mean, of course, but someday you will."

"You made me feel it all at once."

"Creston used to laugh at time. He said the only way to be unaware of time is to change so that time cannot recognize you, a thing out of place. Grow old, he said; grow wise; die. The most pitiful things, he said, are those which do not change when they should or die when they should."

"I think I should have liked him," said Peter slowly.

"Of course you would. Anybody would."

"Do you have a picture of him?"

"No, but I'm really glad I don't, for the picture would not have changed and I have changed, just as he said. I do have something he wrote, though. Would you like to see it?" She got up.

"Yes, I would." He watched her go from the room, and he was aware of all the sides of her he had come to know. He was more aware than that, however, of what an important place she had in his life. She had become in these few months more than Aunt Martha in Birmingham had been in twelve years. Only his mother, even if she was a distant spiritual mirage, could not be replaced so far; yet in time, perhaps—

"It is just a short few lines." Miss Billy handed him a folded sheet of paper yellow with time, and with the sepia imprint of a pressed flower on it. He unfolded it. It was a poem, untitled:

> How quiet the night; how far away the day;
> How slow a lost tomorrow crawls across
> The sleeping rooftops of the midnight mind,
> And dying moon-moths flutter, sad at loss.
>
> Magnolia ladies sleep where they have wept
> Beside unknown and unmet brown-limbed loves,
> And down across the belted western sky
> A summer constellation slowly moves.
>
> You watch, Diana, pale, insomniac;
> Endymion sleeps where he has always slept,
> But white Narcissus (there's another tale)
> Dies waking, counting petals, lone, unwept.

It was signed "Creston Robert" with the same sprawling handwriting in which the poem was written. All the capital letters were printed.

"How curious. What does it mean?" Peter folded the paper and handed it back.

"I have never known exactly. It has a meaning that changes. At times I have thought he meant me, but at other times I have the feeling that he referred to someone before he knew me. Then again it's almost as if it were written for someone he was going to meet after I never saw him again." She put the paper in an old candy box with some yellowed clippings and faded ribbons. "Would you care to take a walk along the cliff with a magnolia lady?" She extended her arm.

8

THE RAIN-THREATENED DAY had almost spent itself along the gray corridors of the afternoon clouds, flashing distant lightning and rolling thunder down the heavens. Lightning etched on the gray slate of sky, and was periodically washed away by drumming rain spilling from swamp to sea like a gray curtain blowing with unseen winds.

On the end of the little wharf the rain splashed on the tin roof of the shed, and the waves dashed a light vapor across the floor. Toward the shore the trees blurred away into nothing, becoming some of the sky, some of the sea. Peter and Karl, rain-blurred, were silent, for the other world usually calm was being heard in its magnificence and triumph. They sat together, huddled on the side where the spray came only with the highest waves.

"This all reminds me of the most beautiful line of poetry ever written: 'When through scudding drifts the rainy Hyades vext the dim sea,'" Karl said, turning his face into the wind.

"'Ulysses.'"

"Yes." Karl looked toward the vague area where there should have been a horizon. "It reminds me, too, of an experience, one that is hard to tell, for at times it scarcely seems real now that there have been years.

"Once—for I shall tell you about it whether you want to hear it or not, like the Ancient Mariner, who had to tell his story—in another world with different times and seasons, I was time caught, circumstance caught, in a city you have never known. It was summer in Boston, and I didn't come home from school, deciding to stay and write in one of the quaint back streets there near the river. I fitfully wrote many things into the pages of something I called 'Fragment,' an attempt to resolve on paper what the random run-on of days and nights could give no reason to.

"One night I was tired of the usual bars and even the river, and I went to that really legendary area called Scollay Square, where the streets and bars are full of rheumy-eyed old men and women with a bawdy arrested tenderness about them— other inerts to keep me company. I found on a back street a bar I had never seen before. The cobblestoned alley looked damp, even though it hadn't rained. It was so out of the way that I wasn't sure how I had found it.

"There was another person, besides myself, who didn't exactly seem to belong there—a tall very handsome man with silver-gray hair dressed like a seaman out of Melville—sitting at a table across from me. I saw that he was looking at me, staring. Usually I look away when this happens, but I found that I needed someone to communicate with. So we stared, and the whole room lost dimension, telescoped to that oneness on which time had snagged itself.

"And then across the smoke hazy, the last-century gloom of the place, he rose and brought his bottle to my table, still staring. He sat down, said nothing. I said nothing also, for there was nothing to say. There was no meaning to this, and yet all the meaning in the world. When I started finally to talk to him, I discovered the reason for the silence; he was a deaf-mute. I was overwhelmed with pity for something worse really than my own incompleteness. I wanted to take his hand and tell words into his ear that he had never heard—tell him that I, too, knew about loneliness and found meaning in silence, tell him that he had a friend.

"He was handsome, as I said, in the normal, healthy way you are. His eyes were gray, and his lips thin and resolute. I knew that he was muscular and strong. I had ample opportunity for memorizing every detail, for we sat and drank silently until the place closed.

"Outside we followed the streets, which once had had names but were now unfamiliar, for this was a world I had never known. Mine had been the world of brittle witticisms at Harvard, intellectual platitudes, and desultory probing into how much someone knew about something. The streets took on the character they were meant to have and which I had subtracted from them with my weary familiarity with them.

"We came to my room, for there was nowhere else to go. There was much I wanted to say, but it didn't matter that I couldn't. We were friends—not just friends, but suddenly dependent on each other in that mystery of silence and mist out the window. Here was someone I could let into my lonely world—someone who fitted there. Oh Peter, I can't make this sound real, for it isn't real when I try to remember it; yet it was more real when I experienced it than anything has ever been in my life. His name, by the way, was Stephen Paul.

"He was old enough to be my father, but I was too old to be his son. Perhaps he felt otherwise, for it was like that always—that same curious detached yet intimate relationship that father and son have. He could read lips, and the summer passed in evenings with my telling him what I was and was not, what the world had decided for me and what I had decided about everything. He would listen, watching my face with his deep and beautiful eyes. His eyes told me when he sympathized, when he was thinking how much I had to learn, when he disagreed.

"Oh yes, he talked. He wrote notes, indescribable notes, for they said a great number of things in a few words, as if it were necessary to get as much as possible in a brief compass of space and idea. My questions he answered indirectly, and I know nothing really specific about him, yet I feel even now as if I know him completely and permanently. He never wrote what he did, where he was from, or whether or not he had always been a mute. When once I asked him if he had ever been able to talk, he wrote: 'We speak with many voices in our life; perhaps with this one I will say what there is to say.' That was all."

Karl watched a long white wave break itself across a row of barnacled posts.

"I remember those evenings and long afternoons as the most completely satisfying of my life. We would sit in my room, he on the bed reading the paper or one of my books and I writing (for I could write during that time as I have not written since). Hours would pass, and nothing would pass between us. But we were content in each other's company. I came to accept him as a full and necessary part of my existence. I looked forward to the times we planned to meet. We ate together at little out-of-the-way cafeterias, and on Sunday afternoons we walked by the river.

"It was he who told me one afternoon about the butterfly tree. I was sitting at my table and suddenly I felt his hand on my shoulder. He had been reading as usual on the bed. I looked up, and he was looking at me in a new way, a look that had something final about it. I thought for a minute—and how unknowingly prophetic I was—that he was telling me good-bye. But still holding onto my shoulder with one hand, he leaned over to write: 'There is between Magnolia Point and Ecor Rouge something you must find again which I once found.' I was startled, for these were places I had never mentioned to him. In fact, I had told him I was from Mobile, for most people have never heard of Moss Bayou, and it takes explaining. He went on writing. 'It is the butterfly tree, and you must find it there. Remember this—it must be the butterfly tree for which you look, because if you find it, that's what it will be.' "

Peter closed his eyes and leaned his head back against the post that supported the roof. He was dizzy from a half-known truth that shouted through him with a muffled voice. He felt the wharf tremble with the beat of a large wave, and he gripped the post as if to tighten on something tangible and unchanging. Karl went on, his voice coming, too, from some sort of beyond to confuse itself with conscious barriers that pleaded for the beyond to come no farther.

"I tried to find out more, but I could only discover that once he had been for a short time in this town. He had discovered a tree of butterflies, monarchs, and then he had left. Nothing more. But after this we talked about a great many other things, and it seemed that my knowing of his having seen the butterfly tree made a lot of difference. I attributed all that he was for me to his knowledge of such a tree; I came to identify my contentment through him with the butterfly tree, and most of all I knew that seeing the butterfly tree had made him what he was. That's how I came to know I must find the butterfly tree. But I would never leave to find it, I knew, as long as he was there. That way I would almost be looking for what I already had.

"This, then, was probably the reason that one evening when we parted by the river he stopped and gripped me by the shoulder and looked at me a very long time. In that instant we became an entity; I was for a trigger-second all he was and had been. In this glimpse I knew he was going. I didn't feel anything as he walked away, for it was too soon for loneliness and too late for any of the might-have-beens. He was gone, and he had left me something between his first coming and his last going. This was important, and this was the butterfly tree."

He stopped and looked at Peter. Peter tried to look back, but he knew that Karl's was a look like all the others with their unfound butterfly trees. Oh god, he thought, isn't there an end. It was as if he were lost in a big house, trying to find a familiar room, and each time he opened a door, another opened beyond and all kept going. "Peter, are you all right?" Karl reached out and touched his arm. He sat up and looked at Karl and then at the water, and he was grateful that the water had not changed but kept moving, driving toward the land.

"Yes, I'm all right. But, Karl, let's go home. You want to?"

"All right," said Karl, getting up. He looked at Peter curiously as they left the shed and moved off down the wharf, the water racing them on either side.

9

IT WAS Saturday morning, and Peter sat in a deck chair in the back yard watching Miss Emmajean slop around in a bucket of water Eulacie had been using to wash turnip greens. The day was hot already, but the trees and shrubs had not lost their springiness. Birds sprang from treetops and dive-bombed at Miss Billy's old gray cat that always lay around enormously chewed up from nights of loose living.

Peter was very content as he surveyed the rear of the old house, once ungainly and humorous but now friendly and home. Tree shadows freckled its back wall. He sat and listened to the neighborhood with its muffled slamming of screen doors, children's voices tearing the diffused calmness, dogs chasing cars, and farther away the snoring of motorboats in the bay.

The back screen slammed, and he turned in time to see Eulacie whack Miss Emmajean, who had had her head completely submerged in the turnip-greens water. Miss Emmajean, undaunted as usual, trotted around the house where there was some more water in the birdbath.

Eulacie came on out to where he sat. She had a coffee pot

and two cups, and she wheezed into the other deck chair, which
grew bowlegged under the weight but held.

"Lord, it sure do get hell-hot in a hurry," she said, pouring the
coffee.

"Where's Miss Billy?"

"I suppose she uptown mouthin' with that post-office lady.
She can't wait to the matinee performance but have to take off
come Saturday mornin' the minute she get through coffee. Lord
love her, I don't say I blame her. What that post-office lady don't
know ain't worth botherin' with."

"But she can't really get much by reading post cards."

"Yeah, but ain't nothin' stops her from holdin' up letters to
the light. Besides, she kind of a trade center. She take what Miss
Billy know and trade it for what Miss Foster know. By the
end of the day she got it gathered, graded, and sorted."

Miss Emmajean had come up and was running in circles around
the chair with extended arms, buzzing like a fat little insect.

"Miss Emmajean, I don't need to remind you if you tromple
any of Miss Billy's flowers you goin' to have health problems."
Eulacie leaned back and heaved a sigh of contentment. She
yawned and slapped her stomach. "Sure feel nice to get all this
mess spread out and off my feet. Don't like to tire myself out
premature on Saturday. This is Bascombe Club night. That place
really eat up all the mileage you got left. You got to outdance,
outdrink, outholler every other lady there or you just a wall-
flower."

They sat for a while longer, and it was pleasant not to have
to be anywhere or do anything. It grew hotter, but the back
yard seemed cool and remote. The voice from the garden was
almost part of the remoteness.

"Anybody here?" It was Karen's voice, and Miss Emmajean,
instantly wild, disappeared under the big camellia bush.

"Sugar, you is bein' paged," whispered Eulacie, watching with
half-closed eyes and a knowing smile.

Karen came on around when he answered. Her blond hair
caught the sun in spots where the rays came through the trees,
and the spots seemed to flash off and on as she walked toward

them. She wore a becoming pale blue play suit and was barefoot. She came up and sat on the grass.

"Isn't is a perfect day?"

"I'll say."

"If you people will pardon me, I better go sweat some more. I wish Miss Billy watched me and counted time on me. Then I wouldn't feel so damn bad about gold-brickin'. Miss Emmajean, get the hell out of that bush unless you want some great big trouble." She gathered up the cups and poked back to the house, whistling and doing dance steps around the uncoiled hose.

"I thought maybe you'd like to go swimming. Have you been yet?"

"No, but come to think of it, it would be fun. It certainly is hot enough. But has the bay cleared up enough?"

"Oh probably, but I wasn't thinking of the bay. I know a much better place, but it's something of a walk."

"Good. Let me run and get my suit. I'll put it on here."

"All right. I have mine on." She snapped her fingers at Miss Emmajean, who had inched cautiously from under the bush, and Miss Emmajean evaporated once more.

When he came back, Karen was still trying to coax Miss Emmajean out.

"You may as well leave her alone. I was here for a couple of months before she'd come near me. But if you want her out, watch." He leaned over. "Miss Emmajean, watch out for that big snake I saw crawl under there while ago."

The bush vibrated, and there was a streak between them and the back door. "She takes after her mother about snakes," he said as they went around the house.

They went down the wooden steps and on to the beach road. The odor of pine needles and salt water was strong, and there was a breeze below the cliff. Their steps made no sound along the road, because the brown needles lay half an inch thick on the ground. Above their heads the trees and vines climbed the cliff, so that they walked through a tunnel of green. The sun scarcely ever touched this road because of the trees on both sides and the thick interlacing of vines.

There was a reaction to the contrasting brilliance when they emerged onto the beach where the road came to an end. The water rolled in slowly and rhythmically, spread out before them in full tide so that no shore line was visible on the other side, only a thin line of smoke and a faraway white boat.

They turned back toward the land and followed the edge of the marsh, where the waxen flowers opened their mouths to the sun. Tiny fish darted before their moving shadows, and circles spread among the reeds as water spiders skated the surface.

"This time of year is the best of all," said Karen lifting her arms and stretching them over her head. "All at once you want to do so much that there isn't time enough in your whole life to do it. You want to coax your life out of all its hidden corners and show it the sun."

"Yes, I know," said Peter. They were following the path through the tall grass. Black and silver last summer, it was light new green now. This was the path he had come the day he had found Miss Claverly. Somewhere along here was where he had seen the lovers, and his pulse quickened at the memory.

Finally they came to the creek, rippling clear and cold through the dense thicket.

"I have been here before," he said. "Last summer. I went swimming by myself. There is an island over there that you can't see from here."

"That's right," she said brightly. "I thought Karl and I had discovered this place, but I guess that's what happens when there are paths to places. People follow them. But, really, isn't it beautiful enough to be a surprise every time you come? Well, shall we?" She started taking off her skirt.

Peter slowly took off his shirt, feeling already the cold of the water. He dropped his shirt on the ground and unfastened his belt, remembering suddenly, as he glanced at Karen, the day of the hurricane. Karen was pulling the blouse over her head and stood in a black one-piece swim suit, slender and golden in a circle of sunlight.

He left his pants on the ground and went with her to the water edge.

"Don't try to wade in; you'd never make it." She laughed. "Let's hold hands and take the plunge. It won't be bad after we get in."

He wanted to wade in slowly, prolonging the torture, but he took her hand and steeled himself, not so cold that he couldn't help noticing how white his skin was compared to hers.

The shock of the freezing water was paralyzing, and when they came up sputtering, his only thought was to get back where it was hot. But Karen pulled him under again. She swam off and then back. "Isn't this magnificent?" She dived, her legs following her in a neat arc.

Little by little the water became warmer, and deep and fresh it was easy to swim in. Pebbles were visible on the bottom, and his white legs seemed outlined with silver when he opened his eyes underwater. Karen was a beautiful swimmer, and in the water she became graceful and truly pretty.

They made their way to the island and lay in the sun on the soft grass and reindeer moss. He stretched deliciously, and his skin felt tight and velvety after the cold water. He lay on his back with his hands locked behind his head and looked at his body. It was almost as if he had never seen it before. It was a nice body, he reflected, perhaps a trifle thin. A tiny pool of water filled his navel, floating the black hairs that ran from there in a curly line and disappeared beneath the tight band of his gray trunks. His skin, still winter-pale, was ruddy and lightly freckled on the upper arms. He looked at the smooth, even tone of Karen's skin, which, like her brother's, showed tiny splashes of color in the sun.

"Karen?" He rolled toward her. She had her eyes closed and had said nothing since they had lain down.

"Yes?" She opened her eyes and smiled at him.

"You're so quiet."

"I know." She turned on her stomach and raised on her elbows looking at him. "Peter, did you ever pass somebody on the street—when you felt so good that you just wanted to do something suddenly about it—and want to take him or her by the arm and say, 'I love you, I really, honestly do'? Nothing to do with sex, of course. But I mean some old man or woman wrapped up in odds and ends of shawls and kerchiefs. Someone who has lived up a great deal of time and life, whose life and experiences are important. Someone who has loved and sorrowed, who has been lonely and happy, someone who will be gone forever after that moment and will never come to you again in all the worlds you will know from that instant."

"I suppose I have and have never quite thought of it that way. That could be dangerous, you know." He laughed.

"Perhaps, but what a beautiful world we could have if people really felt that way. There are so many ways to feel love. Our language should have more words for love than for anything else, yet it has only one. I love my mother; I love my cat; I love you. But this feeling, Peter, it is the one time I am fully who I am. I become universal, almost omniscient, but I become more completely individually me than ever."

The water moved around them, and Peter remembered that the Greeks had three words for love. He knew, though, that three were still not enough for the kinds of love Karen meant. There would need to be all sorts of words for the arcana of spiritual love, for the nuances of sentimental love, for the complexities of passionate love.

"This feeling—this sudden impulse to say 'I love you' to a stranger maybe explains Stephen—oh, but you can't know about that." She got up and, standing, tossed her wet hair back.

"Stephen?" He sat up, surprised.

"Stephen Paul; it's not important. Come on," and she dived.

He got slowly to his feet. Stephen Paul. Then Karen knew about that part, too. But, after all, why shouldn't she? That would be necessary from Karl's point of view to explain the butterfly tree. But something she said about the impulse to say "I love you"—that, perhaps, it explained Stephen. . . . What did she mean? But, after all, what did any of it mean, and should it mean anything? It was, this butterfly-tree business, past the compass of coincidence. Still, there were always explanations. Perhaps—

The cold plunge cleared his mind of everything but the sensation of dropping headfirst into a world of nothing. He opened his eyes and the underwater world was a miracle of altered light values and suspended elements. There was no definite color or lack of color. It was maybe like the way a blind person imagines color. But the curious quality of being suspended in the translucence of air, color, and water was a trick too intricate to be explained right now. And in this translucence she was suspended ahead of him like a Greek fountain-nymph. She swam to him on a shaft of underwater sunlight and lightly caressed him, taking his hands and placing them on her body. White and continuous now, the skin was soft and warm even underwater. Clasped still they floated to the surface and made their way to the shallower water, where a live oak spread its shade halfway across the stream.

His hands experienced the roundnesses and flatnesses of her body instinctively, now finger-tips and then cupped palm, the heel of his hand down the cleft in the long slender arch of her back. He was scarcely aware when he, too, was standing with all his body free in the water. With his mouth against her throat, he felt her entire body shift against his, fitting angle and curve together at once tenderly and violently.

A timeless rhythm, yet counting with the water, the season, the being of two persons with one identity, carried them from the water to the shore beneath the oak. There was no measure to things now, for what had been awarenesses of sight, sound, and motion had plummeted to unknown depths. Only touch remained, but touch charged with new dimensions of the other senses. Touch became a sense with thousands of possibilities; a body was a wonderful thing, every tiny spot of it a part of a relay so that it was different each time it was touched.

This had all been before, else how could bodies know so well what together they were seeking? This was something that had lain quietly through years of becoming, identifying, learning, but it had been there all the time coiled softly and delicately like a new leaf. Now full and taut, the something of mind and body was fulfilling a moment long waited for and never again to be denied. Never again would that other world of unknowing be his completely, for the world, this world, required another person. Dimly, distantly on the edge of silky softness and firmness came a new meaning of the poem Miss Billy's wise fool had written, but this thought was as suddenly gone as time and motion were eclipsed.

Came an instant—an instant like the icy plunge into the water, an instant like torture and ecstasy—when the twins were the same person, for he was seared with a flash of recognition as if beyond them a face moved in the shadow of the tree and was gone. Then it was Karen only, and he was frightened of what he had imagined and experienced. He felt open and exposed, as if space had suddenly doubled in all directions.

"It's as if someone was there," he whispered, trying to get into his clothes before she looked at him.

"No, I think we're safe." She stretched voluptuously and pointed a toe. Peter stood uncertainly, halfway into his trousers, but he changed his mind and removed them again.

"What if Karl—" he stopped.

"Knew? Don't worry, he won't." She reached over and stroked his stomach. "Although," and her voice dropped, "I wish he could know, not about us, but about what it is. This, this what we have had, is the one thing I would not trade or give up to Karl, even if I could have his beauty. It is where love for everything else begins, not a cold materialistic or intellectual appraisal but a deep earthy awareness of what goes on inside things. Nor, I think, would Karl, not having imagined this as it really is, consent to give up his beauty for it. That is why we must find the—" she stopped and looked away.

"Why you must find the butterfly tree?"

"Yes, then he's told you." She raised on an elbow.

"In a way he has told me—the way Karl tells anybody anything."

"We agreed we wouldn't. It is ours to find—together."

"And you really believe?" Peter knew without asking.

"I believe; there is nothing to do but believe. And it is curious, if you know the whole story, that I should so completely believe something a complete stranger to me told my brother, who is a stranger to himself. Yes, I believe. I worship Karl, and what he believes, I believe."

Peter shook his head slowly, the whole year suddenly too much and yet too little for understanding. He thought how Karl had gradually changed for him. The hero had fallen from the stormy steed. Karl was no less beautiful, but it was beauty with a catch in its soul.

"In a way I worship Karl, too. He *is* an extraordinary person. Now this will make things a little different between me and him. He won't know, but I will. Karl and I are friends, and he has told me—"

"Be careful how you feel about Karl, Peter." She gave him a deep, meaningful look. "As I said, I worship him and I always have and shall, but you must not too much. In many ways Karl is an iceberg that floats in a distant unknown sea. Be friends with Karl, but don't let him hurt you. Right now he is incapable of being happy or making anyone happy, unless one can exist on the kind of happiness that thrives with looking at beautiful things. For you this is not enough; for you there must be life to a statue. One part of you is breathless with wonder before marble contours, but the other part feels them breathe beneath you."

She pulled him down beside her, and this time her hands sought knowledge of his body. This time the distances were measured but vaster; and far off it seemed to thunder, yet when he looked finally, the sun was as bright as ever, and it was almost as if the day, the world, had not changed.

10

THIS IS the way through the dream woods then, the long-imagined way, sometimes lonely (for bodies are lonely and bodies are cruel when they don't render what the mind suggests during their lonely times). This is the way, thrusting into cavernous reaches of underbrush, seeking perfection in imperfection. What are the odors and colors of this way, or are they so special that they will have to be sought again and again? They are fragrances that arise from quagmires and colors that flash in raindropped pines and change when one looks back. Bodies don't stop but come hinting of new perfections, smooth flesh tied cleverly with tendons that stretch and contract, clasping limbs that know where to fit one against and into another.

Tree frogs shrill raucously: what is a perfect body, and there along the way through the woods there are answers. A perfect body is a beautiful body, and the striped lizards, biological luxuries, slide beneath logs. A perfect body is a body that knows another body, and the creek slides smooth pebbles across other smooth pebbles, dimpling sibilantly.

The way through the woods has ended at the creek, and it stretches long and narrow, molded between the folded banks. It moves gradually, feeling the banks with its surfaces and depths, faster, slipping noiselessly along a groove hollowed by itself. Faster its motion carries it, dropping it, lifting it, moving it from side to side, spilling it sometimes over the sides wetting the foliage. Faster, until it empties finally into the sea, lost among the other waters.

Back up the way, it is starting again, never stopped starting, and will never stop—the stream—and it will flow again and empty again.

Bodies, round full bodies, bodies with spread limbs, sweating, fragrant, pulsing—

He awoke, and it was just becoming dawn, gray bearing through the window and giving the furniture a luminous unearthly quality. He sat up, not sleepy, for the dream had been noisy, and the gray silent dawning was a welcome contrast.

He walked naked to the window, his body like the bodies in his dream, ethereal, pearl-colored. He leaned to look at the bay. Through the cliff-edge pines it showed hazy and mysterious. There was a uniformity about the landscape, only the closer objects having form and substance. Beyond the edge of the cliff, the world seemed chaotic as if the elements had not discovered their proper places.

He quietly put on his clothes and slipped down the stairs, letting himself out the unlocked front door. Outside, it was different, for distant objects took on form as he approached them. He looked back at the house, and it had become indistinct. There was dew on the grass, and the long flight of wooden steps down the cliff was wet. The boards echoed under his feet, and he stopped halfway down suspended between two misty levels. Beside him a cedar rose, so gigantic he could scarcely see the detail in its trunk and foliage.

At the bottom of the steps he didn't take the beach road but went directly to the water edge. It was an immensely lost and alone feeling to be surrounded by the mist and the unrippled morning. The tide lay flat and full, heaving not in waves but in vast undulations. He turned and walked slowly, paralleling the beach road. Each minute it grew a little lighter, dawn happening rapidly. Ahead of him, a tall pine at the cliff caught a hint of rose, then it deepened and the other high limbs took color from the sunrise. Little by little the other cliff trees caught fire, and it burned over the cliff and caught on a few of the higher beach trees.

By this time he was at the edge of the marsh meadow, and he sat on a drift-log washed up against a small tree to watch the sunrise work its way to the water. Before him in the swell of the tide, a few fish jumped sending circles abroad. In the mist he heard a gull cry like a creaky wheel and then another. This was the most beautiful part of the day, he decided, but maybe it was because he saw this part of the day so seldom.

The mist, still heavy, in spite of the slowly spreading sunrise fire, played tricks on the imagination. Tree stumps resembled people and animals, and clumps of bushes were like houses. He leaned back against the little tree and breathed the moist air, thinking how he would enjoy breakfast. He knew the voices were not a trick of the imagination, and he leaned around the tree to see two figures coming across the narrow end of the marsh.

They passed close, hurrying, and he saw that they were Karl and Karen.

He stifled an exclamation, for suddenly he realized why they were here. They were already disappearing into the mist across the meadow when he decided he would follow them. He didn't try to examine his motives for doing so, except that maybe, this once, this last time (and he wondered why he felt it would be the last time), the puzzle of the butterfly tree might conceivably work out. This was another direction, another season, another part of the day; so perhaps these were the right combination. Even if it was not the right combination, and he knew it wouldn't be, still this time would be necessary to see the whole affair of the butterfly tree to its end.

He walked far enough behind so that their figures were distinguishable from the trees and stumps only because they were moving. Perhaps this would not be an end, after all, for everyone he had known intimately in Moss Bayou seemed to have the knowledge of a butterfly tree in common.

This was a different path. It led away from the one he and Karen had taken to the creek. Through a cedar grove it ran and then across another meadow of palmettos and blackened tree trunks. The mist floated in ribbons, breaking up finally. He had to drop farther back, for the figures ahead were becoming more distinct. Not once had they seemed to turn, though, but went straight ahead. This was another curious thing. In all the times he had followed the different searchers, they had all seemed to know right where to go. Miss Claverly had used a compass, but still she knew which one of the points to follow. And so far, they had all known when they got to a particular spot that they had missed again.

The path curved back toward the bay, running beside a stagnant pond. The misty trees hovered over the pond, peering dimly at their reflections, and on the surface of the water the mist seemed to rise like steam. Rapidly now the air became charged with light, and color began to grow out of the shadow world. The dull gray-green of trees vibrated greener, and as he cleared the thicket, he could see the sun picking out the tops of the trees higher on the right.

Karl and Karen, clearly visible now, were going toward another huddle of trees across a wide flat gully wash. He stopped till they had disappeared into the trees, then he started to cross the sandy bottom which was streaked with red, ochre, and white, part of it drying, part moist. The tracks of the others were the only tracks visible, and he thought that they would see his tracks when they came back. So he detoured to a place farther up and crossed behind them into the woods.

The trees here were all scrub oaks, and the earth was hard packed and covered with wiry grass. It was almost full light now, and the oaks were a moment before bursting into flame with the sunrise. He hurried, walking silently on the grass, for they had not come into sight again. He was about to round a large clump of dense bushes where he would have run dead upon them, for he heard Karl's voice.

"There, there, baby."

Peter's heart skipped a beat, and he worked his way through the wet bushes so that he could see them.

They stood with their arms around each other, looking at a medium-sized oak apart from the rest. At that moment it burst into light as the sun moved over it all at once. But it was just a tree, after all, and, like all the rest had been, not the butterfly tree. Peter swallowed, for Karl's exclamation had sounded so positive. He was disappointed as he felt the wet leaves against his face, not so much because there was no butterfly tree (for he had not expected one) but because the twins had not found one. He turned his head slowly and looked at them. From where he watched, their upturned faces, too, held the light and the greater light of expectancy, fading in this instant where no revelation had come.

They dropped their arms and turned to walk away, not looking back at the tree, which Peter whimsically reflected was still a very nice tree in its own right. Maybe even—and this was not impossible according to all of them—this was the butterfly tree, and the butterflies had either not come or had already gone.

Maybe one of the other trees had been the right one. He wanted to believe that somebody was right.

They were suddenly gone, and he, too, turned to go, looking back at the grove, thinking what a perfect place for butterflies —for anything—for the sunlight was shafting through all the openings between the trees, and this place would be beautiful forever, no matter where the searchers might look next.

Again he was lonely, sad for all the things people didn't find, bewildered by what they were looking for in the first place, and overawed by the magnificent things they did find, after all.

11

"DAMN IT, if I was twenty-one—goin' to be or goin' to be again—I'd get so dizzy-assed drunk, they'd have to shoot me down with a cannon. I could use about twenty years less at the Bascombe Club. The older you gets around there, the louder you has to dress, holler, and shake your charms, and by charms I don't mean the kind you wear on bracelets." Eulacie bent and peered into the oven.

"Eulacie, if you don't quit opening that oven, that cake's going to fall flatter than last month's gossip." Miss Billy folded a piece of paper and cut designs in it with scissors.

"Honey, you just leave me do the cookin', and I won't tell you how to do your art work." She slammed the oven door, and Miss Billy winced. "Just what gossip did you have in mind anyhow?"

"That's what I meant, silly," said Miss Billy. "But you know that little Glover girl that plays organ at the church fainted again Sunday morning right in the middle of the anthem."

"Uh-oh."

"I think people are so wonderful to be always doing things to talk about. What if nobody did? Wouldn't it be a dull world? Wouldn't it, Peter?"

"Wouldn't it what?" he asked looking up from the newspaper.

"Oh, never mind. Eulacie, I'll be right back," she said, getting up. "Put that blue cloth on the table; you know, the one we used to cover up the azaleas the time it got so cold." She went upstairs.

"Lord, that Miss Billy sure keep up with everything. She sure would be popular on Squall Street if she was colored. Miss Emmajean, get that stewer off your head. Sometimes I think I used the wrong psychological in raisin' you. Just as I say, Peter, if I was twenty-one again they'd have to catch me with a net."

Peter put down the paper and looked at Eulacie, who about that time whacked the stewer with a potato masher, whereupon Miss Emmajean's head emerged with bulging eyes.

"Why did you say net?" he asked slowly, thoughtfully.

"Hell's bells, why not? That's what they use to chase down crazy folks, and that's what I'd be if I was twenty years younger and forty pounds lighter. Man!"

"Is that the only reason?" He still looked at her.

"Oh my god, now you gettin' like her and that bunch of numskulls she play bridge with. I mean crazy-net, insane-net, nut-net. And if you don't quit lookin' at me like that, I may just quietly wet the linoleum. Peter, stop." She giggled as if he were teasing her.

But he wasn't; he blinked his eyes and sat forward. "Eulacie, did you ever hear of a butterfly tree?"

"Hell yes," she said, still giggling, "I wakes up every Sunday mornin' after the Bascombe Club with a butterfly tree in my stomach. Whoo, man, you really had too much college. Maybe you need a good through of calomel, keep all that risin' sap from goin' sour."

He got up and walked to the back screen, looking into the shady back yard. Eulacie grunted and went back to the stove.

Miss Emmajean had put the stewer back on her head and was hitting it with a spoon.

"That's the trouble with this little bastard. You punishes her, and she seem to enjoy it. She'll probably grow into a delinquency."

"Eulacie, tell Miss Billy I have to go somewhere. I'll be back for supper." He turned and started to the front of the house.

"Well, you better; it's your party."

He hurried out and up the road, for all at once there was something he had to know. He was dimly aware that all around him the day bloomed with secrets which neither he nor anyone else could ever know, but there were many other seasons to ponder these. Now he must hurry.

12

"Honey, I know you're not going to like this, but I simply don't have any thinkings done up this week. I been so busy with the tourist season almost starting I haven't had a minute. But the coffee's as good as usual." Mrs. Sparrow scratched at a mole on her chin. "Pie's good, too, an old family recipe. My family's been on this eastern shore since the Spanish explorers."

"No, I believe I'll just have coffee." Peter fidgeted and watched the slow-wheeling spokes of the overhead fan. He tried to remember the first night he had come here, a remote night now, remote as the time before he had known Miss Claverly, the Heppler twins, and Mr. Bloodgood. And had he by then—he couldn't remember—known about the—

"Of course, this new batch I'm making up for the tourist trade are really elegant. Strictly trade stuff, you understand," she said confidentially, "but you'd be surprised how many folks write back and want to buy the things by the carton. This new thinking is called 'Moss Bayou Azaleas, We Love Thee.'"

"Mrs. Sparrow, you've been here a long time. I wonder," and he started to stop, but he had to know, "I wonder if you've ever heard of a butterfly tree?"

She scratched the mole again. "Well, I can't say as I have. Wait a minute, I do seem to recall a bush by that name. Looks a little like Turk's cap. Old Mrs. Bromley down on the Marlowe Road has a whole yardfull." She wiped the table around his cup, dripping water into his lap. "Say, that would make a wonderful title for a thinking." She stood upright with her eyes closed:

> "A butterfly tree with blossoms small
> Grew beside my garden wall . . .
> In spring—"

"Pardon me, do you have a phone?"

"Sure, right back there by the ladies' john. 'In spring it smelled with fragrance fair. . . .'"

He walked back to the phone, a much-scarred instrument hanging on the rear wall, dangling a battered directory by a rusty chain. He looked around and was relieved that the only persons in the café were two old ladies eating sherbet over by the potted palm and Mrs. Sparrow, who still stood chanting her thinking.

"Hello, I should like to talk to the owner of Felice's Place at Bayou Honorine. What? I don't know the number. Yes, there is a phone there; I remember seeing one." He waited for a long time, his ear sweating against the receiver. There were clicks and buzzes and persons talking with far-off voices.

Finally, after a very long wait, the operator's voice came back. "Will you deposit fifty cents, please, for three minutes?" He dropped in two quarters and waited again till they had struck tiny bells and springs and bumped through the mechanical entrails of the phone.

"Hello." It was the soft beautiful voice of the octoroon.

"Hello, Miss Felice?"

"Yes?"

"Look, I know you will think I am crazy— This is Peter Abbott, Karl Heppler's friend."

"Yes, I remember. I had hoped you would be back."

"Well, I will, but I need to know something."

"All right, if I can help."

"I want to know if you are looking—I mean—have you ever—"

"Yes, go on please."

"Have you ever heard of such a thing as a butterfly tree?"

There was a short silence.

"Do you mean have I ever read anything about a butterfly tree? Well, I believe Steinbeck—"

"No, I mean around here. Have you ever heard about a butterfly tree on the eastern shore?"

"No, I'm sorry." Another pause. "Look, if this is something Mr. Karl told you, don't worry about it. He has a brilliant, though somewhat extravagant, imagination."

"No, no, it isn't. It isn't important, really—just something I heard from an old resident, and I thought maybe you—"

"I'm sorry, Mr. Peter. Really I am."

"That's all right." He paused. "Miss Felice, please keep this to yourself. Maybe I'll explain someday."

"Your time is up," the operator's voice cut in.

"And please don't mention this to Karl."

"I understand, Mr. Peter; you may depend on me. And please hurry back to see me. I feel I should like to know you better."

"I will, I will, Miss Felice; thank you ever so much. Good-bye."

"Good-bye."

He hung up and walked back to the booth. Mrs. Sparrow was still there. She had filled up his cup.

"You know, hon, I don't think I'll use that butterfly-tree deal, after all. It just don't have the local flavor. People like things they know about and can see all around them."

"Yes, I know," he said, and sipped the coffee.

13

"I've lost a butterfly."

They looked up as Miss Billy entered the room with the announcement.

"What a helluva thing to lose, honey," said Eulacie, pulling on a strap to a miscellaneous undergarment.

"One of those you gave me, Peter. I can't think where."

"Probably hot-footin' it back and forth to the post office. Oh, set down, it's probably around somewhere."

"Well, I certainly hope so. I think so much of them. But I'll wear this one tonight anyhow. Maybe it won't throw me off balance."

"Humph! Maybe it'll throw you back in balance."

"Peter, dear, how wonderful you look. Isn't twenty-one a pretty age, Eulacie?"

"Hoo-ee, I reckon. Enough to have that little Karen number snap her elastic, I bet." She poked Peter with a pan of hot biscuits.

"Why, Peter, I believe Eulacie with her nasty suggestions has finally made you blush." Miss Billy dropped a lump of sugar into her coffee and slapped Eulacie's hand just as it started to reach into the sugar bowl.

"Sounds like I got pretty close to home, huh, Peter?" Eulacie chuckled obscenely and then fixed Miss Emmajean with a warning look to stop picking her nose at the table.

"Eulacie, this fried chicken is a masterpiece," said Peter, hastily changing the subject.

They laughed and talked longer, and the night grew and blackened beyond the screens, obscuring the garden and lighting squares of windows across back yards. They played "The Silver Swan" and "The Twelve Days of Christmas," since those were the only records they could find. Somewhere Miss Billy found a dusty bottle half full of kirschwasser, and when they had filled the liqueur glasses, Eulacie brought the cake.

It was an elegant cake, and Peter's throat caught in spite of the twenty-one years. He didn't tell them that he hadn't had a birthday cake since he was a very little boy, because he knew that Miss Billy would feel sorry for him and that Eulacie would call his father's people bastards.

"Blow these candles out, all of them, man, because whatever you want got to happen. Can't let a few candles stand in your way."

He laughed and blew them out, conscious that Miss Emmajean had helped, whistling through a missing tooth.

"Lord love us, she done learn to whistle. That the end of peace and quiet round here."

"Whatever you wished will come true; I know it will. It usually does when you're young. It takes longer when you get older. I wish the same thing every year, and one of these years—" She stopped and took the piece of cake Eulacie handed her, feeling for the lost earring at the same time.

"When it comes to wanting something, I relies on a friend in Houstonville who does wonders with snakeskins, dried flowers, and a few candles. It's a helluva lot faster than star-bright, star-light and tooths under pillows."

"Oh, Eulacie, voodoo is so commercial."

"Honey, everything have a price tag nowadays. What you get in this world you got to pay for. Even wishin'."

"I guess you're right."

"Damn right. If you don't mind, I'd like a little more of that kootch-vasser or whatever the hell you call it."

After they talked about wishes some more and discussed the relative chances of fulfillment of one kind of wishing over

another, they got up. Eulacie pulled up Miss Emmajean, who
had gone to sleep, her head resting on the cold mashed potatoes
in her plate.

"I'll get them damn dishes in the mornin'," said Eulacie, throwing Miss Emmajean over her shoulder. Miss Emmajean awoke
and grinned a snaggle-toothed grin at Miss Billy and Peter, and
after Eulacie had carried her out, they could hear her whistling
through her gap tooth across the garden.

14

THE HEAT and sky pressed down flat on his back, and the sand
pressed up beneath his stomach. Alone on a curve of beach, he
lay in the sand listening to the steady slap of waves. The landscape lay motionless, for there was no wind. His body seemed
to blend into the sand, his warmth absorbed by the warmth of
the amber sand, his thoughts absorbed by the distance and
depth of water.

He thought of the curious year he had spent in Moss Bayou
and what unimagined experiences had followed his coming here.

He rolled on his back, throwing an arm over his eyes. He had,
at least, figured out one thing. The butterfly tree was not a
physical entity, with the exception of a remote possibility that
Miss Claverly's migration idea contained a grain of truth. But
as for the problems it would solve, the worlds it would open
for its searchers, that was a complex of illusion and coincidence.
The coincidence was the hardest part, for the strangers in all
the cities were disturbingly similar, yet completely different, each
time.

The questions drove in like the waves, and he sat up to stop
them. He realized how overpowering was the idea and its

multitude of possible questions and answers. He looked over the top of the waist-high grass and saw that the beach was still and deserted.

It was a day on the very edge of the tourist season, and one of the last days that the beach would be uninhabited. School was still not out, and the crowds from across the bay would not be over for a couple of weeks. This day, with that knowledge, was not a lonely day such as the end-of-the-season days had been.

His stomach was pink from the sun, and he knew that he was beginning to stay out too long. He reached for his shirt and stood up, feeling a contentment suddenly that he had a little, at least, resolved the butterfly tree. It was a whimsical and delicate idea, compounded of dawn, noon, afternoon, and night, a thing of seasons and strangers. The imaginary butterflies bloomed on cypresses, pines, gigantic unknown night trees, and scrub oaks. And searchers for the tree sought to discover secrets of life and death, not seeing the real, the only, truth—that nobody could find it. So now it could be forgotten.

He turned to the left and walked across the shady grove to the wooden steps. He hesitated before the steep climb, and then his eye caught the metallic glitter. There, almost buried in a sandy footprint, was the missing butterfly earring. He picked it up and stood looking at it. How lucky! Miss Billy would be overcome. He walked slowly up the steps holding it in his open palm. On the third or fourth step he missed his footing, and the butterfly rolled from his hand, bounced from the step and fell among some last winter leaves a few feet below the steps and to one side.

Peter swore at his carelessness and climbed over, dropping into the leaves. He was relieved that there weren't many leaves. He moved some of them and there it was again, still catching the sketchy sun through a patch in the overhanging tree. He took it cautiously and stood up.

Then he saw the butterfly tree.

It was a glimmer of orange dimly caught in the corner of his eye, a glimmer that moved almost imperceptibly, then moved in double, then in multitude. From the tiny spark, the entire tree became illuminated, burning with a silent, non-consuming fire, breathing in flame from gently wafting undulations. From this miraculous conflagration a thousand white flecks of eyes looked out, and there seemed to be a feathery whisper as the etched black-wing patterns melted into the flame. This burning, butterfly-burning, tree seemed to lift from its base of fern and ground-vines and hover above the floor of the woods, giving life to the surrounding trees, reflecting its fire among their greens.

Flames and shadows of flames dropped from the tree and floated to new positions, away from the sun into the sun. From underneath, the wave of orange magic fire moved upward in a sheaf over the surface of the tree and finally off the top to fall and float upward again.

The whisper might have been this tree or another tree; it might have been imagined voices whispering that a butterfly tree existed after all, in spite of everyone and everything and most of all in spite of himself. He stood transfixed, feeling, becoming, a part of the orange-black fire tide that flowed outward and upward, licking at the sky and all his defenses. He was dizzy with the slow, unending rhythm, and he felt breathless and empty as if part of him were reaching out and becoming incorporated with the lift and downward drift of the flaming butterflies.

They were, as he felt himself drawn into the somnolent rise and fall, riding on shafts of air and sunlight toward him, settling down, down, like burning falling fall leaves, to smother and burn him with their own immortality.

He shook himself and looked at the other trees, all still in place with real branches and leaves. Then he looked back, and the butterfly tree was still there, but it no longer burned.

The shade now was on it, and it became cool and deep like clear water with pale pebbles and black lacework moss. It flowed now with water motion, water bubbling from a constant and unknown source, forcing up to the surface. And now it became deeper, more distant, like a night sky with cold remote stars, stars revolving in a galaxy around a fixed, immovable center.

The motion never ceased but continued, as the butterfly tree became by turns water, fire, and sky. Again it was seasons and cycles. He closed his eyes and held them closed for a long time, seeing the whole tree.

When he opened them, the tree was an earth tree, where butterflies had landed to rest. Here was perhaps the kind of tree Miss Claverly sought, and he remembered what she had said about the saddest of human experiences being unshared beauty. He knew he had to hurry and bring someone, all of them, Miss Billy, first of all, before the butterflies flew away.

He didn't want to leave, because the butterfly tree, the tree that was the beginning and end for all the people who had come to have meaning for him, was starting to be something else, and this time he wasn't certain what. He backed away, and when he got to the steps it was still there, fully visible. He walked up the steps backward, making it last, for with all the unknowns about butterfly trees and their searchers, he wasn't sure it would ever be again, especially as now.

He ran from the top of the cliff the short distance to the house and burst on to the gallery, where Miss Billy sat working a jigsaw puzzle at a card table. He was still holding the earring, and he stood before her with his hand open, thinking how he would say it, this biggest moment of her life.

She fitted a piece into the puzzle and smiled up at him. Then her eye fell on his open palm.

"Oh, Peter, you've found the butterfly!"

"I've found the butterfly tree," he said simply.

"What a sweet way to put it. I'm so happy to have it back. Last night—"

"But did you understand me? I've found the butterfly tree—the real butterfly tree. It's right down—"

"Peter, Peter. Dear it's terribly hot. Sit down and we'll have a lemonade." She started to call Eulacie.

"No, no, no, no! I tell you, it's so. I have found it—no, because I wasn't looking for it—discovered it!"

"And I'll bet you have just got too much sunburn. Look at your chest."

"Miss Billy, look, please look. You must! I have—" he half-shouted.

"Peter, dear, please don't shout. I believe you. This is the season for butterflies. Creston and I used to walk on the beach, and they were everywhere, and at night there were fireflies. Now where did you see so many butterflies that you believed them to be—"

"Come on, it's right at the foot of the wooden steps. Right down there," he pointed.

"Oh, Peter, Peter. Don't you know the butterfly tree must be in a beautiful place, a place that you find because you look, not a place you pass several times a week. It's so easy to want it to be in a nice, easy, not-so-pretty place, but that's not the case. Now, let's have some lemonade."

"Miss Billy, for god's sake—"

"Please, dear."

He was weak with frustration. He wanted to pick her up bodily and carry her to the spot. All her life, years of looking and hoping, and now—

"Miss Billy," he said quietly. "I love you, and I wouldn't insist if I wasn't sure. Please, it's just under the cliff. We may be able to see it from the top. You won't even have to go down the steps."

"Now Peter, I know you are sure you're sure. I tell you what, we'll walk down after it's cool, and you show me the place where you saw the butterflies. What kind were they, dear?"

"Monarchs," he said impotently and walked into the house. He went upstairs and removed his bathing trunks and put on a pair of denim pants and a tee shirt. He had to hurry, for Karl and Karen must come, for the butterflies might move away. If it was true that they came to the same tree every year, at least here was the place of (but who could know the time of) the butterfly tree.

15

KARL WAS MOWING the lawn, and Peter looked at him in the thick afternoon sunlight, feeling again the thrill of perfection as he regarded the tanned muscular shoulders and the hair picking up the gold of the sun. Karl stopped the mower when he saw Peter.

"Well, where have you been the last few days?"

"Karl, I have something to tell you. Where's Karen?"

"Whew, it's hot. Come on, let's go up in the shade. Karen? Oh, she's uptown, I think."

They sat in the metal chairs under the trees by the back gallery. Peter was sorry Karen wasn't at home, for it was right that she also should know now. But it couldn't wait. The butterfly tree was there, and someone had to see it.

"What is it you have to tell me?"

"Just now, just a while ago—I hadn't believed it, but, Karl—" He paused, for it was so big one couldn't just say it simply.

"Yes?"

"Karl, I—I found the butterfly tree." His face shone with his discovery, and he knew it did.

"Oh," Karl laughed, "is that all? Well, it happens. What was it like?"

"It is wonderful—thousands of butterflies, catching other colors, other than their own, fluttering, some of them. Others are motionless— But, Karl, come on. You must come and see them, on a tree on the beach. Hurry." Peter stood up and moved toward the gate.

"Yes," said Karl, grinning his unpleasant grin and shaking the hair from his eyes. "Yes, I suppose it happens to all of us who do know and some of those who could know."

Peter stopped and walked slowly back, bewildered.

"Yes," Karl went on, "I guess I have seen the butterfly tree a hundred times." Peter sat back down, still looking at Karl, wanting to go but unable to.

"Once in Boston, when the afternoons were hot and it was summer, I was torn with several desires at once, all of them unfulfillable. It was just after Stephen had gone. I needed, and I didn't know I needed, someone to listen to me. I found (and I couldn't possibly remember the details) an old woman, who sold flowers, loitering along in the Common, who was such a listener. I don't believe she ever said anything to me at all, just listened and understood. While we were sitting there on a bench—I had taken her hand—I saw the butterfly tree glowing like a thousand jewels across the Common. I rushed from my bewildered flower woman and ran to see it, find it. It was simply a balloon man going along Boyleston Street. I remember how sad it made me to think how cheaply the butterfly tree could be imitated. My friend was gone when I came back, and I sat on the bench, knowing suddenly that the butterfly tree could not be there anyhow, there in a city. So I decided then, at that moment, I would come back here, where he said it would be."

"But, Karl, it is, it *is*. It's at the foot of the wooden steps. Please, let's hurry." Peter half-rose again.

"And I have seen it, too, in such places. The seasons have their deceptions. A burst of spring flowers seen through the new green of trees has been for an instant the butterfly tree. Or again the slow and subtle dyes of autumn have made butterfly trees of every tree in the woods. Even winter with its beaten-copper sunsets. One cannot run, Peter, to every sudden brilliance in the hope it will be the butterfly tree. One must wait for the feeling that the time is right and that a certain place is right. Then he must drop everything and go." Karl ran a finger delicately down the long biceps of his arm and smiled up at Peter. "Don't you see?"

Peter said nothing but got up and started to go, then turned round.

"Karl, for the last time, won't you—"

"Peter, when are we going to get together again? We must get back down to Bayou Honorine. The time is good."

"How do you know?" Peter asked and left through the side gate without waiting for an answer.

16

"IT HAS been a long time, my friend. But I knew you would be back eventually. Things always happen, even if only eventually, in my life. You must need tea." Edward Bloodgood turned from the door, and Peter followed him inside. "Do sit down. It has been unseasonably warm today. I am already missing winter."

Peter sat and looked around. Nothing had changed. There was no fan of any sort in the room, yet the room was cool; and the Buddha smiled its cool smile. Mr. Bloodgood was back, after rattling noises in the kitchen.

"Well, and how has life in Moss Bayou been these last months? But I do manage to see and hear a few things. Those Heppler twins are charming, aren't they? The boy, of course, is incredibly lovely, but the girl has always fascinated me. She has artistic possibilities. I believe she could be quite as lovely as her brother with a touch here and there. Unfortunately, though, she would have to be dead. Isn't life sad?"

"Mr. Bloodgood, it has happened. You said the last time that if certain things happened you could see it, and now you can."

"What is that, my friend? I don't understand." He looked at Peter and smiled his slightly taunting smile.

"The butterfly tree. I have found it."

Mr. Bloodgood sighed and shook his head. "It would be wonderful to have such faith again. Once that would have been possible, but—has it really, ever, with me been possible?"

"No, not faith. I really have." Peter pointed.

"My friend, your faith is even making you point the wrong way, away from the swamps. It must be there, you know."

"But it's not; it's at the foot of the wooden steps down the cliff."

"Gold at the foot of the rainbow." Mr. Bloodgood smiled again. "What makes you think you have found the butterfly tree?"

"I don't think," Peter said, his voice rising. "I saw it, can't you understand?"

"Oh, you actually saw it, then? Well, that certainly makes a difference. Were you looking for it?"

"No, I was just walking along, and there it was."

"Interesting. You know, my friend, the human mind is a complex and terrifying mechanism. How on a bright and beautiful day of late spring, you, who have no reason for ghosts, who have so far nothing to find or want, should have a vision. How like Norman you are now, so much and so long ago." He reached over and stroked Peter's arm.

"My friend, why are you crying?"

Peter shook with great racking sobs, unable to speak, wanting only to cry out all the frustration of not being believed; the fantastic impotence; like shouting in dreams without making a sound. Mr. Bloodgood patted his arm and tried to soothe him. "You mustn't. Although it is sad, isn't it, when we suddenly grow up and find our dreams are not any longer real or, worse, more real. Now, now."

Peter stopped crying suddenly and looked at him accusingly. "I am about the only one left in the world who is not dreaming. You don't believe anything you haven't thought of first, any of you."

"What do you mean, my friend? Any of whom?"

"All of you and your damned butterfly trees. I tell you, I have found the only one there is to find." He stood up and

shouted over his shoulder as he moved to the door. "It's there,
I tell you. I am going."

"But, my friend, you really don't have to take it this way. I
should like to believe you, but— Aren't you going to stay for
tea?" Mr. Bloodgood stood up, his hand extended. "But, of
course, if you must go, there will be other times for tea."

"For tea, yes," said Peter and closed the door.

17

WHEN HE had finished sending the telegram to Miss Claverly, he
came out again into the sun. Up and down the street were
people who were unaware of anything except the heat, the
specials at the A & P, and the other people. It would be hard
to believe in butterfly trees for them.

"Hi!" It was Karen with a grocery bag. "Gosh, it's hot. Why
don't you buy us a glass of beer at Marchand's?"

"Good." They walked the half-block, and he carried the bag
for her.

"If it weren't so late, we'd go swimming." She didn't quite
look at him.

"Yeah," he said, but he couldn't feel particularly interested.
They turned into the cool darkness of Marchand's and took a
booth.

When they had got their beer, he turned to her but stopped,
feeling the futility. Then he thought of the creek and how, after
all, they had been so nearly a part of one thing. Perhaps—

"Karen, I—I have found it. Will you believe me?"

"What, Peter? Of course, I shall believe you, whatever you
want me to."

"The butterfly tree!"

She stopped, her glass held midway from the table. Then she put the glass down. "You have, honestly? Are you sure?"

"Of course, I'm sure. I'm as sure as I have ever been about anything in my life. Do you believe me?"

"Why, yes, if you say you have. What, what is it like?"

"Like fire but not like fire. It is—oh, I can't describe it. Like everything that has happened. Maybe it is even like the day by the creek—you and I—"

Her eyes glistened, and he could see that she believed.

"Where, Peter, in all the world to find it, did you find it?"

"That's what I want to show you. It is the most wonderful thing I have ever seen. You cannot see the tree for the butterflies —thousands of them. It is probably still there. I'm sure it is, and if we hurry—"

"Well, let's go, then." Her face was bright with anticipation and disbelief, not disbelief in him but in its finally having happened. She started to get up. "Oh, but—he, too, must—Karl. We agreed. We can pick him up at home."

"Oh, Karl. I've already been there. He doesn't believe me."

"Oh." Karen's face fell. "He doesn't? Well, that's different." She settled slowly back.

"What's different?" Peter sat back down.

"If Karl, I mean—well, Karl knows. He has always known when the time was. You see, it's really through Karl that I even know about the butterfly tree. Naturally he knows more about it than I do. If he doesn't feel—"

"Then you don't believe me, after all?"

"Oh, I do believe you, Peter, but there must be some other explanation. You might have thought—" she faltered and stopped.

"Then, that's it. Don't you suppose Karl could be wrong?"

"Yes, in many things—Karl was born wrong and will undoubtedly die wrong—but not about the butterfly tree, Peter, not about the butterfly tree."

Peter sat still and drank the rest of his beer, while she sat looking at him sorrowfully.

"Peter, are you angry?" She reached out and took his hand.
"No, I'm not angry. But I want to go."

"All right. Do you want to go swimming tomorrow?"

"I suppose so," he grinned, getting up. "There's a lot of summer ahead of us."

"And there is so much to do here in the summer," she said, hugging the grocery bag out the door.

"But," he reflected, "nothing left to find."

18

HE LAY on the cot on the screened part of the front gallery, watching the dusk gather across the road, thickening the air with a vapory grayness. There, just a short drop over the cliff was the butterfly tree still. He had stopped back after coming from uptown, and they were still there, a little different again in the later light. He had stood looking for a very long time. Once he had heard somebody's footsteps on the long wooden stairs, but he had not called out. He had watched alone, for perhaps this was as it should be.

The boy had brought the telegram a few minutes ago, and Peter still held it in his hand. He had almost known without looking at it what it would say: "Deeply touched you want me back so much that you see b.f. tree. Not enough evidence to prove you right. Can't take chance again. Come to New York."

So this was the last. He lay back and tried not to think.

Where does one go from a butterfly tree; what difference do the rest of the woods make now? Here is a tree, a miracle of trees, come upon suddenly, intrudingly. (For one should look for butterfly trees, shouldn't one?) There should be woods, swamp woods and pine woods and woods that grow by water, and there should be dawntime, noontime, dusktime and nightime. At these times one should come stealthily from far-off, far-off times of life, and in these woods there should be—but wait—

Now the people come, vague and shadowy persons from bright-dark times of day, through the strange and secret places of woods. A black dress first and a faded silk umbrella, cautiously, delicately, peering into the arches of vines and the interstices of trees, sandy washes where colored pebbles lie or pine-needled clearings where fairy rings are drawn. Peter, dear, where are the butterflies? These woods are beautiful, so they should be here. Here where other ghosts have been. Somewhere in a gallery once I saw a sad thing, a painting; it was of a child drowned while trying to catch a butterfly. Butterflies are difficult to catch, especially after they have flown away and will come no more. Little girl ghosts in blue sweaters are difficult to find again after they have grown into little old ladies with wrinkled hands. Come, Peter, you will help me somehow to find the tree, because for a while you seemed to resemble— Oh, but now it's gone again; we must hurry. There, there up ahead, where the sunlight falls, where there are magics. (Maybe there it will be where it is and nowhere else. Did someone say that to me or did I dream it?)

No, Peter, my dear, you don't dream butterfly trees, and Miss Claverly leaned closer to inspect the bark of a tree, tiptoing up so that her satin pajama-top blouse pulled out of her slacks. You don't dream anything, my dear. It is all built into the machine that is you, and you have had to put labels on life. But we must hurry to catch the sunset, for my research tells me the how and when of the butterfly tree. It would tell me the where perhaps if I had another lifetime. But hurry, my dear, we must not let the dark overtake us.

But darkness is the time of the butterfly tree. Edward Bloodgood took a fan from the sleeve of his yellow kimono and pointed it toward a constellation. Remark, my friend, the difference in stars. Some are blue, some are yellow, and some are red. If we take such stars and drop them like burning jewels into a night-wood, we should perhaps later find them twinkling on a tree. Do we not take fragments of our life and lose them in forests and then spend the other flying years in search of them? My friend, for a moment as you smiled at me with eyes like glowing stars (not eyes like the butterfly tree, for that is what he said of my eyes), I thought I had found a part of a fragment.

That's what I called the novel I started once—"Fragment" —for persons are fragments. Each of us is incomplete somehow. Beauty, knowledge, talent, spirit, fertility, they can't all go together, but have to be surrendered, one or more, for the highest development of the others. So come, Peter, help me collect psyches, for if we collect enough we will find an absolute. Karl laughed, and his laugh was a happy laugh. But we must hurry. We must run—you and I and Karen—like golden children in the shallow water, and we must later swim like green and white heroes in hurricanes. The car is waiting, and we must run, for we have discovered what parts of us are missing, and only the butterfly tree can discover us completely to ourselves again.

And don't forget, Peter, said Karen, the clear water of streams where silver-white bodies overflow like fountains, like concert music, and sudden dawn. I am coming with you. I am not beautiful like Karl, but then he is the rest of me and I the rest of him. You are, of course, more than either of us, but less than both of us. (The horn sounded at the garden edge.) What, Peter, she asked, running. You have found what?

He ran after, shouting inside, but no sound came. I have found, I have found—but no one could hear him, and now the car was leaving with all of them—Miss Billy, Miss Claverly, Mr. Bloodgood, Karl and Karen—waving to him out of sight around the curve.

The butterfly tree—he finished with his lips in a honeysuckle vine which sprawled over the fence.

Not *the* butterfly tree, but a butterfly tree. I, too, found it once—but only because it was where it was. The man stood a little apart so that he was an old-young man, like everyone and no one. He walked forward, alternately through sun, mist, and darkness, and still he was not clear, blurred like a bad snapshot. But there was still sunshine in his hair.

You—you are Paul Creston.

Probably, yes.

Then you will believe I have found the—a—butterfly tree? They wouldn't listen. How, Paul Creston, can we make someone else understand? How can we know them?

This knowledge is where it is, and most likely we can never know it. The distance between one person and another is the most tremendous dimension in the universe.

But once they listened. You—something—made them listen. Why didn't you tell her, Creston Robert, where it was?

She would still have looked in all the places where it was not, for you told her and she will never look there.

The light shifted, and the man smiled a gentle smile and leaned to examine a leaf on a bush. Years happened to him when he straightened.

And if it is only one tree, Robert Norman, why didn't you tell her there under the crab apple trees so that all the years would not have been lost?

Were they lost? Really, were they? I hadn't looked to see. But again, would not she have measured distances and counted hours? There is much about life you must learn, Peter, much.

He leaned against the fence, and his body was angular and boyish as if he had suddenly been metamorphosed. He looked stark and alone yet not lonely.

And what of him who looks for beauty and death? What of the butterfly tree for him, Norman Stephen? It is not in the night and it is not in death.

Perhaps it is and perhaps it could be nowhere else for him, not now. We are what we have become from what the wind cried to us as children in old houses, blowing outside through the thorn-bushes or spattering rain on the windowpanes. This becoming is subject to a few changes, but the later part is what we shall be forever. Even in our oldest years there is something of the same wind and the same rain; we keep them like the color of our eyes all our life. So what we look for, too, is part of the becoming and being. We find it, if we do, and it is what it has to be for each of us.

Then the face, still blurred, was old, gently old, but the smile was soft and young.

What then, Stephen Paul, of them, the golden ones who look for a butterfly tree that is there if they find it? Where, where is there; where is there for any of them?

The gray man scratched in the sand with a stick.

There is everywhere and nowhere. If we look for anything everywhere it will be nowhere.

And then—then—for me. What of the butterfly tree for me, who have found it nowhere? What is the butterfly tree for me? What? Wait, Paul Creston, where are you going?

Follow along the cliff for he is disappearing down the wooden steps, and darkness is growing along the hem of the bay-edge trees. The wooden steps are soundless, without their hollow echo. There, there, where the earring fell among the leaves.

Yes, here. Here is your answer (if really there can be answers). The tree reached up into a patch of sky made by the other trees, but now there were no butterflies. See, for you the butterflies have flown away and will never come again. For you there never was a butterfly tree—only a tree of butterflies. For you there was not, for it didn't matter for you. Something will matter someday, and then, whatever that something is, you will look for it till the end of your life.

Until then, Paul Creston?

Until then, you will find many things which other persons look for, but none of them will be for you.

How will I know?

You will know, just as the others have known and couldn't tell you how they knew. You will know. And now—

He began to grow dim, and where he disappeared fireflies came alive and moved among the trees. Peter felt a sudden vast emptiness and longing, but it was as quickly gone. He looked at the empty butterfly tree and thought how he was sorry that his something was not going to be a butterfly tree.

The fireflies collected and blinked like fiery jewels among the night trees, and the night was suddenly full of music, music that vibrated about him and drowned him, leaving him struggling out of night and the sound of night.

When he opened his eyes, there were fireflies in the garden, and night lay in the corners of the gallery. He stretched and remembered the weariness of the day, but now as the feeling of the dream came back for a moment it didn't matter. He didn't remember the dream, but he knew that it had helped put everything in place.

He heard voices in the kitchen and got up and went there. Eulacie at her customary place by the stove looked up.

"Peter, you look like you heard a sad song on a small fiddle."

"Dear, are you all right?" Miss Billy looked at him anxiously.

"Sure, I'm all right."

"Well, that's fine. This has been a long hot day. Are you hungry? Eulacie, hurry with supper."

"Honey, that's a damn fine way to get me to take my time. Miss Emmajean, quit messin' with them burners, you goin' to blow us all to eternal, and I'm goin' to make you wish you had."

"Peter, dear, where is Zamboanga?"

He smiled and laid his head on the back of the chair. Nothing had changed, or maybe, what he really meant, everything had changed, and this made the difference.

DATE DUE

OCT 18			
			PRINTED IN U.S.A.